"Reading *Contenders* is like watching a fire. You ~~see~~ glowing embers that fascinate. The dialogue, t~~he~~ everything crackles and pops in this novel. Th~~is is a~~ piece of work."

—**Percival Everett**, author ~~of~~

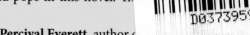

"This book is like watching Lorrie Moore's humor in a glorious street brawl with Ernest Hemingway's bullfighters. Full of heart, spirit, and delightful characters, *Contenders* hits you hard and leaves a mark you'll remember for a very long time."

—**Nick Arvin**, author of *The Reconstructionist*
and *Articles of War*

"Erika Krouse has written a novel as hard paced and surprising as her heroine, the inimitable Nina Black who can beat almost any man in an unfair fight. But *Contenders* isn't only about street fighting. It's also about the spiritual life and the life of the affections, within and beyond family. Can Nina come back from the edge of darkness? I couldn't stop turning these brilliant pages to find the answer."

—**Margot Livesey**, author of *The Flight of Gemma Hardy*

"Erika Krouse's moving novel...gives us a lowdown depiction of Denver, Colorado, reminiscent of the Knoxville, Tennessee of Cormac McCarthy's *Suttree*. And if you know *Suttree* (or McCarthy!), you know that that's no mean feat. What's more, *Contenders* contains within it the most unsentimentalized version of *The Karate Kid* that any good street fighter could want, complete with epigraphs pulled from Krouse's knowledge of the inner workings of Asia...most particularly, Japan. It's a novel that moves with the quickness of a slap to the face, and does what a good slap and good literature always does...it wakes you up. This is an absorbing and rewarding read."

—**Richard Wiley**, PEN/Faulkner Award
winner for *Soldiers in Hiding*

"I've been waiting for Nina Black for a long time. Violent, gruff, and relentlessly female, Nina is the kind of antihero we've rarely seen in fiction. *Contenders* is a one-of-a-kind powerhouse of a novel that further showcases Krouse as a talent to be reckoned with."

"Erika Krouse has penned a fierce and fearless novel about the purity of violence and the necessity of honor. *Contenders* kicks and blazes and jabs, and in all the right corners it breathes with love, with the beauty born of commitment. Her Denver is a pitiless place of forgotten promise, and her heroine, Nina Black, is a twenty-first century American badass, strutting across these pages with uncommon élan. A beautifully crafted novel."

—**William Giraldi**, author of *Hold the Dark*

"A beautiful, brawling book that reminds me of the best of Harry Crews— and there is no higher praise that I can give. I loved every word."

—**Benjamin Whitmer**, author of *Cry Father* and *Pike*

"A sunburst of a novel, one that blazes into your heart and won't let go. Erika Krouse has an uncanny ability to write about the intersection of violence and love, and in doing so she renders a basic and important human truth: that pain and rage are often a response to heartbreak. After all, what is fighting but an expression of desire? *Contenders* is part karate thriller, part zen koan, part mystery, part beat novel, and part love story. Krouse impressively weaves these all together into a deeply moving tale. I'm mesmerized by *Contenders*, and by the exceptional courage and heart contained within."

—**Michael J. Henry**, author of *Active Gods*

"A ferociously taut novel driven with the power of a *shuto* (knife hand), not a mere punch. It is unapologetically on the fringe of everything, which, in this day and age, places it right in the heart of what matters. Here is a novel that does not flinch when facing the sacrifices of what it takes to be human… Nina will burrow into your heart and mind and ask, over and over, 'What matters to you? What would you die for?' But more essentially: 'What would you live for?' This is the toughest, meanest, most compassionate novel I have read this year. I humbly bow to Erika Krouse's brilliance."

—**BK Loren**, author of *Theft*

"The sharpest, most intense romantic comedy you'll ever read. Or a journey deep into the resonance of dark memories and loss. Erika Krouse's *Contenders* is unlike any novel I can remember—it straddles the line of sweetness and brutality like a beautiful, punch drunk, fragile fighter looking for love."

—**William Haywood Henderson**, author of *Augusta Locke*

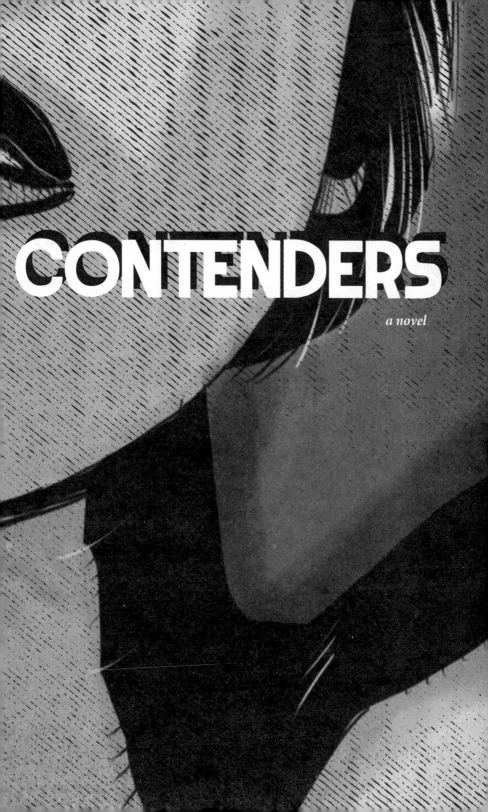

CONTENDERS

a novel

CONTENDERS

a novel

ERIKA KROUSE

A VIREO BOOK | RARE BIRD BOOKS
LOS ANGELES, CALIF.

THIS IS A GENUINE VIREO BOOK

A Vireo Book | Rare Bird Books
453 South Spring Street, Suite 531
Los Angeles, CA 90013
rarebirdbooks.com

FIRST TRADE PAPERBACK ORIGINAL EDITION

Set in Minion
Printed in the United States

10 9 8 7 6 5 4 3 2 1

Publisher's Cataloging-in-Publication data

Krouse, Erika.
    Contenders : A novel / by Erika Krouse.
    p. cm.
    ISBN 978-1940207636

1. Thieves—Fiction. 2. Martial arts—Fiction. 3. Japanese Americans—Fiction. 4.
Denver (Colo.)—Fiction. I. Title.

PS3561.R68 C67 2015
813.6—dc23

For J.D. and K.

PART
ONE

CHAPTER ONE:
THE JOB

If two tigers fight, one is bound to be hurt, and the other to die.
—Okinawan proverb

It's just a job. Grass grows, birds fly, waves pound the sand.
I beat people up.
—Muhammad Ali

NINA BLACK WAITED IN the alley for a fight. It was taking longer than she had hoped. Conditions weren't ideal. A cool wind blew her hair sideways, and she jumped up and down to stay loose. She always forgot how cold Denver could get on summer nights. The graffiti on the bar's back door was blurry; she couldn't tell if it said Courage, Bondage, or Cabbage. She stopped jumping and squinted.

The door cracked open, and the word slid into the dark. A shorn head poked out. "There you went." The man's torso leaned out of the door and his legs scrambled underneath to keep up, until he stood in front of her. In the light from the streetlamp, his hair glinted orange. His souring breath wafted across her cheek. "Were you that woman in there? That woman at the bar? Staring at me?"

Nina pulled her hands from her pockets.

"I think you dropped something." The man was tall, thick, like someone who had played football in high school and watched football ever since. A Rorschach birthmark blotted his face. His movements were exaggerated, yet careful. He reminded Nina of every drunken thirty-year-old she had ever met.

"I said, you *dropped* something," he said.

Nina scanned the ground and patted for car keys, money. The man sighed and clutched his own T-shirt in his fist. It bunched and lifted until a crescent of belly gleamed above his belt. "It was my heart," he said.

He licked his finger, pressed her bare shoulder, and made a hissing noise with his mouth. "You're hot." Then, "I came out here to puke. But now I don't have to." His fingerprint evaporated from her shoulder. "What are you, Filipino?"

"I'm American."

"No, but what *are* you?" His face flashed a frown and went slack again.

"My mother was Okinawan. My father was a white guy."

"Ching chong," he said.

Nina tried to breathe evenly, but instead she hiccupped. Rancid cooking oil dribbled toward a drain hole from the open door of a Japanese restaurant, staining the night air with the scent of bitter, scorched fish. She hiccupped again.

"Gesundheit." For a second, his face was fatherly. "Hey."

"What?"

"You wanna blow me?"

She hiccupped again and pounded her chest with a fist. "You're drunk."

"Nope. I'm high on Jesus. Been saved and everything." He stared at her like she was a twenty-dollar bill he found in the street. "You what? You wanna?"

Nina smelled him, his metallic beer breath, sweat, and the chemical smell of air-conditioned flesh. At some point that night, he had eaten celery. He breathed high in his chest. The canvas of his skin was uneven, with pale jade patches near the veins in his temples. His shoulders strained his jean jacket.

He reached for her. She stepped out of the path of his hand.

"Hey." A sharpness rose in his voice. The alcohol cleared from his eyes, and the capillaries around his nostrils reddened as he sobered up. An updraft brushed their hair off their foreheads. High in the atmosphere, Nina smelled rain.

He said, "C'mere, you little bitch," and grabbed her wrist.

Nina's other arm whipped around and bit into the side of his neck, edging downward into his carotid artery. His knees buckled and his fingers loosened. Before he could recover, she kicked out his standing leg and slammed her palm into his chest, clotheslining him. His surprised face glided through the air, a freckled moon.

He landed on his back with a soft, patting sound. Almost without realizing it, Nina had caught his head on her instep a few inches above the concrete. She cradled it on her foot for a second, just to let him know he had been saved yet again, before sliding it off her shoe to the ground.

It was over. She stood above him, panting. Adrenaline zinged across her chest. The man's neck muscles strained under his skin as his lungs pulled hard for oxygen. Nina flipped him onto his belly, bent his arms into chicken wings, and pinned them high behind his back with her knee.

Her knuckles were turning pink, his imprint still on her skin. She hiccupped again and played back everything that had happened since her last hiccup. How had she hit him? What came first? Could she have done it better?

On his stomach, the man was still sucking air, his face torqued to the side against the pavement. Nina thumped between his shoulder blades a few times to help him get his wind back. His breath rasped against her shoe, and a dab of spittle landed on the toe. "This. Ain't. Right," he gasped between breaths.

Nina shoved his fists higher up his back, and he grunted. The bar door stayed shut. Her vision was beginning to clear, but the graffiti on the door made even less sense than before. The man's pupils jittered back and forth.

"Don't worry," she said. "Nobody's watching."

"Let me go." She could tell that he was trying to sound reasonable, but the knee in his back cropped his words. "Cut me a break. I'm only human."

"But I'm not," she said.

He twisted, trying to see her face. His birthmark was a sapphire shadow. He asked, "Then what are you?"

She reached for his wallet.

CHAPTER TWO:
THE FOX AND THE RABBIT

O N A WALK WITH his student, a Zen master watched a fox chase a gray rabbit across their path. The rabbit hopped in frantic zigzags, and the fox streaked closely behind. The animals disappeared into the underbrush.

The Zen master said, "That rabbit will escape the fox."

The student said, "But the fox is bigger. It's stronger."

"The fox is running for his dinner," his teacher said. "The rabbit is running for his life."

~

NINA WAS A THIEF, technically, although she never defined herself that way. Apart from being negative-sounding, it was relative. The way Nina saw it, if you stole a wallet, people called you a thief. If you stole an election, they called you President.

Nina instead thought of herself as a kind of pool shark, except she didn't play pool. It wasn't her fault that they underestimated her. Men shouldn't be hitting women anyway, I mean, really, what kind of world was this? She was an enforcement officer, collecting small fines from men who violated the social contract. Every animal steals to live. Nina liked to pay her rent on time. She liked to be fiscally responsible.

Nina shoplifted, too, but only stuff on sale. Meat, bound in butcher paper, sunk into a handbag. Filet mignon, fresh tuna, an artichoke. Socks, stockings, underwear, olive oil. If she thought she was being watched, she stood in line to pay for a single box of spaghetti, and walked out cradling a full purse of supermarket makeup and shellfish. She wondered which other shoppers among her were also harboring hidden Oil of Olay and vials of saffron. She suspected a higher incidence of shoplifting for embarrassing things like athlete's foot powder, vaginal itch cream, Beano, or extra-small condoms, so she made sure to purchase those kinds of things outright if needed, in case security cameras were trained in those directions.

No, stealing was sponsorship. Fighting was the passion. She never stopped, never tried. During dry spells, she missed it like it was lost legs or a drifting lover. She knew what she loved.

Of course, like most careers, it's harder for a woman, and easily complicated by standards. Nina had a code: she never hit first. Her teacher Jackson often used to quote an Okinawan proverb, *Karate ni sente nashi*—there is no first attack in karate—and Nina took it seriously. Anything after the first strike, she figured, was fair game.

Besides the first strike rule, she didn't fight kids, women, the homeless or elderly, gangbangers, and crazy people. For practical reasons, she also avoided drug addicts and her neighbors. Basically, she tried not to fight anyone she wouldn't have sex with.

It took work. Nina exercised every day to exhaustion. She dressed trampy, hung out in questionable areas of town. Certain streets, all she needed to do was stand with her back pressed to the wall, knee up, and someone came along demanding a date or worse. On the same streets the next night, nada. The odds sucked. Because she couldn't get around it, no matter how hard she tried: people were essentially good. And she wasn't as good as she used to be.

It was probably temporary, just a series of dumb mistakes resulting in minor injuries—a dislocated jaw, bruised ribs, shiners. They added up. Last month outside a 7-Eleven in the rain, a biker grabbed her and she punched him in the mouth. His front teeth broke and embedded themselves in her hand. He smiled, and blood streamed from his mouth in a silky rope. He hit her, and hit her again, and didn't stop until she ducked and he broke his fist on the wet wall behind her. She heard the bones crack like small thunder, and still he cocked his fist again, a blinking robot. She ran straight home and lay damp and sweating under the covers until the sun came back up.

Men on meth were the worst because they felt no pain, had no morals. She tried to avoid them, but you couldn't always identify them if they bathed. She wore precautionary leather, but she still bore scars on her ribs and arms. She had been cut five times. Her nose was crooked and blunt from breaking. She had fractured four ribs and a pinky. Her jaw was permanently askew and clicked when she chewed. When she groped her skull, her fingers found dents and scars she didn't remember getting.

Sometimes she wondered if she had ever seriously hurt any of them.

Perhaps she should go on medication, and take one of those drugs that sound like superheroes (Effexor! Lexapro! Zoloft vs. Celexa!). She couldn't go on like this forever, winning. Or, at least, not losing. It was mathematically impossible. She wondered if she'd soon start losing when she should win, and if these shitty times were, in fact, her glory years.

Sometimes she opened her desk drawer and counted all the wallets she had taken over the years—folded leather piled one on top of another, mounting evidence that her number was almost up. Nina had survived over ninety street fights. She knew exactly what she was made of.

Her old teacher, Jackson, once said, "The smart thing is never the brave thing." He was five-foot-six. He grew up on Oahu near the military base. On his way home from winning a cockfight, four drunken marines jumped him. He fought them all off, never once letting go of his chicken.

Jackson told Nina that her mother was once assaulted in Okinawa by two Americans. One of the men kissed her, his hands at her throat. She bit off his tongue and spat it at him. It's impossible to know what a person is capable of until that moment comes and passes—who or what they'll sacrifice. That person doesn't know, either.

What will you fight for?

~

THERE'S A LOT TO learn. When Nina was a teenager, Jackson used to take her to Denver on long day trips. He introduced her to Asian men in dirty parts of town who showed them their minor miracles.

One was an Indonesian guy who practiced a monkey style. The story was, when he was young, his teacher threw him in a cage with a wild monkey. The monkey went crazy and tore the boy up. The teacher pulled him out just in time, saying, "Now you know how the monkey fights." Okay, whatever, but this guy did fight like a monkey—crouching low, thumping people on the head, crawling all over Jackson's hunched back. In the monkey man's village in Indonesia, everyone carried knives, and if someone challenged you to the death, you couldn't refuse. They'd kill you anyway.

The monkey man had killed people. The three of them had lunch at a Chinese restaurant. The monkey man's stained pants smelled like motor oil and chicken fat. He and Jackson mostly talked about food they liked, but Nina was too shy to say a word to the old fighter, who had bristly white hair and a long scar down his neck.

After lunch, the monkey man escorted them back into the kitchen. Midsentence, he punched a fist-sized dent into the metal door of a walk-in freezer. The kitchen staff kept working, chopping pork and rinsing bean sprouts. The other freezer doors had similar dents. The monkey man was a regular.

On another trip to Denver, they watched an underground, unadvertised demonstration. A boxer had challenged a skinny Thai guy. The Thai guy held out just one hand, the other still grasping a cheap Asian cigarette. The boxer sent a jab, and the Thai guy hit his arm so hard that an aubergine-colored bruise instantly appeared on the boxer's wrist. Within seconds, the blood vessels broke and spiderwebbed all the way up his arm and neck to his face.

Once, they visited a craggy Chinese man who smelled like ozone. If you stood next to him, your skin vibrated, and static electricity raised the hairs on your arms and legs. In a dusty alley behind a burrito stand, Nina watched him drink an entire bottle of clear Chinese firewater with a snake coiled in the bottom. Then he ate the snake. Then he ate the bottle, tearing into the glass with his teeth, chewing and swallowing. She thought that was it—what else could there be? Then he started demonstrating throws, chucking people around the pavement until everyone just shook their heads, panting, hands on their knees.

He beckoned to Nina, the only girl there. She stepped forward, ready to be thrown against a wall or something. Instead, he wiped his hands on his bald head and gave her a fresh lychee, shell on. She ate it while it was still warm from his pocket.

Jackson used to split open watermelons with his fingertips. He cracked entire stacks of bricks with his palms. He could extinguish a candle from three feet away by swatting in the air. He could split a plank of tossed wood in midair with a punch, and push down trees. He kicked a double layer of baseball bats in half on his fiftieth birthday.

He criticized Nina for being in love with the tricks, but she couldn't help it. She couldn't believe that these people existed— real-life unsung heroes and demons in basements with water stains on the ceiling tiles, in alleys behind projects, in putrid restaurants that served jellied meat parts. In warehouses. She saw an eighty-year-old man throw a college linebacker fifteen feet. She saw a fat Chinese guy make a med school student puke from across the room, by pointing a finger at him.

How is this possible?

Nina refused to believe in a god who refused to believe in her. And Jackson said not to trust anything she perceived, said it was just shadows on the walls of a cave. The physics book she had stolen from the library said that sound was nothing more than vibrations in the air. From that you get language, the barking of dogs, Yo-Yo Ma. Sight—you actually see everything upside-down, and the mind subconsciously makes the flip for you. A mind can do that. An apple only looks like red because it absorbs light in every color *except* for red. So, the sky is everything but blue. What you get is not what you see.

Or what you touch. If you remove the space between particles, a human body can fit on the head of a pin. Same with rocks, same with aircraft carriers. The only thing that gives the impression of solidity is that these tiny pieces of matter are moving fast all the time, carving out space for themselves, saying, "I'm here. Get the fuck out of my way." And everything—every fingerprint, every snowflake—is made of the same particles, doing different dances. These tiny particles are connected by a force that moves at the speed of light, and is, therefore, light. If you could find a way to look closely enough, you'd see that everything is exactly the same, made of light, space, and potential. That included Nina.

So, on this most basic of levels, it was possible to do all these crazy things. Hell, more, even. You could shake a house on its foundation. You could walk through walls of stone, or split diamonds in half. Jackson called it *Areté*, after the Greek— doing that which you cannot do. Nina wanted to figure it out for herself—but with her body, not her mind. She wanted to be more than a story of something that happened to someone once. She would go to the source itself. By learning the exact relation of motion to matter, even the most ordinary person— Nina—could become extraordinary.

～

HER RELATIONSHIPS TENDED TO suffer. Not that she didn't want one. She wanted one. Especially at night, watching her pizza cool on the plate, or sitting alone in a movie theater, baseball hat pulled low. When Nina saw couples going to dinner or bickering in a drugstore, she wondered how they managed to pull it all off. Her most recent love affair had stalled out when her boyfriend answered a call from the girlfriend Nina didn't know he had, from a cell phone she didn't know he had taken to bed with them. He called his girlfriend "Pumpkin" and smacked kisses into the phone, hung up, and tried to roll back on top of Nina.

That was over a year ago. Romance swirled around her and rolled off, like mercury in the palm. One day, she kicked a rug and found herself staring at her half-buried diaphragm, trying to remember what it was. It was a dilemma. She knew she'd never use it again, but it seemed like too personal an item to just toss in the trash with the potato peelings. Was it like a flag— once it touched the ground, you had to burn it? She eventually threw it into the South Platte River and watched it bob away like a legless octopus.

Before the married man, there had been others—men she had met in clubs, at coffee shops. She wasn't a nun or anything. Her sheets had seen plenty of tug-of-war over the years. She had built pillow barricades to muffle nose whistles, endured scratchy feet crawling over her legs. She had eaten morning waffles and drank morning coffee with a bartender, a short order cook, a day trader, a marine, a tollbooth operator. A bisexual clown.

For one windy spring month, she dated the takeout guy from her favorite Chinese restaurant. She sloshed around his sleeping bag until dawn, dreaming out the window at neon signs with letters missing, waiting for him to bring home soggy fried wontons and leftover Kung Pao.

But he dumped her for the dishwasher, who was a man. Then she went out with a guy who believed the Federal Government spent too much money on education. Then she went out with a guy who brought along his ex-wife. Then she went out with a man who tried to sell her Amway.

Nina had never once planned ahead, never taken the person in her bed for granted. She had never walked down the street, humming, "Looks Like We Made It."

She did have occasional good sex, which is easy to confuse with love. She spent hours lounging in bed with men, letting the major muscles atrophy while she thought, *This is it.* She memorized near-strangers. She laughed hysterically at things that were only vaguely funny, awash with desire, certain for the twelfth or nineteenth time that she had never, ever felt this way before.

Then, without warning, the drawbridge went up in the man's face as he realized how precious life is, or how precious he is, or how nothing amounts to a hill of beans in this crazy world, or how he'd always wanted to move out of the state but had never known it until that second, or how he's not ready for love, or how he's incapable of love, or how he's got this, um, wife? Or this, um, disease? Or how he's still getting over this girl, really psycho, who traumatized him, or how he was wondering if Nina ever noticed that she snores a little bit, or how this isn't a relationship, they're just dating, or how he's used to his own space so could she please go home now, or how this is a momentous connection and he's fucking it all up. He knows it, but he can't stop himself, and it's just killing him.

"Fight for love," Jackson used to say, but Nina didn't have any love to fight for. Instead of an actual heart, she had one of those have-a-heart traps: the rats get in, and they stay in. She suspected that she herself wasn't a human being, but some kind of mutated animal. It made sense that she would attract men who could only love her with an animal love—that is, ferociously, and then not at all.

Sometimes, though, she caught glimpses of something, rare moments full of potential when, despite herself, she unfurled in sleep and the men did, too. For a night, they were one person, one breath. Their thoughts blended with their smells and they turned into abstract Picasso selves, more like shapes than flesh, more like dreams than names. Then Nina would love, in the primitive way that sleeping babies love. She loved because she could, and because she needed, and because a hand lay in hers, and, in its careless sleep, promised to stay there forever.

~

THREE BLOCKS FROM THE scene of her latest crime, Nina sat in the driver's seat of her Pinto, ignition off. She still felt the aftershocks of contention, like minor quakes through her chest. She tried to shake the adrenaline from her limbs, but they trembled anyway. It felt bad in a good way, and good in a bad way. The loose window shuddered next to her, and a soda can rattled in its cup holder.

The street was quiet—no police cars, no sirens, just the night traffic playing its one note. She wiped her cheek, and a smear of blood snailed across her palm. She probed until she found the raised outline of a nick on her cheekbone, the size of a grain of rice. She checked the rearview mirror; a new bruise bloomed above her eye.

Nina picked up the wallet she had won. It was blue. They were never blue. She smelled it—real leather. She pulled out his driver's license. He had lied about his height—no way he was six foot one. Men always lied about height. She replaced the license and flipped through the billfold. Fifties, four of them, two twenties, and some singles. That was all right. The credit cards she would sell tomorrow to Jared, a teenager who worked at the Denver Public Library. The folds hid a video rental card. An Eagle Scout card. A punch card for a deli downtown—one more visit and she'd get a free sandwich. She slipped the cards and the cash into her own pocket. Nina was an Eagle Scout, now.

She smoothed her hand over the dashboard of her Ford Pinto. She loved this car, admirably well-performing despite its danger of bursting into flames upon impact. It had somehow missed the recall, and for that reason she had been able to buy it for a few hundred bucks and twenty-five stolen credit cards. She had a don't-ask-don't-tell policy with this car. If she heard a strange sound, she turned up the radio. If she smelled something burning, she opened the window. It was like the old, balding widows who shuffled around her neighborhood—they never seemed to work right, but they just wouldn't die, either.

Nina scrabbled a Strike Anywhere match against the stack of papers in the passenger seat. It ignited, and the list of phone numbers flared under the flame. She lit her cigarette. She only smoked one pack a week, but she couldn't bear to quit. Not because she missed cigarettes, but because she missed *missing* cigarettes—the swift ache, and its instant satisfaction. Besides, she wasn't a quitter. She figured that if she died of anything, it would be in a fight, and the worst thing she could imagine was lying in the street, bleeding to death, and thinking, "Wish I had smoked that last cigarette."

She drove toward Capitol Hill, steering with one middle finger locked over the wheel. She parked near Kitty's Porn Shop and got out of the car. She shifted the stack of papers in her arms, the blue wallet wobbling on top, and walked down the alley to her apartment building.

She loved this alley, her alley. Nobody else ever walked down it, never ever. Maybe that was because it was next to a gun shop, and maybe because it was the only alley in Denver that dead ended, due to an proviso made to an ex-mayor who owned an interfering building at what should have been the alley's mouth. The building had been turned into a gun shop that sold firearms, porn, and, strangely, secondhand shoes. To get into the alley, you had to squeeze past the building via a broken sidewalk too narrow for a bicycle.

Not only was the alley cut off from street view, but no windows faced the alley at this end. It was as if all the adjacent buildings had agreed on a boycott. If you died right there, nobody would find you until garbage day. Maybe even later; the garbage trucks sometimes skipped this alley, since they had to drive in and back out in reverse. The walls looked like the blank, windowless sides of a prison, except you were on the outside, where nothing interesting was happening.

Nina did most of her morning and afternoon training here. She ran wind sprints up and down the alley, her sneakers grinding against the oily concrete, the rarefied air brushing her cheeks. She pounded an abandoned thirty-inch tire with a sledgehammer until her bones ached. She had made a medicine ball out of an old basketball and sand, and she did power crunches with it, bouncing it against the wall and catching it. She whipped chains so heavy, nobody had ever tried to steal them. Likewise with a dirty duffel bag packed with rags and sand, which she had covered in duct tape, attached to a chain, and hung vertically under the fire escape stairs for a heavy bag. Right now, lying on its side in the dark, it looked like a dead body.

Nina mounted the dim fire escape stairs to her second-floor apartment, the metal clanging against her shoes. The building was called The Chessman Arms, its facade originally constructed in careful brick patterns that were now painted with decades of soot. The Arms was one of many apartment buildings off Colfax Avenue—The Cavendish, The Holiday Respite, The Country Squire—designed to appeal to grannies and Section-Eighters, anyone willing to believe in the grandeur of the name despite all visual evidence to the contrary. The hallways were mottled with carpet stains, plaster scabs, and old mold. Inside the apartments were scarred hardwood floors, tall windows of rheumy glass, and ceiling leaks. It was just the right kind of old, and if you squinted and it was dark, the building looked classy with a capital K, at least from the outside.

Nina had moved into this apartment two years ago and stayed out of inertia. The neighborhood felt home-ish, flecked with prostitutes, gallant art deco buildings, and waving trees. Homeless people ambled down hot alleys, magpies squawking at them. She belonged here. The abandoned Guardian Angels Headquarters was two blocks away. She was within walking distance of three, count 'em, three tattoo parlors, and a head shop/bookstore called Leaves of Grass. She was as settled as a person could get.

But tonight, she dumped her stuff in the middle of the floor and scrutinized the squalor. What had she done here except time? She had wrapped rubber bands around doorknobs and subscribed to *The Denver Post,* but she was still a squatter. She saw her neighbors every day, smelled their cooking, and heard them have sex, but she never felt like she could knock on their doors and borrow an egg. She didn't know their names. They didn't know her, or like her. All her furniture had once sat on a nearby corner with a "Free" sign on it. She didn't own anything she couldn't move herself.

She kept a goldfish in a coffeepot. It swam upside down, too dumb to die. And every time she tried houseplants, she was reminded of the phrase, "Death comes to us all." She never understood why they shriveled up, those quiet little guilt-trippers. They seemed so needy, always wanting water and giving nothing back to the world but (huh!) oxygen. Once, she found an abandoned cactus in a terra-cotta pot, sitting on the curb. She put that plant in her window and watered it for a year before she realized that it was plastic.

Home, this wasn't.

Two weeks ago, a drunken ex-wrestler tried to slap her. As she blocked his hand, he followed with a punch to her jaw that she was too late to slip. Nina saw black, tasted aluminum. For a few seconds, she was unconscious on her feet, and her heart stopped in her ribcage.

Her twin brother's face loomed in the ether, just like in cartoons and movies. He was huge, filling every inch of the screen of her mind.

"Hey, Chris," she said. "What's up?"

He looked at her the way a person looks at his own hangnail. Unfettered by consciousness, Nina missed him with the force of a tsunami, with a violent undertow of hope that she hadn't realized was still there.

Then Chris was gone and she was back on the street, her heart beating again, that stubborn machinery. The sweating face of the ex-wrestler had replaced her brother's, and she stumbled backward at the ugly transformation. The man reached into the back of his pants and pulled out a gun.

Nina turned and ran, but he shot at her anyway. The bullet whistled just past her head. The sound punctured a hole in her eardrum. That week, every time she had a cigarette, smoke leaked from her left ear.

What if she had caught that bullet? She'd never see her brother again. She'd never see anything again. She would end up unclaimed in the morgue, her body disposed of like medical waste, dumped from drawer to incinerator. No lover would mourn her. Nobody's life would be ruined by her absence. Isn't that why people had husbands, families, children? Isn't that what everyone wanted, in the end? To be vital enough to ruin a life?

If you've lost your way, you retrace your steps, and hers dead ended with Chris, wherever and whatever he was. As the wind pushed against her windows, Nina studied the list of names and phone numbers she had bought from an elderly private investigator. Hundreds of Chris Blacks, all in California, if that was even where he was.

Nina laid a ceramic plate on the floor next to her phone, unwrapped a Twinkie, and poked a pink-and-white striped candle into it. She struck a match and touched it to the wick, humming "Happy Birthday" to herself and her absent twin. Shy and unaccustomed to wishing, she silently appealed to the water stain on the ceiling.

Then, in the wee hours of her twenty-eighth birthday, Nina Black blew out her candle, picked up the phone, and dialed the first number on the list of two hundred forty-three. A lady answered, voice mushy with sleep. "Hello," Nina began, clearing her throat. "I'm looking for Chris Black? My brother?"

CHAPTER THREE:
ACTING

I N JAPAN, THEY HAVE a river monster named Kappa. He has scaly skin and a turtle shell on his back. The top of his head is a small dish that holds water, so he can breathe on land. His face looks like a monkey's, but with a beak instead of lips.

Deadly sumo wrestlers, Kappa monsters are very polite. If a Kappa challenges you to a fight, just bow to him. He will bow back, spill all his breathing water, and be forced to return to the river. This is a good trick to know, because Kappa is ferocious. He thinks it's funny to pull people's intestines out through their anuses. He also eats children.

While children taste good to Kappa, his favorite food is cucumbers. To ensure that the Kappa won't eat their children, Japanese parents write the children's names on cucumbers and throw them into ponds and rivers. They watch the cucumbers float on the water, perhaps feeling a little silly. Regardless, their children don't get eaten. It still works.

~

I'M BALONEY, ISAAC THOUGHT. *Baloney.*

"Harder, baloney," the director barked into his wholly unnecessary megaphone. "Shake it harder!"

"It" was Isaac's costume, a codpiece made out of real baloney. They called it a loincloth, but nobody was fooled. Isaac jangled his hips until the thing jerked and bobbed in front of him, grease smearing all over his junk, while he belted the chorus of "My Way." Jailbait girls sang backup in string bikinis with baloney breasts and cheese slices flapping at their hips like fringe.

"Cut," the director said.

The cheese slices had unwrapped themselves again in the heat from the lights on the set. The costume director rushed on set again with fresh slices and a stapler. They were now on Take Thirteen. Chaz, the director, shouted at her, "Try superglue," waved at Isaac, and pointed at the ground in front of him.

Isaac approached Chaz, teeth-first. "Hold this," Chaz said and handed him a half-empty water bottle. Isaac took the bottle and Chaz made another note on his clipboard, muttering without looking up, "Frankly, I'm not feeling your commitment." Chaz winced at his watch. "This is an important commercial. It revolves around this damn dream sequence. I need you to really"—he formed little Italian circles with both hands and shook them lightly—"embody the product."

"Got it." Isaac stood straighter. "I am the baloney."

"That's why we hired you, and not any of those other assholes."

"I'm just wondering...why we're wearing the actual product. On our bodies."

"The client wants authenticity, Eraserface. Don't you want to be authentic?"

"Yes. Yes, of course." Isaac cleared his throat. "Just...still wondering who might want to buy baloney if I'm wearing it on my crotch, you see."

"They're marketing to women," Chaz said and walked away, leaving Isaac with his water bottle.

In one swift pivot, Isaac hurled the bottle against a wall.

The bottle just made a popping noise as it bounced off the wall and rolled all the way back to Isaac's feet. None of the people circulating around the studio even noticed.

"Why did you do that?" Kate was standing behind him with her doll. The two of them gave Isaac the same stare with different colored eyes.

"I thought you were waiting in the viewing area," Isaac said. "Kids aren't supposed to be on the set."

"I got bored. And hungry."

Isaac fetched her a sandwich from the catering table. He slumped into a chair next to her, making sure the codpiece covered everything. "Sorry this is taking so long. Your dad probably never made you wait around like this. I'm guessing this isn't exactly fun for an eight-year-old."

"Almost nine," Kate said. Then, "You smell."

"Yeah. I hope they don't repackage this costume after I'm done with it."

Kate clutched the doll he had given her when she was little, one of those bald plastic ones that you can put in the bathtub with you. She had named it "No-Hair," and still translated for it frequently. "No-Hair wants to see a Rated-R movie," she said. "No-Hair hates salad." After her father got sick, No-Hair stopped asking for anything, but rarely left Kate's arms.

"Why did that man call you that name?" Kate asked.

"Eraserface? It's just a nickname, honey."

"It sounds mean."

"Is No-Hair a mean name?"

"No. She really doesn't have any hair. But you have a face."

"Is Kate a mean name?" He tried to tickle her. She squirmed away, but didn't laugh.

Truth was, Isaac was grateful for his nickname, grateful for the work it brought him, especially now. Grateful that he was the only talent in the business who had a nickname. It seemed like every actor in the world was jostling to get in front of the same Vaseline-smeared lens to sell sleep medication, or jock itch cream, or food in a can. His therapist said that gratitude created serotonin, so he was awash in gratitude for a starring role in a commercial for an up-and-coming lunch meat manufacturer, right here in LA.

Half his work was here, but he traveled constantly for acting gigs—commercials, trade shows, bit parts in direct-to-video movies. His agent croaked, "New York," or "Chicago," or "Houston," and off he flew, renting an economy car, staying at a discount hotel, ordering pizza, and halfheartedly watching cable porn.

It was a life, his. After graduating from Northwestern University armed with his MFA, his sincerity, and his acting credits (Wasn't he Hamlet in the Northwestern production? Wasn't he Willy Loman?), Isaac had moved to LA to break into film via commercials. Film faded, but the commercials endured. It seemed that there was an endless supply of crap that Americans had to buy, and Isaac had built himself a reputation—good looking, reliable, and willing to do almost anything, no matter how demeaning. He got corporate gigs, commercials and infomercials, training films and TV-order products. Then the jobs got more upscale—credit cards, fashion designers, car manufacturers. Soon, Isaac found that he had sunk to the top of his field.

In fact, he was on his way to becoming a world record holder for the most TV commercials in a single career. The frenzy had begun when a casting director dubbed him "The Man with the Erasable Face," and *TV Guide* did a short article on him. It was all about how Isaac could appear in multiple commercials for multiple products, but nobody ever recognized him. For every product he sold, he looked like a different person, and directors cast him over and over without exhausting his range.

Bookings increased even more after that article came out. Isaac's agent hired an assistant, bought a condo near the beach. Everyone was requesting "Eraserface" for airline commercials, insurance commercials, luxury vehicle commercials. Proctor & Gamble executives dialed him direct, on his cell phone. They called him "son." Sometimes, though, when extolling the benefits of a new weight loss pill, or dressed up as a giant tube of toothpaste, Isaac wondered what it was all for—if he was doing any good in the world, or just annoying people.

Isaac scratched some dried egg from Kate's upper lip and she batted his hand away. Kate could never act, or even lie. Her pale face and squinting eyes would betray her. She could do some kind of public service commercial about neglected kids, maybe. She glanced at him, looking just like her dad for a terrifying moment before it passed. Unexpectedly, she plugged her hand into Isaac's damp one, as they watched the costume designer scuttle around with duct tape and cheese. At that second, Isaac missed Kate's father with a new ferocity, undaunted by the sorrow of the day before.

He cleared his throat. "I booked us a flight to Denver next Monday."

"I'm scared to fly," she mumbled and started kicking his metal chair leg.

"You're too young to be afraid of flying. Please stop that."

Kate swung her foot in the empty air.

"What are you afraid of?"

"Dying."

Isaac pulled a pencil and scratch pad from the coffee table. He drew a plane that looked like a flying hot dog. He pointed with the pencil. "An airplane's wings are tilted like this, see? When it moves forward, more air goes underneath the plane than the amount that goes on top." He drew a bunch of arrows pointing under the wings. When Kate's face didn't unscrunch, he drew darker arrows. "The air sucks the plane into the air. So it doesn't fall down."

"I've fallen off monkey bars before," Kate said. "The air didn't suck me up. And a plane is much bigger than I am."

"It's aerodynamics. Size doesn't matter."

From Kate's scowl, Isaac saw that no woman, no matter how young, seemed to buy that argument. "The wings don't flap." Kate ate like she was feeding a meter.

"I fly every week for work. If we're going to be living together, even in the short term, you have to fly. Don't you want to try to find your aunt?"

Kate's cheeks bulged, food stashed in them. "I guess so." She chewed and chewed, swallowing several times. "She's my only relative."

Isaac glanced at her and away. That was the issue, wasn't it? In his will, Chris hadn't given custody of Kate to Isaac, his best friend of twenty-three years. Instead, he had given custody to his renegade sister Nina, wherever the hell she was.

Despite a measure of relief (Isaac had never even changed a diaper, and wasn't exactly ready to father a child who wasn't his—not that he'd have to change Kate's diaper, she was almost nine, but even so), he was somewhat baffled by Chris's choice, and he burned with low-grade resentment. Nina was lost. How would Isaac find her to dump Kate on? Which he wasn't even sure he felt comfortable doing. I mean, who knows what the situation was there. Why did Chris choose to give Kate to the Ghost of Sister Past, when it was Isaac who was there the whole time, in the flesh?

Except he hadn't been around much, either.

He had only disappeared at the end. Until then, Isaac had been around plenty when he wasn't working, and on weekends after Chris got sick. He had helped Chris through his wife's death, through Chris's own medications and their failures. He had helped them move to that Section Eight place once Chris got too weak to work at the service station. Isaac had downgraded his own apartment to pay for Chris's. He had handled Chris's mail for him, paid his bills with his own money.

It wasn't easy taking care of an indigent widower with drug-resistant AIDS. Chris had thrown up all the time. He had lost his hair in clumps on the carpet. He had constant diarrhea. Isaac went south every day and cleaned up. He deodorized. He had power of attorney. He was the point person, right up until Chris went into the hospital for his last weeks on earth.

Then Isaac never visited him.

Instead, he went to nine auditions. He had sex with eleven women, once each. He cried on his sofa fifteen times, and six times in bed. He went to a grief counselor seven times. He picked Kate up from the school bus, took her to the hospital for visiting hours, and cried into his hands outside the door until Kate came out. He stopped when she emerged, and drove her to his Hollywood Hills apartment. He fed her dinner every night and tucked her into bed on a mattress made of air, and while she pretended to sleep, he cried some more.

Chris died two days before his own twenty-eighth birthday. Kate was in the hospital room with him when he died, alone.

Isaac heard her howling and grabbed a nurse, who found Kate wild-eyed, pulling on Chris's dead finger, shrieking, "Wake up! Wake up!" Kate kept screaming until they left, and afterward for a time, too.

Now, Isaac tore at his manicure until something broke through the sound barrier and into his head. It was Kate's voice. "What?" he asked.

"I said, is she like me?"

"Who?" He willed his eyes to focus on the girl. Her hair stuck to the side of her dried-out face.

"Aunt Nina."

Isaac's memory flashed on Nina, silent and vicious as a treed raccoon. She and Kate were different species. "I haven't seen her since high school. I don't even know where she is."

"I thought she was in Denver." Kate stopped chewing. "Did you call her?"

"I only have an address. There was a postcard from her old teacher among Chris's things, so we'll try his house. It's a place to start, anyway." Isaac cleared his throat. "Kate, even if we don't find her right away, you can always stay with me. Actually, your father, he said…" he trailed off when Kate stopped eating entirely and looked at her lap.

"Isaac," the assistant director said. "We're up."

"As soon as I nail this, we'll go home to pack," Isaac said. Kate stared at the crusts of the sandwich crumbling in her hands.

Isaac walked to his spot under the lights. He stood with his legs apart, ready to emote. The day before, they had watched Chris get buried. Chris had chosen a cheap cemetery in South Los Angeles, away from their neighborhoods. Neither Isaac nor Kate would pass it on the way to something else. They'd have to go there specially. Chris was one hundred and nine pounds when he died; his wife, Bethany, had been only seventy-five. A nearby grave was decorated with used hypodermic needles stuck into the ground in the shape of a heart. Isaac kept an eye out during the funeral. The cemetery was in a dangerous area of town, and he thought Kate probably wouldn't go back there until she was old enough to buy herself a gun.

~

GRAND JUNCTION, TWELVE YEARS ago:

Isaac pulled over at the Black house on 28½ Road. Chris and Nina climbed into the Jeep. "Take us high above this shit," Chris said. Their mother had left them two weeks before, and Chris and Nina looked like they hadn't slept since. Their father being what he was, Nina probably hadn't dared to.

Isaac drove away from the shacky houses and trailer parks until he hit dirt, curling the Jeep up the Book Cliffs. Under a greenish-blue sky, they crawled along the high desert until they found a herd of wild horses grazing in a shallow canyon crusted with random ridges of snow.

"Just like the Stones song," Chris said. He leaned back and whispered something to his sister, and she ducked her head. It occurred to Isaac for the first time that Chris might tell things to Nina and not him, and he felt briefly jealous of both of them. Even though Chris and Nina were the twins, Isaac was convinced that his and Chris's futures lay in a twisted double helix, an appropriated DNA that comes with the kind of friends you don't know how to live without.

They were planning to go west on the last day of school. Isaac had found his parents' cash stash in a piece of tinfoil they kept in the freezer, and Chris had some money from his job at the gas station. They had almost enough money for the two of them to get to Nevada, or California if they got good gas mileage. Isaac glanced at Nina. Chris was planning to send for Nina once they had enough money. Probably.

"You tell her yet?" he mouthed to Chris through the rear view mirror.

"Shut up," Chris mouthed back and looked at the dirty horizon.

Isaac didn't have siblings of his own, didn't know those social rules. He barely knew his own. He always felt like a guest in his parents' house, like he had to apologize for his existence, his laundry, his need for peanut butter and toilet paper. He wanted to be a given, not a guest star. Chris always took him for granted, which made him feel more real.

He didn't know how Nina thought of him, since she never talked. He had even turned it into a game, asking her random questions: "Hey, Nina. If a tree falls in a forest and nobody hears it, does it make a sound?" or "Hey, Nina. Why can a person be discombobulated but not combobulated?" Every day, he expended valuable daydreaming time thinking of ways to provoke a reaction: "Hey, Nina. Rats can't throw up," or "Hey, Nina. Two roads diverged in a wood. I took the one *more* traveled by. It made no difference whatsoever." She never responded, except for one time at lunch: "Hey, Nina. What's the sound of one hand clapping?" Nina thought for a second, reached across the table, and slapped him loudly in the face.

Now, Nina was the first one out of the Jeep the second it stopped. Isaac jumped out behind her. He had heard about these horses years ago, and had been searching for them ever since he got his driver's license. A cloud of dirt from the Jeep's wheels still hung round and low in the air, like a filthy sun. "You coming?," Isaac asked Chris. Chris, never much into nature, climbed into the back seat for a nap. He pulled his baseball cap lower, and slumped down.

Isaac and Nina crunched across the cracked earth together. The air smelled like pine sap. Furry horses in every color quivered a little in the chilly air, although the sun was strong. Their coats were brushed askew by the wind. They grazed on the tough desert grass, heads slung low.

The only one not eating was a black horse set apart from the herd, his mane ruffled up. Isaac and Nina walked over the mud and brush until something in his dark eyes said, *Stop.*

"See that one, that black one?" Isaac pointed from his shoulder, as if sighting a gun. "Herds always have a sentry. If you scare that guy, they all run."

Nina's thin jean jacket was shiny at the seams, and the cold blurred her lips. "You chilly?" Isaac asked. He took off his coat and held it in her direction, looking away as if he didn't want it. The cold air instantly blanketed his sides, but he was wearing a wool sweater and Nina only had a thin T-shirt under her jacket. He shook it at her, and his hand became light as she lifted it. When he glanced at her again, it was already on her shoulders, flapping almost to her ankles. He sank his hands into his jean pockets, and the cold from his fingers soaked through to his legs.

They watched the horses eat. "What are you going to do after graduation?" he asked.

Nina shrugged. Her black hair rustled against the shoulders of his coat.

"It's only three months away. You really should have a plan." Isaac liked the way his voice sounded, deep and assertive like that. He wiped his cold nose with the back of his hand. "I have a plan. A few plans, actually. My old man wants me go into mining, like him." It sounded as bad outside his head as it did on the inside. He kicked a rock, watched it scurry across the dirt. "There are some jobs in California and Nevada. But I'm not all that interested in it. Dirt and rocks."

Nina pursed her lips, her gaze fixed on the black horse.

"What I wish I could do is something cool, like be an actor. Like Shakespeare. The great tragedies and comedies. Life and death. Something real." Isaac had recently played Stanley Kowalski in their school play, and he had scared himself with his passion for acting out this made-up story in front of people sitting in the dark. Now, he was surprised to be saying this stuff out loud to Nina when he hadn't even talked about it with Chris. She wasn't listening, so he kept talking.

"You can just disappear into someone else," he said. "Someone surprising, except not surprising, because you know the lines. No matter how fucked up they are, the characters, it's not as bad as how fucked up I am. Because, you know, their fucked-upness is art, and mine is just…here."

A horse tossed his head and nickered. Nina clicked her tongue at him.

"Of course, it's not like I really could do that for a living. Become some great actor or something. Only one percent of one percent of one per*cent* of actors get acting jobs." Isaac didn't know if that was true. It sounded true. He kicked the cold dust and watched it scuttle across the ground toward the hazy horizon. "Maybe even less than that."

The wind gusted, and if he hadn't been so surprised by her speaking at all, he might not have heard Nina say, "Someone has to do it, though."

"What?"

She raised her voice. "Someone has to get those jobs. Or there wouldn't be any Shakespeare. Or plays, or movies. Right?" The wind whipped her hair over her face.

"Sure," he said. "Someone gets those jobs."

She asked, tilting her head, "So why not you?"

When she didn't laugh, Isaac blushed, baffled and angry. He wanted to tell her, *Because I'm nothing. I'm from the Land of Nothing. I can't. It's impossible for people like us, from the sticks, broke, and stupid.*

She waited in his coat.

He wanted to shake her, push her down, kiss her. Instead, he just cleared his throat and said, low, "You have no idea how hard acting is."

A smile hit one corner of her mouth, lingering like a smudge. Nina turned and began walking away from him, her feet swishing through the frozen grass.

The sentry horse turned to face her, his front legs twitching a little. Nina didn't break her stride. Isaac said, "Nina, these horses are feral," but she ignored him and walked closer and closer. The sentry snorted at her, his tail flipping. She paused, as if taking his opinion into account. Then she continued her forward march.

"Nina, what are you doing?" Isaac hissed, but she couldn't hear him anymore. He took a few steps toward her retreating, fragile back.

Now, she stood right in front of the horse. Its black mane stood up like a Mohawk. She leaned forward into the stiff wind until they stared face to face, not an arm's length apart. Isaac was afraid that the horse would bash her, knock her out. He was afraid of a stampede. He was afraid of…he didn't know.

With a whoosh, Nina grabbed the sides of Isaac's coat and yanked them high above her head, like a bat.

The black horse reared onto its hind legs above the girl. She didn't move, her black wings flapping in the wind. The horse's crumbly front hooves pawed the air above Nina's tiny head, and he whinnied hard. Isaac imagined Nina's head smashing to pieces as the horse landed on her, her body crumpling to the ground under his hooves, irreversibly lifeless. He shouted and ran.

The horse twisted at the last minute. His hooves landed next to Nina's worn shoes. He pushed off, launching his body away from her as she stood motionless, still angled forward.

By now, the entire herd was galloping toward the ridge, moving as one beast, the black horse holding the rear. The ground vibrated under Isaac's feet, and the dry air filled with dust and the thumping of their rough, worn hooves. Their backs rippled as their muscles stretched and contracted under their hides, over and over in perfect action.

Isaac knew he should be watching them. He'd never see anything like this again. But he couldn't stop looking at Nina, transformed. Nina, with her smudgy smile, Nina with her black wings.

He caught up to her, panting. She let her scrawny arms drop to her sides. Suddenly small again in his coat, she grinned up at him through the din and dust.

"Acting," she said.

CHAPTER FOUR:
COPS AND ROBBERS

DONG HAICHUAN WAS BORN in China in the early 1800s. The youngest son of the youngest wife, he was the bullied runt in his family hierarchy. He left home as soon as he could.

At a place called Crouching Tiger Mountain, Dong Haichuan spied a broken-down temple. He tried to cross the river to get there, but the current was too ferocious. He was stuck. Just then, two monks approached and crossed the river as easily as if they were walking across a bridge. He asked them for help. They carried him across the water, lodged him, and taught him martial arts for almost two decades.

When he crossed the river again eighteen years later, trouble returned. Fighters fight, and Dong Haichuan, now thirty-six, was now the best fighter in China. He killed someone, which created vendettas, and more killings. Things got complicated, but nobody could touch him. Dong Haichuan was a wanted man, an uncatchable criminal.

Finally, the Imperial Court offered him a deal. They would clear his record and give him a job collecting taxes. He would teach martial arts to royals, and live in the Forbidden City. The catch was, he had to be castrated.

Many boys and men decided to become eunuchs at that time. There was good money in it. Only castrated males were allowed to live inside the Forbidden City. Life there was preferable to life outside, where you could be killed or beaten for no reason, by people just like him. Outside, open sewers tunneled the sides of the roads. Inside the Forbidden City, all was peaceful, even if you couldn't hold your urine.

Dong Haichuan took the deal.

After he recovered, he worked for the Courts. Then, with his top student Yin Fu, he traveled north. He extorted taxes from tyrannical authorities in the outer reaches of Manchuria, fought off bandits, traversed the Chinese countryside, and had a great old time. He was still beating people up. He was still undefeated. He was still doing the same things as before—roaming around, fighting, stealing, and killing people. But now he was a cop.

~

PUNCHING HER DUFFEL BAG in the early morning alley, Nina worried about the downturn in violent crime. Summer was usually her most lucrative time, when people loitered outside, drunk and angry at global warming. She socked away enough money to see her through the cold and snow season, when she often found herself shoplifting to eat, taking the odd factory shift, and ignoring increasingly urgent telephone calls from her landlord until summer's cash rained down again.

But this summer, everything was backasswards. Nina blamed the economy. She blamed psychotherapy. She blamed Oprah. She blamed herself. All she had to look forward to was yet another meal of lunchmeat and bananas, when this was the time of year for king crab and gourmet potato chips. Was this what happened in normal careers?

She gave the heavy bag an extra-hard punch, and stopped to adjust the sweaty tape over her knuckles. A staph infection had taught her to protect herself from her own gear, especially this bag, which was probably alive with bacteria, MRSA, tetanus, and hantavirus. She had split it open so many times it was, by now, constructed almost entirely of duct tape. The sand had settled to the bottom, where it felt like she was kicking solid rock, and the damp insides added to the weight.

Still, there was joy in it. She punched it for another twenty minutes, snaked her belt around the railing overhead, and began a set of pull-ups. The walls were beginning to collect the day's heat, which enveloped her body like a shell. Sweat was in her eyes when she heard from below, "Hiya."

She dropped down, panting. Nobody ever came into her alley, and definitely not at seven in the morning. She wrapped the end of the belt around her hand, staring at the man, who was standing alone in a wife beater and jeans, with a holster at his side.

His smile sagged. "You don't even remember me?"

Nina squinted, never good at faces. This guy was huge and blond and bristly, with a boxer's stooped shoulders. His eyes were so pale they matched the glare from the clouds. Acne as a teenager, but now he was coming up on thirty. He had plucked his white unibrow into two distinct eyebrows, but they were already growing back into each other, like twins conjoining. His nose had been broken until the cartilage was crushed smooth. Both of his ears had transmogrified into a permanent state of cauliflower. And, of course, there was that gun.

Nina's right foot slid back automatically, but the man seemed too clean to be a threat. She decided to slip past him, but he sidestepped, blocking her path. He grinned, but what his mouth was doing was disconnected from the blank expression in his eyes. "So, you punched me in the face." He pointed at his left cheekbone, which looked the same as the other one.

Now she remembered him. Months ago in a bar, he had reached for her breast, like it was his beer mug. She felled him, slipped his wallet out of his pocket, and ran out the back door. In her car, she opened the wallet to discover it had a police badge in it. The thing scared her so much she ran home and threw it into the depths of her desk drawer without looking at it again.

So she was finally going to jail. Confused by her own feelings of relief, she stretched her wrists out.

"I'm not going to arrest you." His voice was pleasant and sonorous, as if it had picked up momentum on its way from the inside to the outside.

Was he going to shoot her instead? Nina put her hands in the air. She wondered if she should run. But this cop just retucked his wife beater into his jeans and smiled. The holster remained snapped and untouched. Nina dropped her arms and pulled a cigarette from her shirt pocket.

"Filthy habit," the cop said. "Have you ever seen the inside of a smoker's lung?"

"How would I see that?" Lighting her cigarette, Nina glanced at him. "You're really not going to arrest me?"

His smile vanished so quickly she saw it had been fake. "Give me my badge back."

"I left you your gun," she said. "You still have your gun."

"I want the badge." He didn't say "need." He smiled again.

"If you had been in uniform, I would never have hit you," she said.

"Oh, that. I'm a detective. It's like, business casual."

"Get your boss to give you a new badge."

The cop laughed.

"You can probably get a counterfeit one on Colfax for fifty bucks," she said.

"I already did. Thanks. But I can't have my badge in the wind. It's traceable to me." When Nina shrugged, he asked with unnerving gentleness, "Do you even know who I am?"

"You're the cop I…from a few weeks ago, right?"

"I'm also Cage Callahan." He grew an inch, but his shoulders slumped. "Maybe you saw me fight on TV about eleven years ago? MMA?"

"I don't have a TV." Nina blew out a clotted stream of smoke. "Is Cage your nickname?"

"What?"

"Don't you guys all have nicknames?"

"Oh. No. It's 'Killer.' Cage 'Killer' Callahan." He half-shrugged. "A fighter retired right before my debut. So 'Killer' became available."

Nina remembered how he fell on her first punch, like a diving falcon.

Cage's upper lip tightened into a ridged line, transforming his fleshy face into a hard thing. "You caught me off guard. And I was hammered."

She tried again to mount the stairs, but this time Cage swung his whole body in front of her. The charge radiating from his skin was vaguely acrid. The white hairs on his arms glinted, and hers stood up. His skin smelled strong, like Lysol. She sneezed, and then twice more.

The smile worked its way off Cage's face. He snarled and "Bless you" wrested itself from his florid lips. Then he said it twice more, "Bless you bless you," his face etched with despair.

That was interesting.

Nina squinted at the glare from his immaculate sneakers. The cuffs of his jeans were ironed. His perfect shave shone in the sunlight. A drop of sweat appeared on his brow, and he pulled a plastic pack of tissues from his pocket, picked one out, and dabbed at his face with quick motions.

And she thought she had seen everything. "I never met a fighter with OCD before. Or a cop, for that matter."

Now that he was all cleaned up, Cage's ever-present smile was back. "It's a mild case."

"It must be. Blood and murder and all that."

"I work in the Robbery Unit." At Nina's face, Cage said, "The irony is not lost on me."

"What's it like, going from fighting to crime fighting?"

"Oh, it's fine. Like being a garbage man, except the trash is human. Better than being a junkie, anyway."

Nina agreed. Then she realized he was talking about her. "I'm not a junkie."

"Then why rob people?"

She flicked ash. "We can't all be cops. The world needs robbers, too, or there's no game." Apart from their guns, she wasn't afraid of cops themselves. The only real difference between a cop and a criminal was one bad day.

Cage said, "Your casual demeanor with me is interesting."

"You already told me you weren't going to arrest me."

"No. But." Cage leaned against the wall and sighed. "The thing is, there are rumors now."

"What rumors?"

"That I'm a tomato can and got knocked out by a bitch," he said pleasantly. "The night I met you, remember the people I was with?" Nina did. They had cheered. Cage said, "You hit me in front of the VP of Talent Relations for the biggest fight promotion company in the world. He poured a beer on my face to wake me up. That's not the kind of thing Antonio Ricardo Ricardito Gino Joseppe Irving Spina forgets."

"Who?"

"Antonio Ricardo Ricardito Gino Joseppe Irving Spina? The biggest fight matchmaker on the planet?" He shook his head at her blank look. "We were discussing my comeback."

People are always better in their imaginations, Nina thought. Cage might think he was just on a bad streak, but Nina could see his future, and it didn't hold a comeback. His eyelids puffed at the corners from occasional dabbling in whatever—confiscated drugs, veganism, urine drinking, creatine, condomed hooker sex. His skin was ruddy and bloated, as if it held too much sour blood and steroids for his body to effectively contain. He was flaming out. The rough terrain of his face was flushed bright with the changing season, summer to autumn, but he was going out in a quieter blaze than he had anticipated.

Cage said, "I'm asking nicely."

It was a reasonable request. She should give the badge to him, make a friend.

But if he had his badge back, he would then be free to arrest her. She'd be nothing to worry about. Now, she was a nothing with a stolen police badge. Jackson used to say, "It's not strength—it's leverage. Grab a pinky finger and you can move an entire man."

"It's in an undisclosed location," she said. "Not hard to find, but not easy, either. If something happened to me, it would certainly pop up. But until then, it's perfectly safe." This was all a lie—the badge was in her desk drawer at home.

Cage probed her face with his washed-out gaze. "Tell you what. Why don't we fight for it? Nina."

Her breath caught. "How do you know my name?"

"I'm a detective, dumbass." He smiled above Nina's head. "You know, I've never been in this alley until today. This place feels…exempt."

She knew what he meant. It was in-between. The oil slicks were more variegated, the bricks held more contrast, and the smog cleared away, just here, as if this particular alley had its own source of air and light.

Nina didn't like Cage in her alley. "I'm not part of your story," she said.

"Just fight me, chica. If I win, I get the wallet. If I lose, it's yours."

"It's already mine." *And I already beat you*, she thought. "I fight for money. Not hate, or whatever this is."

"I'm not sure if I hate you or love you."

Saying the word "love," Cage suddenly looked bigger, handsomer. He stood tall, relaxed, his eyes clear. His shoulders were big enough for her to rest her head on, without him even feeling the weight. He was a police officer. He was a smiling keeper of secrets, an armed person in an unarmed world. Could she rest there in his Lysol cloud? Or anywhere?

"This is already an unhealthy relationship," she said. When she lit another cigarette, her hand shook. Summer buzzed against her skin, itchy.

Cage stepped closer, looked in either direction, and kissed her.

His kiss was matter-of-fact, a prerequisite, like taking your pants off before sex. Nina tried to lean into him, but couldn't find her angle into his enormous body. She touched his cheek, and it slid from her fingers.

Cage disengaged from her mouth with a soft pop. He plucked the cigarette from her hand with perfectly groomed fingernails. Then he turned his back on her to stub it on the wall behind him.

Nina decided to choke him out.

She grabbed Cage's big shoulders for leverage, hopped up and jabbed both feet into the hollows of his knees. They buckled. The air sharpened as he thudded to a kneel.

The cigarette fell from his fingers. Before it touched the ground, she had already launched off the ground again onto his back, piggyback style. She locked her feet around his waist. He was already twisting toward her, a giant boa constrictor. Sweat had sprung to his skin, lubricating Nina's rear naked choke as she snaked her arm around his neck.

The sun poked Nina in the eye. Cage's Adam's apple chugged against the soft crook of her inner elbow. Realizing what had just happened, he yanked at her arms, but her other hand was already shelved against his head. He clawed backward at her face. She buried her face in his neck. He smelled of dandruff shampoo, expensive aftershave, and the kind of cheese you don't have to refrigerate. She was wondering what his diet was like when he whirled around and thrust himself backward against the wall.

"Oof," she said, sandwiched between brick wall and high-velocity Cage. Something happened to her ribs, her hip. But she held on.

He did it again, but she tucked her chin and braced for the impact. It came, harder than before, and she held on. She always held on.

Cage reached for his pocket holster, but his arm was slow, limp. He fumbled with the snap. By then, his head must have felt like a grape, about to pop out of its skin. The tiger tattoo on his flailing shoulder roared, retracted, slept. His body sagged downward. The gun rested, cupped in his hand. He relaxed in her arms. Whites lined the cracks of his partly-shut eyes.

Nina laid Cage down flat in the dry, hot street. She checked his sluggish pulse, his hot, wet breath on the back of her hand. She picked up the gun. It was so heavy. She caressed it for a second, then threw it in the dumpster. Washed in adrenaline, she climbed the fire escape to her apartment.

Nina didn't feel bad about what she had done. She felt as neutral as a bowl of water on a ledge. She was just showing him. Nobody really loves anyone, not really. It wasn't a constant, or a quality. The truth as Nina knew it: when your life is on its thin edge and you're on your last breath, you only have enough room in your heart to love one thing. Air.

~

ISAAC DROPPED THE PHOTOGRAPH and postcard onto the dashboard of the rental car, and Kate immediately snatched them both up. The postcard featured a movie still of Ronald Reagan tucking a chimpanzee into bed. It was from the film, *Bedtime for Bonzo*. The printed handwriting on the other side read: "Dear Nina. I am sorry about your tooth. I have a house here with an extra bedroom for you, and I turned my basement into a dojo. I will wait. Jackson." It was followed by an address, no phone number.

Kate put the postcard in her overalls pocket before pulling it out again to read it.

"Your hand's sweaty," Isaac said. "You'll smear the ink."

"Who is this man again?" she asked.

"Ronald Reagan. Ex-President of the United States."

Kate examined the card. Then, "No, the person who wrote on it."

"He was your aunt's teacher."

"Was he your teacher? Or daddy's?"

"No. I saw him occasionally, and Chris wasn't interested in karate. Nina mentioned him a little, when she talked at all. Which was never."

"Karate, like karate chops?"

"Yeah."

Kate karate chopped the dashboard. She karate chopped Isaac's arm. She karate chopped her bagel, which was already stale in the dry Colorado air. She flipped the postcard over. "The President of the United States was the daddy of a chimpanzee?"

"No, Kate. He was acting. It was fake."

"Like you?"

Irritated, he said, "Like his presidency." Then he realized that she had been talking about his acting. Not about his fakeness.

She studied the picture up close until she was cross-eyed. "Shouldn't you be nice to him?"

"Ronald Reagan? He's dead, honey," Isaac said, and instantly regretted it. "He had Alzheimer's disease, and bankrupted our country. His presidency led to George Bush's presidency, which led to George W. Bush's presidency, and the only good thing I can say about that is that I got to reuse my 'Impeach Bush' bumper stickers until I sold my Jeep, and they probably increased the value." He looked at Kate, whose mouth was open.

"You're weird," she said.

Isaac wondered if Nina even knew that her brother had been sick, was dead. AIDS is such an isolating disease, but even before that, Nina had been excised from Chris's life so completely, her silhouette remained in the space left behind.

So why did Chris will Kate over to a ghost? Isaac glanced at the little girl, who was narrating the sights of Denver to No-

Hair. "This is a gas station," she whispered. "This is some dirt." Her legs were strewn about the seat like a couple of Pick-Up Sticks. Shadows encircled her eyes. She still wasn't sleeping.

"If we don't find her this time, we can come back again, right?" Kate pushed and pulled on the automatic door lock button. The doors made a *chunk!* noise over and over.

"Stop playing with the car."

"Why?" She *chunk!*-ed it one more time.

"Kate," slow, rising. But at least she wasn't whispering and cowering, which, frankly, got on Isaac's nerves.

"Why don't we just look her up in the phone book?" she asked.

"She's unlisted. Or, she doesn't have a phone."

"Everybody has a phone," she whispered to No-Hair. She started licking her hands and smoothing down her own hair like a cat, straightening her overalls. She pulled down the visor mirror. She pinched her cheeks and bit her lips to make them red. "Why don't we look back in your old town?"

"Grand Junction?" Isaac tasted dirt, the way he always did when he thought of his hometown and 28½ Road.

It took until Isaac's adulthood to realize that normal towns don't have fractions in their streets. 28½ Road is exactly twenty-eight and a half miles from the Utah border. There is also 29⅝ Road, 30¼ Road, and so on. He always thought that if Grand Junction had a motto, it would be, "We're Not Utah." But it looked like Utah—stenciled with canyons, dry as alum. The valley was made of sawdust and petals, sunshine and frost. Despite the heat and thirst, in Isaac's day, there was a feeling of imminent prosperity in the air. See, there was oil in them there hills.

It's hard to imagine prehistoric whales and dinos swimming above Colorado's snowcapped peaks, but it's also hard to imagine that humans would come to burn the remains of these gargantuan animals in Kia Rios. When the prehistoric sea retreated, the lagoons filled with peat, coal, sand, and dinosaur corpses. This witches' brew turned into oil shale, which rose like bread and turned into the Colorado Rockies.

It wasn't until the 1970s that a hundred million years of causes and effects presented a one-time solution for the oil crisis. Exxon moved into the Western Slope with the objective of mining petroleum from what the Ute tribe used to call "the rock that burns." The plan was simple: strip mine the hills, and squeeze serviceable oil from the shale.

Grand Junction grew big. Then oil prices retreated in the early eighties. Oil shale was more trouble than it was worth. On a day locals called "Black Sunday," Exxon laid off their employees and skipped town.

Over the next year, Grand Junction dwindled to a third of its size, as people moved away to wherever there might be jobs. Home values halved. Partially-built office buildings sat fallow on their foundations. Banks sued, frantic. Schools sank into disrepair. Grand Junction turned into Grand Junkyard, and stayed that way for over a decade. Even after the town finally recovered, the Black family didn't.

The problem with poverty is that there's nothing to do except beat your children. Isaac remembered Chris's black eyes, the finger bruises on Nina's arms. There was no way to explain any of this to Kate. "Nina would never go back there," he said.

The address on the postcard led them to a yellow ranch-style home with purple petunias in front. As soon as they knocked, an older man poked his head out the door. Three feet below him, a beagle poked out his head, too.

The man was short and compact. He wore a faded, tight-fitting Hawaiian shirt and dress pants. His sparse hair was dyed a startling shade of black, the kind that absorbs light instead of reflecting it. He was Caucasian, with a perma-tan that had faded to a mottled yellow. His skin had an astounding number of wrinkles, like a piece of paper that had been repeatedly crumpled and smoothed out again. Isaac couldn't remember Jackson's face before, but he now recognized him immediately. The dog sniffed the air.

"Hi," Isaac stuttered, "Mr. Jackson. I-I was wondering if, ah. Um."

"I don't believe in your God," Jackson said and began to shut the door.

"No, I'm not—it's Nina, I'm looking for Nina. Sorry to intrude. Mr. Jackson, please." He snatched the postcard from Kate's hand and stuck it through the narrowing crack in the door.

Jackson picked the postcard from Isaac's outstretched hand. It took him so long to read it, Isaac wondered if he hadn't written it after all, or if he could, in fact, read.

Finally, Jackson waved the card in the air. "How did you get this?"

"Chris had it. Her brother. She had already left by the time it came to their house. I know it was a long time ago, Mr. Jackson, but we were hoping you might know where she is."

"Just Jackson. It's my first name." Jackson motioned them inside.

Isaac felt oversized inside the low-ceilinged house with its geriatric smells. The beagle thwacked his tail against the legs of the furniture. He crouched on the carpet and began peeing.

"No! Hank! Stop it!" Jackson shook the dog by his collar with a surprising strength. The dog stopped peeing, eyes round. Jackson threw a dishtowel over the spot and stepped on it with his slipper. "Submissive urination. He pees like a girl when he sees visitors. It's embarrassing." Jackson had a singsongy, truncated way of speaking, like he was distracted by the beat of a song in his head. His yellow shirt was tucked into his khaki pants so smoothly, his outfit almost looked like a bodysuit. Every remaining hair on his head was in place. Nina had said that he had gotten blown up in Vietnam. She said that he had killed twelve men with his hands. It was hard to believe from this man with a potbelly and freckles on his bald spot.

Kate held out her hand to the beagle, who tongued it. Jackson pointed at a distended couch. They sat on it and were instantly enveloped. It smelled like wet dog and old scrambled eggs. Jackson scrubbed at the pee spot on the floor and sprayed half a can of deodorant on it, and then the house smelled like deodorant, too.

"Now, then." Jackson finally sat on a folding chair. His mouth was an upside-down crescent moon. "Nina left her daughter behind?"

"Kate is Nina's niece," Isaac explained. "Chris's daughter. I'm Isaac."

Jackson looked so relieved, Isaac thought he was going to pee on the carpet himself. Jackson studied Kate, who squirmed under the weight of his gaze.

"Stop looking at me," she whispered.

"Kate!"

"That's okay," Jackson said. "I think I have something to eat." He trudged into the kitchen, Hank licking his leg all the way across the apartment.

Left alone, Kate got up to study the framed cross-stitch picture of a cowboy riding a horse. She poked her finger in the empty candy dishes.

Jackson padded back in, bearing a tray with coffee cups and a chipped plate with little round, flattish balls on it. He set the plate on the table. Cornstarch trembled on his fingers as he poured green tea.

Kate climbed into a chair, waggled her legs, and grabbed one of the round balls from the plate. She sniffed it and studied it at close range until her eyes crossed. She bit into it.

"Squishy," she said, mouth full. "What is it?"

"Omochi," Jackson said.

She squinted at the smooth, white cake before taking another minibite. "What's inside? Chocolate?"

"Red bean paste," Jackson said.

Carefully and immediately, she placed it down on the coffee table.

Isaac smiled at the old man, who didn't smile back. "I was friends with the Black kids," he said. "I remember seeing you with Nina sometimes. Do you still teach?"

"No. I quit karate. I'm retired," Jackson said.

"You seem young for retirement."

"I'm sixty-three. I get a VA pension."

Isaac lied, "You look much younger. What do you do now?"

The lines in Jackson's face multiplied. "This and that."

"Do you still practice Chinese medicine?"

"Here and there."

Kate said, "I know a girl in my school who's allergic to her own spit."

"What happens to her?" Jackson asked.

"Her mouth swells up."

"That sounds uncomfortable," Jackson said.

"She uses special toothpaste."

Jackson wiped something invisible on his pants. "So."

"Yeah. Okay." Isaac sat up. "We're looking for Nina. Her brother died."

Jackson's face elongated, his creases sharpening. "I'm very sorry to hear it. He was a nice boy." He looked at Kate. "Your father died, then."

"He died in the hospital," Kate said.

"You were there?" he asked. "With him?"

She nodded.

"It wasn't your fault," he said.

Kate's eyes grew wet, and then dried instantly in the arid air. She tugged at her sleeves, wiped her nose, stared at the dog.

Isaac leaned back, exhausted by his own failure. How did Jackson understand Kate better than Isaac did, after just a few minutes?

"How do you fit in?" Jackson asked him, sipping from his cup. "You're taking care of her?" He nodded at Kate.

"I have power of attorney over her, but not guardianship. That's supposed to go to Nina, wherever she is. I've had the power of attorney for two years, but it expires in about a month. Chris didn't think he'd last that—" he glanced at Kate. "We all want this thing to be settled." Isaac realized that he had just called Kate a "thing." "This...custody matter."

Everyone drank their tea.

In the silence, Hank started biting at his leg, and licking it over and over. Kate asked, "Why is he doing that?"

"The same reason dogs do everything. Because it feels good, smells good, tastes good." Jackson looked wise then, a doctor of obscure medicines. Isaac rested his bleary eyes on Jackson's still form. *I want to be a dog*, he thought. *I want to be his dog*. Isaac understood why Nina spent so much time with this man. He was sinking lower into the man-eating couch. He wanted to lie down and sleep for a hundred years among the yellowing lead paint and bean paste.

Jackson said, "I don't know where Nina is. I haven't seen her since I left Junction. We had a fight."

"About what?"

Jackson drank his tea. Kate kicked the chair harder and harder.

"You knew their mother, right? Before she vanished into the ether," Isaac said.

"Not the ether. Tokyo."

"You knew where she was?"

"I gave her the money for the ticket."

Something curled up inside Isaac. "You *what*?" After his mother left, Chris slept in Isaac's cluttered basement for days, peeing in cups and leaving them on the stairs for Isaac to empty. Nina stared for hours and hours at the sheets on the clotheslines. "Why?"

"She wanted to go."

"She had children! How could you?" Isaac was now yelling, yelling at a man in his own home.

"I didn't want her to do the things that desperate Asian women do."

"What? Something terrible, like stay and raise her family?"

"Ritual suicide."

Isaac's jaws flapped open, then shut. "Oh." His gaze hooked on a photo tucked into a mirror. It was the same one he had brought from LA, of the three of them. Isaac leaned over and pointed at his image with his thumb. "That's me. In the middle."

"I know."

The refrigerator hummed.

Jackson said, "You like to talk about yourself, don't you?"

Isaac cleared his throat. "Did, uh, Nina ever contact you after your falling out?"

"It wasn't a falling out. It was a fight."

"You didn't try to find her again? After you wrote this postcard?" Isaac picked it up off the coffee table and waved it in the air. He felt oddly invisible.

Jackson leaned back in his folding chair and glanced at the clock on the wall.

Kate tugged at Isaac's shirt, but he ignored her. "I mean, you were best friends. You were her only friend." Isaac opened his palms. "So you have no idea where she is. Or why, in twelve years, she never once looked you up."

"I don't know why!" Jackson suddenly shouted, his Hawaiian accent thickening. Kate shrank in her seat. "Sometimes people leave! Sometimes you leave, too, and nobody knows where anybody's going, and just like that, you lose them forever! This is America! It happens all the time!" Jackson popped up and clenched his hands into gnarled fists. Isaac's stomach contracted. He didn't want to be Jackson's dog anymore.

"I lost my friends, too! I lost everyone in my unit! You're asking me why?" The old man loomed, sweating. "Do you still keep track of everyone you once knew? Everyone you loved? Your favorite teacher? How about your first girlfriend?"

"No, sir."

"No! Sir! She's gone, or dead, and you don't know 'why' either! Huh!" Standing in profile, Jackson downed his tea, his throat chugging. Isaac held his own scalding cup in his shaking hand, wondering how the man could drink it like that without burning his throat.

He and Kate jumped again when Jackson slammed his empty cup down on the coffee table. A ceramic chip flew into the wall. Jackson pointed a crooked finger at Isaac's face. "You find Nina? Send her to me. I mean it. Or I'll find you." Jackson gave Kate a look Isaac didn't understand, and then stomped to the back of the house.

To hide his shaking lips, Isaac sipped the bitter tea.

After a minute, Kate whispered, "Is he coming back?"

After another minute, Isaac called out, "Mr., um, Jackson?" and then, "Sir?" He waited one second, two, before snatching the postcard and photograph from the coffee table.

Kate stared at the half-eaten rice cake on the table, picked it up, and put it in her pocket. She whispered toward the open door, "Thank you for the…thing."

They crept out.

As they drove away, Kate said, "You blew it."

CHAPTER FIVE: THE THEFT

James "Quick" Tillis was the first heavyweight boxer to last ten rounds with world champion Mike Tyson. When Quick took a Greyhound bus to Chicago to begin his fighting career, he was just a young cowboy from Tulsa. He disembarked from the bus in front of the Sears Tower, a cardboard suitcase under each arm. He dropped them, looked up at the skyscraper and shouted, "I'm going to conquer Chicago!"

When he looked down, his bags were gone.

~

Nina made some of her best money at happy hour, especially in the bars near the Financial District. It was like stepping into a different era, one where people still wore shoulder pads and thought the Republican Party was moral. Filled with bankers and lawyers too scared to go home to their frigid, mean wives or empty apartments, the preppy bars were rife with opportunity—plus they always had fancy french fries. Parking was a bitch around commuter time, though, and her Pinto was starting to make a clacking noise the radio couldn't mask, so Nina caught a bus.

Colfax Avenue is the longest continuous city street in America, and back when Nina had nowhere to sleep, she took the Colfax bus back and forth, dozing just short of REM. She had gotten to know the regulars—commuters, prostitutes, other homeless people. A man with bloodshot eyes and gray skin sometimes sat in the back, reciting the entire story of his life in relentless detail: how he lost his toes to frostbite while ranching outside of Gunnison; how he gutted salmon in Juneau until he cut off his index finger. Piece by piece, she heard about broken and lost limbs. She got occasional reruns, but she saved enough money for an apartment before she heard the whole story.

Nina didn't fear other people anymore, but she feared that kind of poverty. It also made her sentimental. Life was simple when all she had was one duffel bag in a train station locker, when her armpits smelled of powdered hand soap and brown paper towels. She didn't want to be hungry again, but she wanted to feel the lightness hunger brings. She didn't ever want to be poor again, but she did want to hear the rest of the homeless man's story.

The bus spit her out on Tremont and pulled away, vomiting exhaust. The street's heat radiated through the thin soles of her shoes.

She stopped in front of a chrome bar called Nemo's. Muffled noises leaked from inside—nasty laughs, tinkling barware. The windows showcased shadows of men with dark suits and loosened ties. A dirty boy in dreadlocks squatted next to the door.

"Aren't you out of your neighborhood?" Nina asked him.

"Working." He scanned her outfit and lit a hand-rolled cigarette. "Like you." Crouching, his weight was on his toes. It would be easy to kick him onto his back.

She pulled out a cigarette and said, "Got a light?"

"I am the light. Baby, what you need is fire." He clicked a purple Zippo and she leaned in. "So, chica, for a donation, I'll create an original poem just for you."

Lucky, Nina thought. She pulled a crumpled dollar from her pocket and dropped it into his hand. The boy looked at the dollar and recited, "Cheap chick gave me a buck. Fuck."

Unlucky. She tried to snatch the dollar back, but his fingers closed over it. She kicked him onto his back, dropped her cigarette on him, and went inside.

Inside the bar, it was a sausage fest. Eyes lit on her from the neck down, and dotted away. A poppy-faced happy drunk kept smiling at everyone, his suit riding up in front. Another man with skidding eyes ordered another tequila. He stared down the shot like it was an opponent before swallowing it neatly, wiping his lips with a napkin that never left his hand. He had frayed cuffs, though, and Nina's rent was due.

One guy at the bar, though—perfect. He wore a platinum Rolex with a pale blue watch face, which he flashed with a quick arm-jerk before asking his friend, "What time is it? Party time." His shirt was tailored, and a bloated diamond ring swung on a chain around his neck, as mesmerizing as a pendulum. Nina wanted it.

Rolex man tipped the bartender twenty dollars for his dirty martini, pinching the bill on either side and tugging it tight before laying it flat on the bar. Nina thought, *I'd better get things started before he blows all his cash.* "Are you using this chair?" she asked.

Rolex's friend leaned over. "No, ma'am, it's using us."

Nina flashed the friend a brief smile and sat next to Rolex, whose back was turned to her. He swiveled her direction partway and raised his voice so she could hear him over the bar noise. "...I told him, 'Don't sell the yacht. You might need it someday. With all those earthquakes, California's going to break off the continent and the Pacific Ocean will wash onto your doorstep.'

That's why I still have my little baby." He glanced at Nina. "Not that it's little. It's big. Very big."

"California isn't next to Colorado. It's next to Nevada." The friend glanced at Nina. "Where's Rhonda today?"

"Dumped her." Rolex guy fingered his necklace. "You know why I wear this diamond ring around my neck?" He turned his face so Nina could view his profile.

"Yep," his friend said.

"I wear it to honor the love of my life."

"I know."

"It was right after college, ten years ago. I got a job working at my dad's stock brokerage firm, making obscene money. Nothing like what I make now, of course."

The friend's smile drooped as he glanced at Nina, sensing that he had already lost the girl to the schmuck, as usual.

Rolex raised his voice. "I was twenty-two, and in love with the most beautiful girl in the world, Penny." He glanced around the bar, his gaze lingering on Nina. "Penny could have been a model. She had skin like, like," he shook his head. "Anyway. It was great skin."

"I know. I knew Penny," the friend grumbled.

"She wanted to get married. So I said, 'There's no way you can tame me. I was born here, and I've got cowboy blood.'"

"You were born in Connecticut."

"When she got pregnant, I bought her this diamond ring, but I couldn't bring myself to give it to her. I told her, 'Forgive me, for I know not what I do.'"

"Christ."

"I wear it as a reminder of the man I am, the man I can't help but be." Rolex turned his back to his friend, leaning in on Nina. "What about you? Married? Kids?"

"None that I know about," she said. She could see why he hadn't turned his face until then. He had a scar on his other cheek. It wasn't a knife fight kind of scar—more like a fishhook scar, puckered like an anus.

Rolex nudged his friend, who looked down at the oily surface of the bar. Then he said to Nina, "I'm better looking than you, so why don't you buy the next round."

Nina shook her head and tapped the bar in front of her, right where a drink should be.

Rolex smirked and pulled out his wallet. "I can tell you're the kind of girl who gets what she wants."

"And I can tell you're the kind of guy who'd insult me and ask for something in the same sentence."

His friend laughed. Rolex man said to him, "Stop laughing or I'll tell her about your herpes."

"I don't have herpes," the friend said. Then, to Nina: "I really don't."

"That's really douchey," Nina told the Rolex man.

"A what?"

She shouted over the bar din, *"Douchey."*

The corners of his mouth pulled downward. He said, more quietly, "Nobody talks that way to me."

"Not to your face, maybe."

His nostrils flared, one and then the other. "If you were a man, I'd kick your ass."

"If you were a man, I'd kick yours," Nina said. But this felt wrong somehow, like she was taunting a caged animal. *Ugh,* she thought, and spun away on her barstool.

Rolex pulled on her shoulder and turned her around again to face him. She wiped his hand off her shoulder. "Don't touch me," she said.

He wedged his knees between her legs, spreading them. "I'll do what I want to you," he said.

So she punched him in his open jaw. Every bit of her meanness exited her body through her fist as his jaw clacked against it. It was in him, now, and his face slackened at the impact. He fell off his stool.

The bar fell silent. Rolex blinked on the floor, but didn't get up.

Nina slipped off her seat. The friend's mouth was stuck open. Nina drained the rest of Rolex's dirty martini and wiped the brine from her mouth with her wrist.

"Forgive me," she told the friend, "for I care not what I do."

The wallet lay on the bar. She flipped through it. There must have been five hundred dollars in there. The bar collectively murmured as she deftly pocketed the wallet and then bent down to slip the Rolex from the man's damp wrist.

A flat male voice said, "Someone stop her." Nobody did. Nobody ever did.

She reached for the diamond ring. The chain left a red crease on his neck before snapping and snaking from her hand to the floor.

The Rolex(less) man opened one eye and said, thickly, "Not the ring."

The female bartender reached for a phone.

Nina looked at the diamond in her hand. "But I'd like a reminder of the man you can't help but be."

"I misspoke." His voice rasped so hard, Nina had to lean forward to hear him. "I found my girlfriend in Ohio, but she told me to fuck off." He groaned. "I keep it with me in case she changes her mind. Don't take it."

Nina spun the ring once around her finger. She dropped it onto his chest.

The man closed his eyes, just as if he weren't lying down on a barroom floor. "Everybody needs a little redemption," he said.

The crowd parted to let Nina pass through the bar, their hands up in finicky gestures. Untouchable. She erupted out the back door into the bright street, sirens in the distance. She couldn't breathe.

The air above the street condensed in the heat, making straight lines curve. Nina felt like she was swimming. She ran through a parking garage. As the sirens grew closer, she took a shortcut through a hotel where she had once spent the night with a German tourist, through an alley, through a back kitchen, and out the front of a pho restaurant.

She couldn't wait for the bus—she'd have to zigzag back to Capitol Hill on foot. What had she been thinking, anyway? The bus? This wasn't a desk job. You don't commute. She couldn't take success for granted. Jackson used to say, "Tether even a roasted chicken." A swell of loneliness mingled with the backwash of adrenaline. The sirens took a lateral turn, but she kept moving. The Rolex cut into her palm. She hoped it was real.

She caught a flash of red in the dusky air, a man carrying a big bunch of red roses, "I'm sorry" flowers. You can tell a lot about a person from the back of his head. He had an expensive haircut, the kind you have to blow-dry. *Same asshole, different pants,* she thought. This man would bring the flowers home to his wife. His wife would smell the roses, not the perfume on his neck, which he'd shower off the minute he got home. "Racquetball," he'd tell her. "I'm disgusting."

Later, Nina would remember the other details caught in the dirty filter of her memory: that he was smiling back at someone through a window, that he looked scared, that he looked familiar.

But right now, she only noticed flowers, crimson against the gray concrete. They were some other man's redemption, for some other woman, someone loved. Nina wanted them, too.

~

"WHAT IF SHE'S DEAD?" Kate asked, carefully carrying her fast-food tray.

"She's not dead." Isaac pointed with his elbow at an empty table by the window. "Sit there."

On their way to the table, a boy Kate's age with froggy glasses stuck out a foot to trip her. Isaac opened his mouth, but Kate had already stopped. She looked down at the foot, and then at the kid's freckled face.

"I'm an orphan," she told him.

He withdrew his foot slowly, sneaker scudding against the carpet.

Jesus, Isaac thought.

They sat, and Isaac rubbed his forehead. Kate leaned over her beige tray, which was covered with food in varying shades of beige—beige bun, beige french fries, Sprite. Isaac squirted ketchup on the tray for color, and went back to rubbing his temples.

By day three of their trip, they had gotten lost eleven times, and were no closer to finding Nina than when they started. Isaac checked his list, scarred with cross-outs. They had visited every Nina Black listed in the Denver-Boulder metro area. Each person at the door was exactly wrong—a short African American woman, a sixteen-year-old girl, a housewife with a lazy eye, a shut-in who weighed at least four hundred pounds, and an elderly woman who kept saying, "Actually, I don't know *what* my name is."

They tried other approaches. Isaac's ideas: the courthouse, DMV and Voter Registration. Kate's idea: asking strangers on the street if their name was Nina. Both methods yielded nothing.

Maybe she was dead after all. A seventeen-year-old runaway from the sticks—what were the chances she had survived that? Or, she could be anywhere in the world. She could be anything in the world. She most likely wasn't a veterinarian, or a stay-at-home mommy. Probably drugs, or porn, or jail. Nina had always been on the outside of things. She used to cut her classes, not out of rebellion but out of shyness. She was only good at bad things—the trumpet, math, the Dewey Decimal System. She was a spectator to slow disasters. Chris and Isaac had been the ones to dream freely, driving with the top off the Jeep on those dusty nights in the desert, breathing the changing air, believing that their lives were bigger than they had originally thought.

"What about her?" Kate pointed at a prostitute in a plastic skirt. "Or her? That looks like her." She pointed at someone in an evening gown walking an Afghan hound, carrying a knotted bag of dog shit.

Isaac shook his head. "That's a man in women's clothes."

"Maybe her?" An earth mother wafted past, robes floating in the breeze.

"She's just one of the archetypes." He sipped bitter coffee from a Styrofoam cup. "The average American moves twelve times. There's no guarantee she's here."

"You said this was the best place. If it's the best, that's where she is."

Isaac sighed. He forgot that Kate couldn't discriminate between theory and practice. "I think we have to give up for now and go home." Kate dug her chin into her chest. This obviously wasn't what she wanted to hear. She wanted to hear that Nina was just around the corner and ran a candy store, was what Kate wanted. "I have a job back in LA next. We'll look there, too."

"She's probably not there, either," Kate said. "Probably she's not anywhere."

"How can she not be anywhere?"

"I know people die," she said. "You don't have to lie to me."

Her face looked like spring snow, white powder with a clear, hardening crust on the surface. It made him uncomfortable. "She just moved, is all."

"I'm so mad, I want to eat my whole hamburger!" Kate tried to stuff the entire thing in her mouth.

"Oh, come on. Cheer up," he said. "Tell a joke."

She said, mouth full, "Why did the monkey fall out of the tree?"

"I don't know. Why?"

She swallowed four times before all the food went down. "It was dead."

Okay, so she was a little upset. Isaac, on the other hand, felt tentatively elated. These few days were like a karmic do-over. By acting the role of parent, he had convinced even himself. He had bossed Kate around, and she (magically) did what he said. Eat your vegetables, don't jump on the bed, stay quiet for sixty seconds, do it, do it or I'm going to count to three. Hey presto, he was a father! Isaac! He tried a smile on her. She grimaced back. He was Kate's new dad, one who would honor the traditions of the old one. He thought of the fathers he had seen, his own father. His father had worn flannel shirts and baggy Levi's. Isaac could wear that. Nina was gone, and Isaac had done everything reasonable. He was a big, happy, reasonable man. An ideal father.

"Would you feel better if I bought you a beige apple pie?" he asked.

Kate's face was retracted into a full-blown scowl. "No." Then, when she realized that this meant that she wouldn't get any, she amended, "Yes."

He walked up to the counter and ordered from an old Asian lady, glancing back to make sure that nobody touched Kate. Was this what parenting meant? Always wondering if strangers were pedophiles? "That's my daughter over there," he tried saying to the cashier. It sounded okay. "She's mad at me."

The McDonald's cashier pointed out the window at a flower stand on the sidewalk. "Buy her flowers. Every woman loves roses." Tan powder flaked off her face when she smiled and handed him the apple pie.

Come to think of it, Isaac had never bought a female person flowers. "Does that actually work?"

"I've been married for forty years to the same sonofabitch. So, yes."

Isaac walked back to the table and dropped the cardboard-wrapped pastry onto Kate's tray. He watched her eat.

At age eight-going-on-nine, Kate was a blend of newly discovered likes and dislikes. She liked cheese, but only if it was orange. She hated shoes, stockings, and the clips girls put in their hair. She liked dolls in antique stores, lamps where you pulled a string to turn them on, and record albums, which she called, "big, black CDs."

She liked Isaac, but he was no Chris, and they both knew it, no matter how much TV Isaac let her watch. Chris used to tell him that he wished he could die at his best, so Kate could remember him as a better man. As it was, she only remembered him sick with, as she called it, "the AIDS."

Kate did not like the AIDS. She was afraid of catching the AIDS. Isaac tried to explain to her that you only get it from sharing blood. One day, Kate heard her teacher say that she and her parents "share the same blood," and she ran home screaming. Chris had been sleeping, so Isaac tried to contain the problem. "Kate, that's just a metaphor."

"What if the metaphor came true?"

"It can't. For example, if someone says your cheeks are like apples, it doesn't mean that you can eat them or make pie out of them."

"You *could* make pie out of them." She picked at her dress. "Do you share blood with anyone?"

"No. I use protection."

"Can I have some protection?"

"You don't need it. You don't sleep with anyone."

"Sleeping gives you the AIDS?"

"No. Sleeping with—listen, forget it, okay?" Even as she said, "Okay," he realized that, in her eyes, he was already as good as dead, too.

Right before Chris died, Kate said, "Grownups are like one bag of candy." She liked candy and Isaac had thought she meant something good by it.

Now he realized he had been wrong; it was *one* bag of candy. No matter how big the bag, there's only so much to go around, and someday, the bag empties out and drifts away.

With the side of a thumbnail, he scraped at a smear of pie on her chin. "Kate. I understand that you're afraid. And maybe you think—just a little—that by finding your aunt, we're going to get Chris back."

Her eyes ticked to the side.

"Chris is gone, honey. I wish it weren't true, but it is. There was nothing you could do."

"That's what *you* say."

Her voice was so tiny he had almost missed it. "What?"

She looked out the window.

"You couldn't save him, honey. Didn't anyone ever tell you that?" But who would have told her that besides him? "It wasn't your job to save him."

She turned back toward him, her face red and hot. "Whose job was it? Yours?"

Her gaze threw him off, made him blush. "No," he stuttered. "Nobody's job. Nobody saves anyone. Nobody can do that."

"You're wrong," she shouted. "Anybody can do that! Anybody!"

He was not wrong. He was male. He hadn't been fed the pink plastic princess diet since birth. *That's the problem with relationships,* he thought. *Girls grow up on Disney bullshit, and boys never grow up at all.*

Best to prepare Kate for heterosexuality now. "You can't go around trying to save people. They call that 'codependency.' Which is bad. It's better to just save yourself." He hated the grim feel of his own mouth, so he tried another smile. "We're on our own. Together."

"What about Nina?"

"Exactly. She's gone, who knows where. It's time to give up and go home."

"There are gangs there," she said.

What did Kate know about gangs? She was eight. She thought gangs wore leather jackets, snapped their fingers in front of their chests, and chanted, "When you're a Jet, you're a Jet all the way." "Our life is in LA," Isaac said. "It's warm there. It's happy."

"I'll kill myself," Kate said.

"What?"

"I'll. Kill. Myself." Her face was flat and ordinary, as if she had said nothing at all.

Isaac felt dizzy, like he was going to pass out on the disgusting carpet. "I'm stepping out for just a second, okay? I'll be right outside. Just for some air. Don't talk to anybody."

Isaac walked outside and took a deep breath. Away from Kate, he felt instantly better. *Ten more years of this,* he thought. He walked to the flower vendor. *She's eight. She wouldn't kill herself. Every woman loves roses.*

Isaac reached into his pocket for money. This would require a change, being a father to a semisuicidal orphan. A guardian, he meant. He could fix this. He'd just have to find a woman to help, the kind who made to-do lists and carried a banana in her purse. The roses were pretty, but Kate would have to watch out for the thorns. He picked out a red bunch and handed a twenty to the vendor, glancing back at Kate and waving through the window. She didn't wave back.

No, he'd just have to consider Kate first in everything. He'd no longer be able to take a woman home on a whim, a woman he didn't like much. He wouldn't be able to buy a motorcycle. He'd have to go to PTA meetings and maybe get a subscription to that Martha Stewart magazine for the recipes, although that might send a bad message, Martha being a felon—

The roses were snatched from his hand and gone with a blur of black legs.

He looked down at his palm. He could still feel the imprint of the plastic wrapping. He scanned the street right and left, but he couldn't see his flowers. It had been too fast.

The Mexican vendor held up his hands. "No es culpa mia, señor."

Isaac frowned and adjusted his tie. Was this some kind of scam? *Fuck it,* he thought, and dug his hand into his pocket for another twenty. He turned around to reassure Kate that he'd buy her another bunch, but the window was empty.

He shaded his eyes and squinted. Kate wasn't at her table. He walked to the window, peering through—where was she? He had told her not to move. Then he tracked a blur to his left.

Kate's green knee socks pumped like pistons, outside on the city street, away from him.

It took a second for him to react. "Kate!" he shouted. "Stop! Stop—there! I'm counting to—" She disappeared around the corner.

He ran after her.

By the time he turned the corner, Kate was far ahead of him, running up a hill toward the Capitol building. Her skirt flapped behind her. She was chasing a lady in a black miniskirt, black stockings, black leather jacket, black hair, white face. The lady was running with a bunch of red flowers in her hand, brushing her leg with every stride. Isaac's roses? Kate ducked her head and picked up her knees higher. Isaac was already gasping from the altitude, but he kept after her. She was a stain on his eye. She turned a corner and vanished again. "Shit," he panted.

As he rounded the corner, he caught sight of Kate's dress. Magenta is a color you can see for miles. She was way down the street, hair flapping at her sides. "Kate! Kate!" he yelled. "Stop! I'll buy you new flowers!" She turned into an alley and yet again he lost sight of the two figures, the lady in black and his child, his…guard? His charge? Whatever. Kate.

Isaac skidded into the alley behind Sancho's Broken Arrow, sprinting past openmouthed dumpsters, the brick backs of buildings, car bays. He tried to dodge a slick spatter of oil, but caught the edge of it and almost fell in his dress shoes, his sports coat, his Dolce tie. "Shit," he muttered again, slipping, and then he got some purchase on a patch of dried mud. Sweat slid down his spine.

A turning bus obscured his vision for one terrifying second, and there she was again. She was beginning to lag behind the woman in black. The woman's inky figure streaked down an alley, looking back, leaking petals, eyebrows up. Kate clutched her side as she ran.

By the time Isaac caught up to her, Kate had stopped, her chest heaving, bent over. She was looking up at the lady, who was taking the creaky steps of a metal fire escape two at a time. Isaac skidded to a stop, gravel crunching.

Kate's breath jagged in and out of her body. Isaac crouched over, also panting. So quickly he had lost her and recovered her, he was still feeling it all—the loss, the elation, the anger, the seven stages of grief and their instant nullification. He worried that he would burst into sudden, useless tears. He rested a hand on her shoulder.

A voice from above said, "Hey. You." The lady in black leaned over the fire escape rail. Her hair surrounded her pale face like an oil spill. She dropped the roses over the side. They fluttered through the air, petals flashing as they fell.

Kate reached up and caught the bouquet in her arms like it was a baby. When they looked back up, the woman had already slipped inside.

Kate turned to Isaac, clutching the crimson roses to her chest. Her cheeks were smudged with dirt and sweat, and pushed up in her face in a funny way. She looked strange.

Then Isaac realized that she was smiling. Kate hadn't smiled since before her father got sick. She had a new missing tooth. She pushed the hair from her bright face. Isaac forgot everything he was planning to say.

"That was her," Kate said.

~

"WE ARE NOT GOING up there. Out of the question," Isaac said. He reached for Kate's hand. "March."

Kate crossed her arms, the roses pressed against her chest. One beheaded itself and dropped to the pavement. "Why can't we just ask her?"

Isaac felt gritty and sweaty. "First, we're going back to the hotel to clean up. Then we're taking a standby flight back to LA. Now throw those flowers away. They're dirty."

Kate clutched the roses tighter, and silently pointed with her elbow at the fire escape.

"That's not even her," he said.

Kate blinked hair out of her eyes. "You don't know that."

"You're forgetting that, out of the two of us, I'm the only one who's ever seen Nina." He wiped his forehead. "Listen. If we're going to get along, there are a few things we have to settle. First, you do not, and I repeat *not*, run away like that. What if a car hit you? What if someone abducted you? What would I do…then?" Isaac stuttered to a stop.

What would he do? He had a brief vision of his old life returned to him, free of charge. Sleeping with whomever he wanted. Traveling at will. No obligations, no inconveniences, no kid menus. No daily, minute-by-minute reminders of Chris. No Kate, ever again, for the rest of his life. He would be completely cut from every tie, every point of connection in this world. He would disappear.

"She looks just like my dad," she said.

He tried to focus his eyes on Kate's. "Kate, when you miss someone, sometimes you see their face a lot. I see Chris's face all the time. Sometimes I almost chase after strangers, too."

Something in a mouth, or a set of ears, and he was reaching forward, almost touching a stranger for the sake of whom they were not. "It's normal. But it doesn't bring him back."

"Are we talking about you again?"

You brat, he thought and looked away, down the odd dead end alley. You could hear the street beyond it, but all you could see was the back of a brick building, "Guns 'N More" scrawled on the back door. He said, "Regardless, that isn't Nina."

When he turned back to face her, Kate was already scurrying up the fire escape.

"Hey," Isaac barked. By the time he reached the railing, she was halfway up the steps. "Kate, get down here. Right now." She was at the top now, peering down at him. "I'm going to count to three. One. Two."

She was already inside.

What had happened to his wimpy child-mouse? That was it. When they got to LA, he was going to send her a child therapist, a chubby one with puppets and juice boxes and Rorschach blots of cows and horses and crap like that. That'd fix her. He ran up the stairs and swung through the door.

He tried to ignore the hallway stench bomb of old curry and dry mold. Kate was already talking to a large African American woman in a doorway. The woman pointed down the hall. "Number three, I think," closing her door. Kate ran over to apartment three and knocked frantically, glancing at Isaac as he strode over, index finger out. "That's it. You're grounded."

"What's grounded?" she asked.

Isaac grabbed her shoulder but she wriggled free. The door opened.

The first thing Isaac noticed was the delicate hollow between the woman's collarbone and her neck. Her shirt almost covered it, but he could see the shadows there, highlighted with a light sheen of perspiration. He found his hand twitching, almost reaching out for that soft space. *Jesus, I need to get laid,* he thought, and glanced at the woman's face.

He knew her with his body before he recognized her with his mind. Her lips, her eyes, her forehead. But older, more put together, as if her awkward teenage features had finally learned to live with each other. Her hair was the same as Chris's: lampblack, coarse and straight, with blue and red shining in it. A wisp drifted into her eye. She blew it away, like Chris used to, like Kate still did. It had to be Nina—other people didn't look like that, all angles and witchcraft. She had that scar on her chin. She looked like Chris. She even smelled like Chris did, like someone's lawn. He hadn't expected this, the relief at seeing his dead friend's eyes in another person's face.

Isaac was suddenly sick with missing him.

"You made a mistake," Nina said. "This is harassment. And, if I may say so, ridiculous."

"Nina. Is it you?" He felt like he was speaking a foreign language. *You? You?* echoed in his head. "It's you, isn't it?"

She was quiet for a moment. Then she said, "I don't know." She stood first on one foot, and then another. It was the signature of his hometown—always keeping your feet moving in hot weather so the ants didn't crawl up your legs.

"I can't believe this." Isaac was grinning like a clown. "Nina Black."

God, she was pretty. Well, not pretty. Striking, though. When they had been kids, softer looks were popular—aqua eyes and tan skin. But Isaac's tastes had changed in the bleached light of Los Angeles. He preferred Nina's contrast, the chiaroscuro of her face. Twin pink spots flushed her cheeks and highlighted her cut eyes. Now that she was here, real and slightly sweaty, it seemed ludicrous that they had been looking so hard, that she hadn't been with them all along.

"Who the hell are you?" She stepped closer and squinted, still a little nearsighted.

Just as he was about to say his own name, her eyes swelled and she said, "Isaac?" She seized both sides of his face. "My God." He felt himself solidify in her eyes: Isaac Dickson, friend of Chris. He grabbed her.

He held her tight, surprised by her warmth, and the response that jolted through his body. All this time, he had forgotten that she had been, well, his friend, too. She was solid and vibrant in his arms, like an animal. He didn't know if he had ever hugged her before, but he now wanted to climb inside this familiar stranger who knew him better than anyone else did anymore.

They broke apart and stepped back. Kate, not to be outdone, gave Nina a miniature football tackle herself. "Wow, you have a daughter," Nina said. "Jesus, it's been, what?"

"Twelve years."

"Twelve—" Kate was still hanging on tight to her thigh. Nina looked down at her. "Hi." She scrabbled the top of Kate's head with her fingertips. "What are you doing? Why are you in Denver? Where are you living?"

"Los Angeles. I'm an actor."

Nina smiled, politely trying to dislodge Kate from her leg. "So you did it. One percent of one percent of one percent. That's you."

"That's me." He was surprised she remembered. "What do you do?"

"Oh, I'm, I'm in finance." She started, as if from sleep. "Sorry, I'd invite you in, but it's a mess in there. Maybe we could go somewhere for a drink," she glanced at Kate, "of juice." She stepped into the hallway. Isaac caught a peek at the unopened junk mail carpeting the floor inside. "You know, it's the strangest thing, because I just called your number in LA. A few times, actually. I've been looking for my brother. I didn't want to leave a message." She laughed like she was embarrassed. "I tried your old house before that. Your mother never picked up."

"She's still kind of reclusive."

"I remember." They were quiet, thinking of the stacks of old newspapers and dented cans covering the windows, the apocalyptic hoard that had conquered his parents' house.

Nina placed a slender hand on the doorframe, gripped it a little. "Is Chris in LA?"

"Um, he's, yes, still there. Technically."

"Is he still mad at me?"

"No. I think it's safe to say that he's not still mad at you." The fluorescent light buzzed overhead. Kate stood on one leg like a stork.

Isaac hadn't planned this part out. In fact, he hadn't really planned on seeing Nina at all. Now she was standing and breathing in front of him, he didn't know what to say. He had never told anyone that her brother was dead before.

This was going to suck.

He mentally inventoried the plays he had been in, movies he had seen. Maybe he should go to a quiet place somewhere, get her to sit down, buy her coffee. Give her lots of verbal warnings to warm her up. Offer his shoulder to cry on once the crying started, which it would—after all, she was his family.

Of course, she should have been there.

She was his sister, whatever that meant. As an only child, Isaac didn't understand it, siblings. So they had common ancestors, spent some time together as children. He thought of all the women he'd lived with, spent intricate time with. He didn't even remember their middle names. They could be dead, too.

He looked down at Kate, studied the white part dividing her smooth hair in two. Nina didn't even recognize her brother's daughter, who was now staring at her aunt with a terrible hunger, like she wanted to take a bite out of her. Nina didn't even know Chris had been sick. Her eyes held only questions, no answers, no sorrow, yet. He studied the exact shape of her mouth, the top lip curved like a bow, the bottom lip the slash of a thick, fallen arrow.

Isaac had missed her, too.

Why hadn't she been there, taken some of the burden off him? He felt so guilty that he hadn't visited Chris in the hospital, when it should have been Nina instead, all along. It wasn't his responsibility, but hers. Did she really think she had the luxury of time? People die, fast, while you're looking away. He glanced at her scuffed boots, her short fingernails, her black shirt pilling along the seams. He had needed her. *He* had. He was furious. He wanted to grab her, to slap her. He hated her, her smile, her dark eyes that had seen nothing at all.

"This is his daughter," Isaac said.

Nina looked at Kate.

"Chris is dead," he said.

PART
TWO

CHAPTER SIX:
SEVEN TIMES DOWN, EIGHT TIMES UP

THERE IS NO BEGINNING or end to fighting, but the official history of martial arts began with Bodhidharma. He was born in 482 CE to a warrior-caste family in India. After his father died, he requested ordination as a monk. The twenty-seventh patriarch told him to spread the teachings of Buddhism to China, one thousand miles away.

It takes a long time to walk one thousand miles. Bodhidharma experienced it all—the Himalayas, bandits, thieves, starving people, the kindness of strangers. He ended his pilgrimage at the Shaolin Temple in northern China, where he taught an intense form of meditation now called Zen.

The monks tried to do it, but they were too weak for the rigors of the practice, so Bodhidharma started them on a schedule of exercises based on animal fighting techniques. The monks practiced and practiced, perfecting and augmenting their moves. Renegade resistance fighters often took refuge in the monastery, adding secret fighting techniques of their own. The fighting style evolved into Shaolin. The monks were rumored to be unbeatable.

After a while, Bodhidharma decided to teach no more. He retreated to a cave, to end his days in meditation. Pilgrims visited from all over China, begging him for instruction, but Bodhidharma ignored them. For nine years, he sat facing a wall all day and all night. It's said that his shadow became permanently etched into the cave wall. Some say that he grew so frustrated at himself for falling asleep during meditation, he cut off his eyelids. Where he cast them aside, the first tea tree grew.

Others say that, because Bodhidharma sat in meditation for so long, his limbs fell off from disuse. He is often depicted as an armless, legless orb. The Japanese call him "Daruma." They make dolls of him—round, red papier-mâché balls with blank disks as eyes.

On the New Year, you buy a Daruma, make a wish, and draw an eyeball in one of the empty circles—only one. Daruma inspired the proverb, *Nana korobi ya oki:* Seven times down, eight times up. The dolls are weighted at the bottom, and if you get frustrated by your thwarted desires, you can smack the thing and it'll topple back upright, one-eyed and infuriating.

When your wish comes true, you color in the other eye.

When your wish doesn't come true, you turn Daruma's face to the wall. At the end of the year, you float it down a river, or burn it into nothingness. This is how you give up a dream.

~

ISAAC'S WORDS FELL INSIDE Nina's ear and slid along a track until they fell into their proper slots inside her, like pachinko balls. Without sound, it would have just been a man's mouth moving in a doorway. What congealed the words into meaning was the sound wave they traveled on, which was physics, which was theory. Isaac's drawn face hovered in front of her. Nina had loved him once. She had once loved a boy named Isaac, and now he was in her doorway, a man in an orange tie. Orange was just a specific use of light, which was again physics, which was only theory. He leaned forward. She could punch him. It would be easy. It would be nothing.

She slammed the door in his face.

The wood felt cool against her back. It vibrated as that Isaac impersonator knocked on it from the other side. She heard his little midget kid ask something, her high voice curling up at the end. Nina locked the deadbolt and turned toward the glaring window, the light there. Chris wasn't dead, not when she had yet to get her shit together. If he was dead, he could see her right now. He knew all about Nina, and that was impossible. Nina didn't even know all about Nina.

"Wake up," she said. She punched her leg, hard. Nothing. She punched it harder, right in the belly of the muscle.

Now she couldn't walk right. She limped into the kitchen and grabbed a fork from a drawer. She jabbed it into her arm. The tines made plucking noises as she pulled them from her skin. Four red dots grew and smeared little trails down her forearm.

Blood, bruise, and pain, and a fist still banged high on the door, with small, polite knocks clustering below. What was it going to take to transition this nightmare into her waking, everyday one, full of blunt force trauma and possibility? Real or not, she knew what she had to do. In dreams and horror movies, you always open the door.

There they still were, their fists poised in midair— theoretical Isaac and the little girl. She wondered why these particular people were in her dream. Did Isaac represent Nina's animalistic desires, her past, her fear of rejection? Was the little girl a manifestation of her guilt, or her lighter, brighter shadow self?

She'd figure it out. She'd see a shrink and analyze the shit out of this one. She waited for Isaac to turn into a moose or a chest of drawers, or start flying around the room quacking, or any of the usual things that happened in her dreams. Her arm was starting to hurt, and some blood dripped onto the floor.

"Nina," Isaac said.

Maybe it was a hallucination, not a dream. Maybe you can have LSD flashbacks without ever having done drugs. She wished she had done drugs. Maybe she could do them now, and this would be a premature flashback. Or maybe the space-time continuum had curved just for her, just for now.

But Nina knew she wasn't that special. This couldn't have been her imagination, even if she had one. Isaac's image was his own, in ways she hadn't remembered until now, like the way his shoulder hitched up to his ear when he felt bad, and the dimple that formed in one corner in his mouth when he frowned. He vibrated like a cello. He smelled like home.

"No," she said. The word must not have made it out of her mouth, because this Isaac kept on talking, saying words and more words, advancing, backing her into her apartment, the little girl dragging behind.

Why don't I feel anything? Nina wondered. Then, *Why don't I hear anything?* Because Isaac was still talking, eyebrows shifting around his face in expressions that were supposed to mean something—concern, sadness, remorse—but she couldn't hear anything besides the sound of rushing water. She didn't feel right. She clutched her shirt above her heart, which was cracking open, bloodless, an empty eggshell. The air pixilated and turned white. Isaac stopped talking. He reached for her.

She blacked out.

~

NINA WOKE UP WITH a finger in her face.

She lay on her lumpy futon sofa in a position so uncomfortable she could tell someone else had placed her there. A little girl poked her cheek over and over with a finger as sharp as a knitting needle. Groggy, Nina batted the hand away.

At first, the kid looked like she might cry. Then she shouted, "She's alive!"

"That's good," someone male yelled from the vicinity of her kitchen. The little girl stared at her.

"Who the fuck are you?" Nina asked.

The little girl recoiled and bolted up the stairs to the loft.

It took a moment to realize that the male voice in the kitchen was Isaac. He was really here.

Nina tried to sit up, and sank back down on the sofa. Her head felt like the inside of a diaper. That girl softly rustled upstairs in the loft. Isaac, on the other hand, was making crashing noises in the kitchen. He was either looking for a pot or making a bomb.

Nina felt cored, like a leaky, rotten apple. Everything looked different, but not. Her apartment had the same dirty dishes on the floor, the same squashed bug on the wall. She suddenly felt empathy for that bug, the bug she had herself crushed the day before with a shoe. The same furniture was here; the same pictures hung crooked on the walls. But now they existed in a new, backward world where her brother was dead and Nina was alive.

Isaac emerged from the kitchen and handed her a mug of steaming water, a teabag drowned in it. It was even worse that he was nice. "Are you okay? Should I call an ambulance?"

Nina shook her head at the bloated teabag. Her body trembled. She marveled at Isaac's low voice, his man-body in expensive clothes, moving around her living room. He looked as beautiful as a Michelangelo, or maybe she just had a concussion.

"How's your head? You smacked it on the floor pretty good when you fell."

Nina groped her skull. A lump swelled in back.

"Have you ever fainted before?" Isaac asked.

"I don't faint. Didn't."

"It's my fault. I should have been more…subtle." Isaac's gaze traced her face, then he picked up her orange phone. "I'm calling an ambulance."

She admired the take-charge tone in his voice, the way he turned his back on her to dial. "No, don't." When he didn't hang up, she said, "Please. I won't go."

"You should get your head checked out."

"What else is new?" Her voice sounded weird, as if she were her own ventriloquist dummy.

Isaac hung up the phone, wiped off a chair, and sat on it. He glanced at the dust bunnies in the corners of the room, the crooked lampshades. He leaned over and picked up the list of Chris's names, filled with cross-outs and notes scribbled in the margins. "There sure are a lot of Chris Blacks."

"That's just California. I was going to try Chicago and New York after that."

"How did you know we were there?"

"I didn't, but California was the only place he ever talked about. Does he still have that car?"

"The Oldsmobile? No, that broke down in Nevada. We hitched the rest of the way." Isaac flinched, as if from an old injury. "That was pretty cold, stealing his money and leaving him with your father like that." When Nina started crying again, he said, "Aw, shit. I shouldn't have come."

"I would have found out anyway. Someday." She was glad he was there. His face was the only thing that kept the room steady. Something in the loft clattered. They both looked at the ceiling.

"That's Kate," Isaac said. "His daughter. Katrina Black."

"Chris has a daughter?" *Had,* she thought, *had, had.*

"His wife's name was Bethany."

Chris with a wife. That made no sense. Nina remembered when he thought girls were boys with their penises cut off.

"She died when Kate was four," Isaac said. "Bethany contracted AIDS first."

"How did—Bethany—get it?"

Isaac looked out the window. "She never believed in tests. She said, 'If I die, I die.'"

"So, she killed him."

"It's not like that. When she found out, she was wrecked. We all were. She was a good person. You'd have liked her. She was likable."

"You slept with her, too."

"No. No, I did not." His chest rose and fell inside his shirt.

"What did Chris do over there?" It felt funny to ask about her own brother.

"He was an auto mechanic. Oil changes, mostly. He took online courses in Italian. He met Bethany playing Ultimate Frisbee when he was twenty, got her pregnant, then they got married. They were happy, though. For a while."

This was a Chris Nina had never met. She still thought of him as a little kid, shooting her with a finger gun from behind a cereal box fort at the breakfast table. "Well. I can understand how he never looked for me, with his heavy Frisbee schedule and all."

"He did look for you."

"He did?" She sat up, fighting a dizzy spell.

"About five years ago, after he was diagnosed. He called your dad to tell him, and to find out where you were."

"My dad would be the last person to know."

Isaac paused, but not to think. "Nina, your dad had lung cancer. When Chris called, he was coughing a lot. Like, he could barely muster the breath to call his son a faggot. When Chris called again a few months later, the line was disconnected." He interlaced his fingers. "I'm not sure if I should say I'm sorry or not."

Nina picked at the sofa. The piping felt comfortingly solid under her thumb.

Isaac said, "When Chris couldn't find you, we wondered if something had happened to you, too."

"No," she said. "No, I just took a train." A family full of the dead and missing. Nina wondered if there was an afterlife, and if Chris now had to wait in purgatory with their father as he spouted conspiracy theories, stubbed brown cigarettes on couch upholstery, and farted.

"Well. It's all too late now," Isaac said. He wasn't being cruel—he was right. Nina and Chris had simply scattered in opposite directions, saving their breadcrumbs for themselves. Just like that, her family, never much good to begin with, had disintegrated into nothing.

Isaac pulled a postcard from his pocket. "This is from your friend."

She took the card, read it, and read it again. It felt weird to see Jackson's handwriting again. She touched the scar on her chin. "I wonder if he's still in Denver."

"He was three days ago."

"What?"

"We went to see him."

"You saw him? What did he say?"

"He said to—"

"No, *exactly*. What exactly did he say?"

"He said, 'Send her to me.'"

Nina could imagine his voice, probably yelling. She wondered if he still dyed his hair Ronald Reagan black. She wondered if he still smelled like American cheese and ate Japanese food and quoted ancient Greek ideals. Pointing at the address on the back of the card, her finger shook. "He was here?"

"Yeah. He lives there." Nina memorized the address and handed back the postcard, but Isaac waved his hand. "Keep it. It's addressed to you." She traced her fingers over the words, "I'm sorry." Jackson was a Vietnam vet. He never said he was sorry.

Isaac said, "There's something I never got. Why did he take care of you like he did? And not Chris?"

"Chris was scared of him. Jackson did some bad stuff in Vietnam."

"Were you scared of him?"

"No."

"I always wondered," Isaac's eyebrows twitched. "Was there anything…sexual between you two?"

"Jackson? No! Gross. He's like my father." *Was*, she thought. *Was, was, was.* "It's hard to explain."

Isaac glanced around her dirty apartment. "So. You said you work in finance?" He kicked aside the gym sock with her money stashed inside.

"I work with, with cash." Her head hurt.

"Like, a bank teller?"

Nina had never been inside a bank, and wasn't even sure what bank tellers told anyone. "It's highly confidential." She rubbed her temples. It felt like the inside of her head was bigger than the outside. "Tell me about LA."

Isaac needed no further prompting. As he talked, Nina listened to the sounds of his words, rather than their meanings. Something in his voice soothed her, reminded her of sleepovers when they were kids. Isaac always talked and talked (and talked) until the three of them fell asleep on their blue corduroy sofa that smelled like feet. She had dreamed of him even then.

She had fallen in love with every one of the characters in his stupid school plays—Mercutio, Danny Zuko, even Stanley Kowalski, the rapist. A low buzz emanated from him, the peculiar frequency Isaac ran on that always made her want to lean in, wondering if proximity could ever alchemize into love. When he teased Nina in class or in her driveway, she wanted to crack sarcastic jokes and look pissed off all the time, like the girls he took to the movies and Homecoming. But she was not that girl.

Well. She owned ninety-two IDs. She was any girl she wanted to be, now.

"—lots of hard, scabby sores everywhere," Isaac was saying. "He got shingles for a while, and thrush in his mouth, candida. So he had this weird discharge. That was hard on him. He threw up a lot, so his apartment always smelled like—"

"Okay. Thanks."

"—vomit. Sorry. I probably should have kept that to myself. I just haven't had anyone to talk to about this, except Kate, and that's inappropriate." He half-smiled. "It's been a little lonely."

Nina couldn't imagine Isaac lonely. "Were you with him when he died?"

Isaac looked away.

"If you hadn't come here, I'd still think he was alive," she said.

"Is it better or worse to know?"

"It's more real."

He smiled. "Which means worse, right?"

"Still. I appreciate it." Nina held out her hand.

Isaac took her hand and, confused, shook it. He let go and unthinkingly wiped his own on his pants. "Well. It's important to know. Besides, there's the custody thing."

There was a loud thump upstairs. "What?" Nina asked.

"An issue we need to talk about. Regarding Kate's future." Glancing at Nina's face, he clarified, "Your niece."

"My niece." At that particular moment, she couldn't even remember what Kate looked like.

"Maybe this isn't the time."

"You tell me my brother's dead *in a doorway*, and suddenly you're worried about timing?"

"You don't have kids, do you?" He scanned her living room, as if there might be a baby hiding out somewhere.

"Custody. You said custody."

"Do you, um, like kids?"

"Isaac. I am going to beat you with a stick."

"Okay." He opened his messenger bag and handed over a sheaf of papers, shrugging with one shoulder as if to say, *I didn't write it*. Nina turned them right side up and read: *1. Will. This is my Will. I revoke all prior Wills and codicils.* "This doesn't sound like Chris at all," she said.

"A lawyer wrote it. Skip to the end."

"*Each of us is now age 18 or older, is a competent witness, and resides at the address set forth after his or her name…*"

"No. Here." He pointed at a paragraph with his middle finger.

She read, *Guardian of the Child's Person. If I have a child under age 18 and the child does not have a living parent at my death, I nominate Nina Black as First Choice as guardian of the person of that child (to raise the child). If the First Choice does not serve, then I nominate Isaac Dickson to serve.* She looked up.

"Holy mother of God. So, *that* girl—" she jabbed up with her thumb "—is supposed to live with *me*?"

"We could split her."

"What, you take the top half and I take the bottom?"

Isaac flung his hands up. "Hey, it was a surprise to me, too."

"I can't be a mother," Nina said.

There was a thump from upstairs.

Isaac glanced again at the ceiling, and then tapped the will. "Not a mother. Just a guardian, it says here. See? Guardian."

"Same shit, different toilet." Nina stood and started pacing. "Isn't there anyone else left? How about Brittany's family?"

"Bethany. And her family is worse than yours." Isaac was standing now, too. "We can work out whatever is comfortable for you. Or I can take her to LA with me while you think it over."

"I just thought it over, and the answer is no. So take her with you and get thee to LA or wherever." She handed the papers back. She wanted her brother, not some leftover kid in green knee socks.

Isaac didn't take the papers, but instead looked again at the silent ceiling. He said in a low voice, "It's just that she has her heart set getting to know you. After Chris, you know? Maybe she could just connect with you a little first. If we left now, it might be a problem for her down the road." He whispered, "Therapeutically."

"Are you shitting me?" She sank down on the sofa. "A child? Stay here?"

Isaac glanced at the spot next to her on the sofa, and instead sat on the floor. "You'll like her. She's funny. Like you were."

"I'm not funny."

"Are you kidding? They broke the mold *before* they made you," he said.

"You were weirder than me. Leaping around the stage with Vaseline in your hair."

"Remember when you were little, how you used to try to fish by tying red yarn to a stick and dipping the tip of it in a puddle? Remember when you put on your dress sideways? Or when you made coffee by melting brown crayons in a pan?"

"Yeah, well, *you* drank it."

"And karate?" He picked lint off the carpet. "Pretty weird for a girl."

"Jesus. A few days, all right? That's it." Nina gave no shit about the girl, but she did like the sight of Isaac Dickson on her floor.

"You still do that stuff, anyway?" Isaac made obscure arm movements in the air. "Martial arts and all?"

"Yeah."

"Why?"

"I don't know. Same reason you act, maybe." Then, despite herself, she said, "Areté."

"Areté? Like, the Greek Areté? Excellence, reaching the ultimate human potential, Plato's allegory of the cave, all that? How do you know about that?" The way he was staring at her made her feel stupid.

"I don't know. Jackson liked to quote the Greeks, to show off his semester at community college."

"Areté." Isaac shook his head. "I haven't thought about that in lifetimes."

Out the window, light pollution reflected orange against the low clouds that raced in from the mountains.

"It's still strange to train your whole life for something that may never happen. Fighting and all," he said. "Although I guess with your dad, it helped to be prepared."

"Shut up," she said.

Fear crossed his face and dissipated. "Okay."

"I mean, shut up. Who are you, anyway?" Nina said. "You walk into my place after twelve years and say, 'Your father sucks, your brother's dead, you have a kid now.' Just shut the fuck up."

Isaac sat up slowly. "You sure talk a lot more than you used to."

She could kick him in the head. She could push him over and do whatever she wanted. She saw it in her mind.

"Anyway, your dad's gone." He picked at the carpet again. "You're safe now, right?"

Nina's body began to shake—first her legs, and then her arms. The stirring coursed up her middle, radiating outward like a sunburst. She had to leave or she would explode all over him. She grabbed her keys. "I'll be back."

ᔕ

NINA DIDN'T START DRIVING with a plan, but found herself pulling up to the address she had memorized from Jackson's postcard. Jackson lived on the top of a small hill in the Highlands neighborhood, across from a neighborhood 7-Eleven near Viking Park. His was a Colorado-style ranch, a typical squat thing with a small front porch and Lego-ish construction. She couldn't tell what color it was in the dark. A *makiwara* sprouted against the wall. Behind blinds, the windows of the house leaked yellow light. She couldn't see Jackson, nor the shadow of him.

The last time Nina had seen him, it was the day after her mother left them. Nina was seventeen. She had banged on the door of his trailer until he appeared, a stippled ghost against the screen door's dirty mesh grid. "You're early today," he said.

"Where's mom?" She tried to push the screen door open, but it was latched. "Tell her to come back. The house is a mess."

"She went home."

"That's her home." Nina pointed down the street at their scruffy house with the dead lawn. Her arm fell. The house was stripped bare inside, with most of their belongings in various pawnshops around town. That was nobody's home.

Jackson said, "She went back to Japan."

Nina rattled the screen door. "Come on. Let me see her."

"She's in Japan, Nina."

"She can't be. No money."

Jackson rubbed his eyes with a spotted thumb and forefinger. "I gave her my money from the coffee can in the freezer."

They stared at each other through the mesh cage, like two animals.

Nina punched through the screen door, unlatched the latch and slammed it open. She swung at her teacher. As he ducked, his black hair left a stain on her eye, like a brushstroke.

She whirled and punched him with her other hand, just as he did the same to her. Their fists crossed, passed each other. Either of them could have blocked the other's punch, but neither did.

Jackson's dry tooth gave way under her knuckle, as her own head snapped to the side.

Nina fell down, panting through her nose. Blood dripped onto her shirt. She touched her chin, felt the gash there. A molar was loose in her cheek. Her jaw no longer fit together. Jackson had hit her hard, and she went down. But she didn't go out.

Jackson was also on the ground. His throat chugged as he swallowed his broken tooth. Still the student, Nina rolled her own molar onto the center of her tongue. But she was already crying, and she choked on it. She spat it into her palm, ringed with blood.

"I hate you," she said thickly, and meant it.

That tooth and her brother's wallet were the only two things she had taken when she left home. Now, outside Jackson's house, Nina picked the tooth out of the ashtray of her car and held it in the center of her palm. It still felt alive, a hardened part of her.

She cracked open the car door and slid out. The night air smacked her cheeks, clearing her head. A shadow passed in front of the front curtain and left. Jackson's lawn absorbed all light from his windows, which told her that it was mostly dead. Hawaiian, Jackson never believed in watering. Monitoring the windows, she lit a cigarette as a raindrop fell on her toe. Nina liked smoking in the rain; she liked the contradiction. She liked the thought of something burning feebly in her hands, despite the odds. Defiance isn't always a strong thing.

Jackson's light blinked out.

She couldn't summon him to the door in his pajamas after twelve years. Why had she come? She looked down at her body, clothes, the general mess she had made of herself. She was everything he hated.

She tapped the loose tooth against her still-fixed ones, wishing what was outside was still inside. Then she threw the molar as hard as she could into Jackson's yard. It landed in the dead grass without a sound.

She turned and laced her fingers through the chain-link fence. Look at that, a view: Denver, flat and sleepy, lights twinkling on. She hated it and loved it, the way she hated and loved a cigarette in her mouth, the taste of tar and fuel and bad luck and glamour. Even now, in August, the edge of winter lurked like an old threat, saying, *You'll forget about me, but I'll always come back.*

She squinted at the lights. She was all alone. There was nowhere she couldn't go, nothing she couldn't take. The city was hers, laid out like an open palm. It was not enough.

CHAPTER SEVEN:
DESIRES OF THE HEART

No man should think of getting satisfaction today concerning something he felt chagrined by yesterday, or gaining this year an ambition that was frustrated the year before. If we do act in this vein, the desires of our hearts will rise up one after another like dust in the wind.
—Shiba Yoshimasa (1350-1410)

All war is based on deception.
—Sun Tzu, *The Art of War*

FOR THE FIRST TIME in her life, Nina had actual houseguests. Isaac had suggested a hotel (begged, even), but the girl refused. He even tried to pick her up and bodily remove her from Nina's apartment, but Kate kicked so much, he just set her down with a sigh. "Okay if we crash here?" he asked, clearing a space for his bag with a finicky toe.

So Nina stuffed pillowcases with sweatshirts, and unrolled a musty sleeping bag for Kate, who insisted on sleeping upstairs in the loft, despite the heat. The next day, Nina shoplifted new sheets and, with some difficulty, an air mattress for Kate, which she inflated at home with her foot.

Kate liked to spend an inordinate amount of free time sitting at Nina's desk in the loft, which made Nina nervous. She relocated her stash of wallets to the dead space under the bottom drawer of her desk when the two of them were out getting takeout, just as a precaution. Her new guests settled in. Kate ate Happy Meals every time she asked for them. Isaac found the atrophied vacuum cleaner, cooked bland food, and kept asking how Nina felt.

Nina felt like she had the flu. She ached and sniffled. She spent long periods of time staring at a spoon in her hand, or a shoe she hadn't gotten around to putting on. Sometimes whatever she was staring at got puddly and crooked, and she realized she was crying. Last night she woke up crying from a dream that hadn't even been bad. She threw up a couple of times, casually. Her head felt like a small, hard toilet bowl, with her brain swirling around and around, never flushing.

Time, always a fluid concept for Nina, was now a dual thing, a boomerang that whirred between now and a time that she had tried to forget. She traced the faint half-moon scar on her forearm where Chris had bitten her. They had been five, fighting bitterly over a cupcake. She had grown, and the scar had stretched.

To make matters worse, Kate had gotten it in her head that she was staying indefinitely. Her first evening there, she dusted off an empty shelf on the bookcase and folded her clothes onto it. Kate's toothbrush was now in Nina's bathroom cup, the kid-size green toothbrush resting against her red one, bristles interlocking.

Didn't it take a village to raise a kid? It's not that Nina was against parenthood in general, or even in specific. She used to want children. She still did, in the abstract. She could imagine herself saying something wise at crucial moments, or holding a newborn baby against her miraculously flat stomach, or singing well-chosen foreshadowy lullabies to be remembered sentimentally after her premature death. Nina would be a fun, carefree parent, carrying her (sleeping, always sleeping) baby to cafés and restaurants like a cute, animated purse.

But even Nina knew this was fantasy. She had watched new mothers in the grocery store with their (screaming, always screaming) babies, frantically jiggling them while trying to read a label with manic eyes rimmed pale pink, before just giving up and chucking the can into the cart. Nina could tell that the babies were the only ones who got to sleep, ever, and they chose when and where, while their mothers walked around in Disney T-shirts smeared with food and snot that wasn't their own. The kids wailed in the checkout line, sitting in the child seat of the grocery cart where Nina usually put eggs, bread, and a magazine. High-pitched siblings wanted every toy they saw and fought like demons, ignoring the woman who had pulled them out of her body and, at that moment, was wishing she could stuff them back inside.

Nina rarely saw the dads trucking the kids around alone. There might be the occasional man with Saturday custody, talking to his girlfriend on his cell phone and shuttling the kids from the park to McDonald's Play Place, while the kids were so afraid he'd up and leave them (again), they just shyly followed, saving up all their laundry and meanness for the woman waiting at home who loved them enough to stay. Not leave, just stay.

So what was this? Kate's toothbrush, Isaac with a spatula full of pancakes? Both of them maneuvering around her in the hallway like she was made of paper? Evenings, Nina watched Isaac watch Kate watch Nina. Nobody spoke as they all chewed through their hangnails. Nina felt like she and Isaac were estranged spouses on the therapy track. She felt domesticated, like a cow. She hadn't worked a single night. That wasn't what she wanted—the tyranny of the family. She didn't want Saturday cartoons and Sunday bagels and trips to Mount Rushmore with a kid she had just met.

She was also getting paranoid. After the three of them came back from a matinee, she could swear that someone had been inside her apartment, even though nothing was missing. The place smelled foreign, clean. Maybe that weird smell was her own life, disinfecting itself from within.

To keep up her bank job charade, Nina made sure she was gone for a good six hours each weekday, which was actually a relief. She left her house in the most conservative clothes she could find, with her shorts and tank top underneath. After working out in the park all day, she put her skirt and blouse back on and returned home, smelling awful. She missed her freedom. She missed her shower. She missed her alley and her sledgehammer and her tire.

So she should have been glad when Isaac said in the kitchen one evening, "I was thinking I might take Kate back with me this week. We could work out a visitation…thing."

Nina's knife paused as she listened for Kate, but the apartment was silent. "Yeah, that's the thing—" but she wasn't sure how to finish the sentence. She looked down at the steak she had been mincing.

"It was a kind of crazy idea, anyway. You just met her," Isaac said.

"It would help if we knew why Chris gave me custody in the first place."

"No idea. Maybe—"

"What?"

Isaac's shirt was open one button, and soft wisps of hair showed through. "Forget it," he said.

"Why are you blushing?"

Inexplicably, he reached out and touched her collarbone, the broken one. His touch was gentle, and held twelve years of experience Nina had no access to. His hand dropped. He said, "I'm not blushing. It's hot."

Nina tried to meet his eyes but didn't get farther than his mouth, which was parted and a little pale. His cotton shirt rustled.

"It's not that hot," she said.

Isaac cleared his throat and half-turned toward the carrots on the cutting board. "Okay. So it was about eight years ago. After I broke up with this one girl, Marcy. Chris and I were talking about how I couldn't find anyone to—to keep my interest." The pink on his cheeks spread down his neck. "Chris said, out of nowhere—I mean, I hadn't seen you in years. Many, many years. So he asked, 'What about Nina?'" Isaac laughed a little. Nina forced an identical laugh, wondering, *Is he laughing because being with me is ridiculous?*

Abruptly, they both stopped laughing at the same time and watched each other sideways, wary as cats. "Yeah, it's a terrible idea," he said.

"Terrible." Nina hacked harder at the raw flesh. When Isaac touched her shoulder, she twisted from his reach. *I want these people out of my apartment*, she thought.

Isaac sighed out through his nose. "Anyway. Kate's probably better off with me."

"What do you mean, 'better off'?"

He gestured with his knife, a small, looping circle. "Look at this place."

Everything suddenly looked duller, dingier. She glanced at the brown fingerprints on her refrigerator, the dust rimming the windowsills, the spider web she hadn't wanted to ruin because it was pretty. "Okay, I'm no June Cleaver."

He pulled her coffeepot out of the coffee maker. "You have a half-dead goldfish in your coffeepot."

"He's just uncoordinated." The dull knife skidded off her finger.

"The other day, I opened the refrigerator and found a shoe in it. When you have kids, you have to set a good example— dress the way you want them to dress." He glanced pointedly at her ripped Bee Gees T-shirt. "Act the way you want them to act. You have to keep your house clean. Have you ever even worked with children?"

Once, Nina had volunteered for the Red Cross. She thought by working there, she could burn off some of her bad karma, maybe giving her more luck when she was out stealing wallets.

Instead, it turned out this Red Cross just taught CPR classes. After each class, the resuscitation dolls needed to be sterilized and reassembled, and that's what Nina did for almost a whole day until she quit. The dolls had full-size torsos and heads, with absent arms and legs, like victims of Nazi amputations. The most disturbing were the baby dolls, with their sleepy, Down syndrome faces. Their legs and arms splayed at right angles, like fleshy human spiders. Nina disemboweled them and peeled off their baby faces, Hannibal Lecter-style. She arranged them on the racks of a dishwasher and ran the cycle hot. When they were done, the rack of steaming baby faces stared up at her.

"I've worked with children," Nina said.

Isaac paced around the kitchen, rubbing the back of his head until his hair stood up like it used to. "A kid needs shoes, and books, and special foods. A clean, stable house." He pointed at the filet mignon she was mincing. "She's not going to eat that, Nina."

"But it's steak tartare."

"Kids like hot dogs. Almost exclusively. And they need vegetables."

"These are vegetables." She showed him the little bowl of olives and marinated mushrooms she had set out.

"Those are pizza toppings."

"Listen." She slammed her knife down. He glanced at it. "You pop up, tell me my brother died, and now I have to think about vegetables and everything?"

"I don't understand why we're even arguing about this," he said. "A minute ago you told me you don't want her. Now you suddenly do, just because I insulted you. Which I didn't mean to do." When Isaac was confused, he looked ten years younger. "It's about Kate, not us. *Her* needs and well-being."

"You're trying to poach her."

"She's not an object. She's not money you found in the street. She's a human being." This time the electricity around him was sharp, not his usual warm hum. "I was there, Nina, when Chris was sick. Where were you?"

"I didn't know about it."

"You didn't want to know anything about us. You just left town without looking back."

"Wait a second. You think I wanted to drop out and leave one month before graduating? None of that was what I wanted."

"Then why did you leave us?"

The "us" almost caught her. "Because Chris was leaving *me*, you fuck, to go to California with you. I wasn't invited. What was I supposed to do? Stay behind with a father who wanted to—who would have—" Nina was clutching the knife again, in a stabber's grip this time. She barely recognized her own voice. "Things were different once my mom left."

Isaac's arms were crossed over his chest, knuckles to his teeth. "I know. And I'm sorry," he said through his hand. "I really am. But you're not suited."

"Yeah? Well, it's not your decision to make. It was Chris's, and he made it. She's mine if I want her." Nina looked into Isaac's ignited irises and felt the old thrill, the electricity through her knees.

This was better than any wallet. She was stealing a person.

"What about Kate? What she wants?" Isaac asked.

"I think it's pretty clear what she wants." While they were talking last night, Kate snuck outside and threw her suitcase in the dumpster. "You could stick around if you're so worried."

"I have work obligations. You could come to California." He glanced around her apartment. "Make a life there."

Besides never having mowed a lawn or experienced a simultaneous orgasm, Nina had never ridden on an airplane. She once bought a plane ticket to Cancún and went through the bewildering process of checking in and finding her gate. Then when she saw the big, metal airplane out the window, she blanched. She just couldn't imagine how anything that big could fly without flapping. "I'm afraid to fly."

"That's where Kate gets it from." He sniffed. "Maybe you just need some time alone. To make up your mind."

Panic flooded her chest. "No! I don't want to be alone!" This surprised her. She always wanted to be alone. "I'll get some hot dogs," she said.

That night at the table, Kate poked at the steak tartare and asked Nina why her hamburger wasn't cooked.

Isaac leaned over. "None of ours is, sweetie. That's how you eat it." He pointed his fork in Nina's direction. "It was *her* idea."

Kate leaned over her plate and sniffed. "It smells funny."

"It's got seasonings in it," Nina said. "It's French. Your grandpa was French, French Canadian, Kate. Your dad's dad."

"It's got raw eggs, and onions, and anchovy paste in it," Isaac said.

"What is anchovy?"

"They're little, smelly fishes." He eyed Nina. "Mashed up in your raw meat."

Kate raised her eyebrows and looked down at her plate. "Fishes?"

"Sort of like fishes," Nina said. "Not really…fish." She glared at Isaac.

Kate swallowed hard. "Ketchup?" she quavered.

Nina hurried to the refrigerator and grabbed a bottle. When she came back, she heard Isaac whisper in Kate's ear, "We can get McDonald's afterwards." Nina cuffed him upside his head. He looked up at her with round eyes and asked, "What?" Kate uncapped the bottle of ketchup and shook it until a big sploodge covered her plate.

"Kate, honey, you don't have to eat that stuff," Isaac said.

Kate glanced back and forth at Isaac's smirking face and Nina's frowning one. She sighed with the despair of the ages, and piled a mass of meat and ketchup on her fork. She shoved the fork into her mouth.

She gagged.

Isaac and Nina reached for her simultaneously. Kate instead grabbed her milk. She gulped the whole glass and wiped her mouth with the back of her hand. She picked up her fork again and dug the tines into the meat. Tiny dots of perspiration popped onto her forehead. Her hand shook as she lifted the fork to her mouth.

Nina snatched the fork from Kate's hand and whisked her plate away into the kitchen. She dumped the contents into a frying pan and turned the heat on high.

Flipping the world's most expensive hamburger, she wiped her own forehead. She felt embarrassed at this display of love (or loyalty, or desperation, or whatever it was) from a little girl she barely knew.

Still, Kate looked like Chris in certain lights, and the gash in Nina's chest zipped up the smallest bit when she was around. Maybe it was the innocence with which Kate wanted things—a Popsicle, to win at Candyland, to wear Nina's sweatshirts. Nina felt something pull at her, an imaginary fish on a line made of red yarn. This kid actually wanted Nina. Who wanted Isaac. Who wanted Kate.

It didn't take a genius to do this math.

So the next morning, Nina shoplifted hot dogs, two cans of RavioliOs, American cheese, organic toothpaste, and Hershey's chocolate syrup. With money, she bought a carton of whole milk, and schlepped the whole mess home. She arranged everything in the refrigerator, the hot dogs in the front, flabby in their package. She dusted, vacuumed, washed the windows and walls, scrubbed out the refrigerator, and cleaned mold from grout with a toothbrush dipped in bleach. In the bathroom, she placed toothpaste on end next to the two new toothbrushes in their shared cup.

Isaac watched her, and frowned.

~

IT WAS NOON, AND time for Isaac to do what he did best—leave. There was no reason to stay. Mission accomplished, right? He had buried the friend, found the missing woman, and delivered the orphan. *Ta da.*

He had even transformed Nina overnight into a domestic goddess. She polished wood trim with lemon oil, swept out the cabinets, disinfected the refrigerator, wiped the crumbs from the silverware drawer. She scoured the bathtub tile in cutoffs, with her hair tied up in a bandana. On her, it almost looked perverted. She even pulled out the appliances and cleaned behind them, as if Isaac would inspect there. Which he did. It was hard to ignore the effort. The place smelled like vinegar and salt. With all the grime removed, the apartment actually looked nice.

And although Nina only worked part-time at her consulting job, she clearly made decent money, enough to bring home steak or lamb almost every night. She cooked with things like truffle salt and saffron. She left cash all over the place. She had bought Isaac a beautiful platinum nearly-new Rolex as a gift, which he weakly tried to refuse. It was gorgeous, worth a month's pay, even used. She pressed it into his hand, saying it was to thank him.

Clean lodging, financial stability, above-average personality. Wasn't that all you could expect from a parent? It was more than either of them had grown up with.

It was good enough for Isaac. Now, he chewed a cuticle as Nina trounced Kate at a game of Go Fish, watching her shoulder muscles contract as she pulled a card. He was just a couple of hours from a blank slate in his old home.

But instead of looking forward to the trip, he found himself dreading it. Kate was lying on her stomach on the fresh carpet, her pointy chin in her sweaty palm, legs waving back and forth. She smelled like shampoo. Nina studied her cards, perfectly still.

Both of their existences felt miraculous, extraordinary. Nina's hair stuck to the back of her neck, and Isaac had to restrain himself from lifting it and letting it sift through his fingers.

It was probably just a passing feeling, a byproduct of living with someone he used to know. Well, not really living with. Sleeping on a couch, dressing out of a Pac-Man-jawed suitcase and awkwardly orchestrating bathroom time wasn't really living with a person. Still, they were sharing space, time. He smelled the lingering smell of her cooking, her deodorant. They shared air.

He had lived with women before, one after another, in fact. The women formed a long, interlocking train in his mind, with his best friend trailing behind, a sick caboose. Except for Chris, all his relationships felt like projections on a movie screen. None of them lasted, for the same reason he failed shop class in high school; he could never conceptualize the connections— how spark turns to flame, how electricity lights a lamp, how sound travels across a wire. How a touch turns to love. After his last breakup, he looked up "love" in the dictionary. It had nine definitions. Nine was manageable, even memorizable. Why was it so hard for him?

Maybe, despite all his ardent declarations, he had never been in love. Maybe he had confused love with relief. Each relationship, he waited too long, until the woman started glaring at him like he was a car engine that wouldn't start. Isaac had learned that a dream can languish for years, but when it dies, it dies fast, and a woman can fall out of love with you while you're eating a sandwich.

"You just act like a prototype," his ex-girlfriend Marcy had once told him. He had come close to proposing only once, when Marcy had told him to "shit or get off the pot." He got on a knee, held Marcy's trembling hand, and said, "Okay, baby. Let's shit."

Isaac picked at the stubble of Nina's newly shampooed carpet, still crusty with dried soap. It's not that he withheld information; it's just that people see what they want to see. He was an actor, not a liar. He had never cheated on anyone, except for that one time, and that other time. Still, he wondered if Marcy was right, if he was just a little bit…fake. And as he got older, he found himself giving less and less to women who deserved more and more.

It all seemed so exhausting and ridiculous now. Could he go back to LA and start it all over? A new woman, with different foibles that he'd initially find charming and later find intolerable? During their breakup, Marcy nicknamed him "Monkey Bars," in a voice slathered with scorn. "You can't let go of one woman until you've grabbed hold of another," she said.

Maybe, but Nina was nothing to grab hold of. A high school dropout/bank worker with an instant daughter: not someone he'd pick off a dating site. No. He'd better leave Denver—and Nina—before anything turned serious, and then fatal.

The only glitch was Kate. It's just that he had gotten used to the idea of keeping her. He had visualized himself in that role. It was *his* part. As much of a relief as it was to shed it, he hated to give it up to the understudy. He glanced at Nina squinting at her cards and sizing up the kid for decimation. She wiped at her cheek, completely missing the smear of toothpaste there. She laid down her last pair.

"No fair," Kate wailed. "You won last time."

Isaac patted Kate's shoulder, then pressed it. "Honey, do you know what day today is?"

"No." She turned her skinny back on him.

Nina's gaze scuttled back and forth, maintaining her poker face for this, a game of Fish. "What?"

"I'm going back to Los Angeles."

"California?" Nina asked, as if she had never heard of it. "When?"

"I told you a few days ago. Our plane leaves at four," he said to Kate.

"I'm staying here," Kate said.

Isaac picked up his shirt from the floor. Kate's sock clung to a sleeve. It was pink, with orange stripes on it. He stuffed it into his pocket.

"That's my sock," Kate said.

"I know." He concentrated on the lines in the carpet for a few seconds until they straightened out. "I'm taking it."

"You can stay here, too," Nina said. "You don't have to leave."

"We need to stay together," Kate said. "All of us."

"It doesn't work that way, Kate."

"It does. It does! Don't leave us!" Kate's voice escalated to a shriek. She threw her cards at his face. He tried to duck, but caught the corner of an ace in his eye before it fell in his lap.

"I'm not leaving…you." Isaac glanced at Nina with his remaining good eye. "God, Kate, that hurt."

Kate took a deep breath and shouted to nobody in particular, "I hate you! I hate you I hate you I hate you!" Her eyes turned into two black circles. She ran upstairs.

Nina flicked the edge of a playing card over and over with her forefinger. "Well, at least she's stopped whispering."

"Everything's a joke to you." He trod upstairs after Kate, misgivings gnawing at his stomach.

Up in the loft, Kate had dismantled Nina's desk. An empty drawer was pulled out, wedged against the wall, and Kate's head was buried deep in the hole it had left.

"What are you doing?" Isaac asked.

Kate jumped and scooted over until her back pressed against the hole. "Nothing."

Isaac frowned. "You shouldn't snoop, Kate. What are you looking at?"

"Nothing." He thought he heard her mutter, "Not wallets, anyway."

"Not what?"

"Nothing, I said." She glanced back at the desk. "Not anything."

He felt confused. He realized that he was towering over her, and sat down. He tried to peek into the drawer on the floor, but Kate shifted to block his view.

Isaac said softly, "I just wanted to tell you that you don't have to stay here if you don't want to. We could do fine, the two of us. We don't need Nina."

"She needs me," Kate said. "She really, really does."

Isaac tried to hold Kate's face in his hands, but she shook him off. He said, "Nina legally has the right to keep you. I don't. So if you want to be with me, you have to make it clear that you want to come to LA."

"But I don't want to go. I want us to all stay together."

"Okay, then." He felt mean. "I have to go."

"So go!" Kate shouted.

"Fine! I will!"

"Go already!"

Isaac didn't know what to do until Kate kicked him in the shin. "Ow!" he said and limped down the stairs. Kate started crying upstairs. He paused on the stairs, and then kept walking down. He wasn't her guardian anymore.

Nina was shuffling the deck, practicing a magic trick on herself.

"Kate's crying," Isaac told her. "She's pretty upset."

"Oh." She chewed on a hangnail. "So, what's so important in LA? You have a girlfriend there?"

"I have auditions there." He roused himself. "One is for a movie. The villain. He has a mechanical heart. Not a big deal. B flick, straight to video."

Nina was trying to spin a playing card on one corner. Upstairs, Kate stopped crying and started sniffling.

"Then a yogurt commercial. I've worked with the director before. Most recently for baloney, and once as the lead ghost in a cereal commercial. You've probably seen me."

"I don't have a TV, Isaac."

"That's right. Well, the cereal looks like little ghosts. It's a scary cereal," he wound down. "What?" he asked, when the silence got uncomfortable, which was immediately.

"Doesn't it ever make you feel cheap?"

He remembered bragging to his agent about being a good bargain. "Like, inexpensive?"

"No, like a hooker."

Isaac could not believe this woman. "I love acting."

"There's a big difference between loving something and making it your bitch."

He stiffened, and not in the good way. "I'll have you know, I went to school for acting. University of Illinois and Northwestern. I have an MFA."

"That and five bucks will get you a fish sandwich." Nina picked at a paint scab on the wall. "No, let me rephrase that. That and five bucks, they'll give you a job *making* a fish sandwich."

"I think I liked you better when you never talked." His breath came out in short bursts. "You're just like the rest of the people in Grand Junction, you know that? Pissed off at anyone who gets ahead."

"You're not ahead. You're a ghost in a cereal commercial."

He couldn't help himself. "*Lead* ghost."

"And I'm not pissed off. You're pissed off because you think you're Laurence Olivier, just because you're on TV,"—she pronounced it "Oliv-ee-er"—"and I still remember you as the little boy who tried to smoke a cigarette, and ended up setting his Underoos on fire."

This was the opposite of what Isaac needed. He didn't need a reality check. He needed a double Scotch, and a night with a woman. He needed a quart jar of Valium. "Shit, Nina."

"Understatement is overrated," she said. "All that talent and you're just...professionally cute." She flicked a playing card.

Wait. "You think I'm cute?"

"I think you're *talented*, you dumb fuck."

Just like twelve years ago, her faith in him inspired rage. "You know what, Nina? Sometimes you just have to fake it 'til you make it. You can hardly judge my choices when you've spent half your life wearing white pajamas and punching the air."

"I don't punch the air anymore." Nina's voice was so frigid, his balls retracted.

This wasn't right. When they were kids, Isaac had always delivered all the insults, the implied critiques—not Nina. He said, "There's a legitimate market for what I do. Maybe it's not as lucrative as finance, but I'll triple-bet that I make more money than you do." He stuck his finger in her face, and she looked at it cross-eyed. "You know what directors call me? 'Convincing.' 'Charismatic.' You'll trouble yourself to remember that in high school, while you and Chris were pumping gas, I made bank selling vacuum cleaners door-to-door to people who didn't even have carpets." He wanted to shake her. He knew she was probably feeling traumatized and everything, but there was no call to attack his profession, which was a noble one, the Greeks did it, and who was she—

"But what about Shakespeare?" she asked.

"Who?"

"When we were kids, you used to say you wanted to act out something real. Something life and death."

Why did she even remember this stuff? "What about you? What did you want back then?"

"I wanted to marry you."

His voice caught before he got his second wind for another rant. Nina's face was blank, as if she had given the weather report. He took a breath to keep from stammering, his habit whenever he had no script. "Then I guess that illustrates my point. Because you don't anymore, right?"

She looked out the window. "Sometimes I dream I'm getting married."

This conversation was traveling in the exact wrong direction.

"I dream I'm wearing a big, white dress." A scrim of pink cast over Nina's dark features, and she looked down. "Then it starts to look like one of those Chagall paintings—the groom's head turns blue, and violins start floating in the air, and suddenly there's this giant chicken hanging around—"

"Okay. Thanks."

"—and then everybody's naked. But I don't know. I've never even attended a wedding."

"They're not like that, unfortunately." His ex-girlfriend Marcy dragged him to tens of them. She was a maid of honor six times. She said it was like being a Sherpa in heels.

Nina said, "I read somewhere that if you're married, your husband can commit you to a mental institution."

"You're not crazy, Nina." Isaac thought about her chicken dream. "Well, maybe you are."

"Crazy is a grown man pretending to be a tub of yogurt." She picked at a cuticle. "Doesn't it feel undignified?"

"For that to happen, I'd have to have some dignity."

"You're in there somewhere, Isaac."

Again, he wanted to shake her. "I'm going to miss my plane." He stood up. "If you need anything, I'm here for you."

"No, you're not. You're in Los Angeles for me."

Isaac flinched at the emotional draft.

"Stay," she said.

"You're not a financial consultant," he said. "You're just an ordinary bank teller, aren't you?"

It only took Nina a second to get to her feet. "You're a coward," she said, and then slammed into her bedroom. Upstairs, Kate's sniffling finally stopped.

This is what's bad about getting away, Isaac thought as he dragged his suitcase to his rental car. *It upends everything.* It's like when you're really tense, and maybe running late, and you have a show opening and you might be coming down with the flu, but if you just keep the tension levels up, maybe that flu or whatever will pass on to the next person. But if you stop, look around, relax, smell some flowers, all the furies will scorch you, obliterate you and everything you stand on.

Isn't that how they found Nina in the first place, by smelling flowers? Which she then…stole?

But, no. Nina had denied it with such unblinking flatness, Isaac had to believe her. She had no reason to steal flowers. She didn't even own a vase. She didn't steal, or she would have pocketed the fifty he had tested her with, left leaking from his open wallet every night he stayed there. She would have kept the twenty he "accidentally" dropped in the street, instead of tapping his shoulder with it. He started the car and drove off, headed east. He couldn't even recall what kind of flowers they were. Roses? They were red.

What he remembered instead was the sensation as they were ripped from his hand. There was the touch of a dark woman, a messenger in black, leading him to Nina and the end of everything. The woman had grazed his shoulder before snatching the flowers from his hand, and he had started to turn at the touch, only to catch the black back of her. She wasn't a woman at all, but an idea. There were petals and a chase, the little girl running between them. It hadn't felt like a theft. It felt like a game, like they were three people running on the same track. It felt like the passing of a torch.

CHAPTER EIGHT:
THE BUTTERFLY AND THE FLOWER THIEF

Meditation on inevitable death should be performed daily. Every day when one's body and mind are at peace, one should meditate upon being ripped apart by arrows, rifles, spears and swords, being carried away by surging waves, being thrown into the midst of a great fire, being struck by lightning, being shaken to death by a great earthquake, falling from thousand-foot cliffs, dying of disease, or committing seppuku at the death of one's master.
—from the *Hagakure* (1716)

Ha! The butterfly
It is following
The flower thief
—Unknown haiku poet (c. 1800)

SAAC REMEMBERED HOW, SHORTLY after Bethany's death, Kate had stood on his couch, yelling as loudly as she could. When Isaac and Chris asked why she was making so much noise, she answered, "That way I know if I'm alive, or just dead and dreaming."

Back in LA, Isaac felt like he was dead and dreaming. He walked through his auditions, the skin stretching taut over his face as he made himself look happy, sad, confused, tortured, angry, or cagey. Inside, he was as blank as dirt.

He had thought it would feel good to cut his last remaining tethers. Freedom! He imagined he would hit the town until it was black and blue, meeting girls like he was in a beer commercial, a car commercial, a Viagra commercial.

Instead, he was miserable. He found small stray socks in his stackable clothes dryer. He picked up his phone to call Chris twice before he remembered that he couldn't. A magneted crayon picture of the three of them—Chris, Kate and Isaac—fluttered every time he walked by his refrigerator.

When those you love die, you never forget them, yet you constantly find yourself remembering them. Isaac cried at unexpected times, suddenly, like a sneeze. He cried when he took a deep breath, or when he passed a burrito stand Chris liked. One bright day, even as he was crying behind his sunglasses, he saw a poster of Chris's favorite local band and thought, *I should get us tickets.* Who hasn't felt the sudden stab of losing the dead all over again, in a billion minuscule ways?

It's the apartment, he decided.

He was tempted to pretend the whole situation of Chris's apartment didn't exist, but he was still paying for it, and it didn't make sense to rent empty space in shitsville. Besides, after watching his best friend slowly implode, sifting through old T-shirts and magazines should be cake.

So on a Sunday, he made his way to South LA, armed with cardboard boxes and burgers in a bag. He tromped up the stairs past the unemployed moms and dirty kids. He opened the door with the key that was still on his key chain.

He staggered back. The sick smell had amplified with the lack of air conditioning. The place smelled of bleached vomit, old sweat, rancid spills. He had forgotten that this was what his best friend had smelled like at the end.

Everything was where Chris had left it—his reading glasses still upside down on the kitchen table, a mug of tea where Chris's hands had last touched it. Mold floated inside the cup, and a crumpled tissue rested near the handle. Wheelchair tracks embedded the dusty, gray-white carpet Kate had stained regularly with grape juice. Sheets in the laundry basket were still marked with Chris's pus and leakages. A part of Isaac wanted to walk back out, lock the door, and keep paying the rent for the rest of his life. The place could be a shrine to Chris, where his ghost could blow its nose and wheel around in peace.

But, no. Isaac taped up boxes. He threw everything in: letter openers, a bone-dry plug-in fountain, paperclips, wicker baskets, extension cords, a dead and rattling ficus, a leaking snow globe, about two dozen unread *Newsweek* magazines, and a month's worth of newspapers. Clothes, clothes, clothes into garbage bags—socks, pants, shirts, underwear, and a tux Isaac had never seen before. Furniture so cheap, he could carry it himself. He dragged everything downstairs and emptied it all into a dumpster. *When the going gets tough*, he thought, *I am not a recycler.*

Zen to the extreme, Isaac himself rarely kept so much as a letter. His parents had been notable hoarders, saving everything—periodicals, expired coupon books, unopened bags of rice and flour. Isaac's whole life, they had kept an intact slaughtered sheep in a storage freezer. It was all in one desiccated piece—head, woolly torso, legs bent up like it was running away from there.

Isaac was afraid of the sheep. A grown man, he still couldn't bring himself to face the sheep. He knew he should visit his mother at least once in his adult life. But the sheep would outlast any connection between the two of them.

His mother had been forty-seven when she got pregnant with Isaac, clearly by mistake. His parents kept him, but they also kept every magazine they had ever owned. They ignored him, like the magazines. Even his name—what had they been thinking? Isaac Dickson? I Suck Dicks-un? Why not just name him "Kick My Ass At Recess"?

As a kid, Isaac had navigated his crowded, cluttered house, talking to himself and making stale potato chip sandwiches, while his parents obsessed about nuclear war and ordered giant, dented cans of tuna and beef stew. The couch was stacked vertically. Isaac patiently heaped books, clothes, and milk crates in stiff piles against walls to clear a path from the refrigerator to his room to the bathroom. After he left home, his parents didn't notice his absence until he called a week later.

There was one thing to be said for growing up with hoarders. It made it easy to chuck out the crap that circumscribed a life. It took him just three hours to strip Chris's apartment bare. Once he was done, he sighed at the blank floor and bare walls. This was how a place was meant to be: completely devoid of ownership.

He sat on the empty floor, pulled his cold lunch from the bag, and called Nina's number. After a ring, there was Kate's hot voice on the line. "What?"

"Hi, peanut."

"Hi, penis."

"No. Peanut. Not penis." The *boing! boing!* noises of a cartoon filtered through the receiver. "And say 'Hello' when you answer a phone. Not 'What.'"

"Nina wants you."

The phone was rummaged from hand to hand until Nina's suspicious voice asked, "What?"

He felt such relief at hearing her voice, he could almost hang up now, except he hated eating alone. "What's happening over there?"

"No-Hair is President today. So far, she's declared war on the sofa, the TV, and the goldfish."

"Has she been sleeping?"

"No-Hair?"

Instant irritation. "No. Kate."

"Oh. Not really."

"Are you doing anything about that?"

"Should I drug her or something?"

"No. *No*, Nina."

He heard her smile. "I was kidding."

"Oh. Sorry. I'm at Chris's. A little on edge. I'm moving his stuff out." In the background, someone in cartoonland was either falling off a cliff or blowing something up with Acme dynamite. "All the junk is in the garbage. The cabinets are scrubbed out. I mean, it's South LA. I doubt they're expecting perfection."

Just breathing. Typical Nina—all action and no talk. *Aw, screw it*, he thought and started to hang up, but she said something. "What?" he asked.

"Could you—would you send me something of Chris's?"

"Oh. Um. Oh." He looked around the barren apartment. He hadn't considered that she might want something to remember him by. *Of course she would*, he thought. *She's his sister, and I'm an asshole.* "What do you want?"

"I don't know. Anything. A shirt."

"I threw them all away. I could fish one out of the dumpster."

"That's okay."

"They smell funny. Because he was sick. And now, they probably smell worse. Because of the dumpster." A bug bumped against the iron bars of the scratched window, and he couldn't tell if it was trying to get out or trying to get in.

"Don't worry about it."

"I miss you," he blurted. "You guys." He looked down at the cold burger in his hands. "Kate, I mean. You, too. It's weird."

She laughed, one quick breath shooting across the line. "That is weird. Nobody's ever missed me before."

Sudden hoots, chants, and grunts leaked through Chris's wall. His neighbors were either having sex or watching a football game.

"I hate this," Isaac said. "I hate Los Angeles. I hate going through his things. I'm mad at him for making me. I'm mad at myself for getting mad at him. And you know what? I hate, hate, hate all this junk." He kicked a last half-filled box he hadn't yet dragged down to the dumpster. "It's stuff for poor people, cheap stuff. Why hang on to crap like laminated placemats with pictures of cherries on them, or filled-in coloring books?"

"I don't know. Maybe they meant something to him."

"But in the end, it all means nothing. All this crap will go into a landfill next to some other dead person's stuff. Who needs three boxes of toothpicks? Dirty extension cords? How about..." He rummaged through the box. "How about this: *The Collected Works of John Lennon*. Wait, that's actually not so... Okay, I'm looking at a Bic razor, one pink shoe that belongs to an extinct Barbie doll, a shiatsu massage machine, three copies of *Sunset Magazine,* and a Speedo. A Speedo, and Chris can't swim. Couldn't swim." When would he get used to the past tense? "I thought I'd like being in LA again. But it's like going to an apartment where you used to live, and all the furniture's different and there are different pictures on the wall."

"I thought you were at Chris's apartment."

"It was a metaphor." *But what if the metaphor came true?* he thought.

Nina said, "It's the grief."

They were quiet for a while. Her ability to read him, even over the phone, made him uncomfortable.

"Why don't you move here?" she asked.

"You don't understand. You're a bank teller, you can live wherever you want. You could move here."

"This is home."

He was surprised at the sudden heat of his anger. "Bullshit. You live like a homeless person."

"Homeless people don't have apartments."

"You know your red chair? The one with the broken springs? Someone died in that chair, Nina."

"That's probably why it was free."

"You're only joking because your life is a joke." He felt like banging the phone on the carpet. "You don't have any friends there. Nobody calls you. The only photo in your house is of *us*, twelve years ago."

"Isaac, you know that thing where a guy tells a girl what her big problem is and she falls in love with him? That only happens in the movies."

"I don't think so. I think it's happening right now."

No sound but water dripping in Chris's sink. Isaac pressed his phone against his ear, as if what came out of it would somehow lead him home.

And it did. "Come back, Isaac," she said.

And it didn't. "No," he said.

ᴗ

ISAAC WAS GONE, AND Nina was fucked. Children were complicated. "I need school clothes," Kate said. "You have to sign me up for school."

"Can't you just show up?" Nina asked.

"I don't think so."

"Where do I find a school?"

"Yellow pages?"

"Where do I find the yellow pages?"

And Nina thought her plastic cactus was needy. Kate was always wanting food, juice, sandwiches, television, hugs. Last night, Kate had a nightmare. Half-asleep, Nina ran to comfort her with a clanking bottle of Scotch and two glasses. Her face still painted with tears, Kate started giggling. "Nina, I don't drink alcohol. I'm eight." Kate asked for a lullaby, but Nina didn't know any so she sang "99 Bottles of Beer on the Wall" until they both dozed off on the air mattress.

That was actually kind of nice.

Regardless, Nina clearly lacked the maternal instinct. This morning, as they crossed the street together to get orange juice, a car ran a red light and sped toward them. Instead of yanking Kate out of the way, Nina stepped behind her. Not in front of her. It was only after the car swerved to miss them that she realized what she had done.

That was the way she was made—always covering her own ass. She had never fought anyone she didn't think she could beat, and she never had never thrown a single, uncalculated punch. When she really thought about it, through all the bruises, split lips, and high machismo, she was basically a coward.

And it was becoming increasingly difficult to hide the overwhelming evidence that her life was a mess: the angry notes from her landlord, the fake job, the fact that all her underwear was ripped. Isaac had printed out the forms for Kate's guardianship, but all those blanks stumped her.

She just hadn't thought this thing through. She had wanted Chris, not his genetic leftovers. She had wanted Isaac. And it turns out, Isaac hadn't wanted Kate as much as Nina had banked on. His daily phone calls were about smog and award ceremonies and a bunch of other things Nina gave no crap about. She felt him slipping away word by word into a life that excluded her. Yes, when he was here, she had rapidly and repeatedly gotten sick of his jaw-clenching, and how he resonated his voice all the time. But even as her mind thought he was full of shit, her whole body missed him with a force that surprised her.

He knew how to handle Kate's paralyzing questions: "Why was Jesus Christ named after a swear word?" "Why did George Washington chop down the cherry tree in the first place?" "Do worms have eyes?" "Who is God?" "What's for dinner?" "Do you love me?" He was much better at the games Kate invented on the spot, with ever-changing rules: "Okay, okay, so I own a store and you're buying a loaf of bread. No, you're, you're a fireman. The store's on fire. But it's a house now, and you're a loaf of bread. No, you're the babysitter. No, no, I'm the babysitter..." Nina mostly just stood around, the babysitter/fireman/loaf of bread, trying to remember how to play at all.

Nina couldn't find her black PVC boots anywhere until Kate clomped down from the loft with them on. Kate also managed to steal Nina's lipstick, false eyelashes (which she wore on her eyebrows), leather jacket, and a pair of clip-on dangly rhinestone earrings. Nina sat her down on the kitchen counter. "You can't keep wearing my clothes." Kate had on a pleather cap Nina had bought at an S&M store. Nina pulled it off her head.

"But I miss you when you go out at night. You leave me here alone and I'm scared."

So Nina gave her a silver bracelet she boosted from a department store. It wrapped around her little wrist twice. Kate lost it in negative time, and cried until Nina surrendered her leather jacket, cutting off the sleeves so it turned into a vest. It was still huge and hot, but Kate wore it everywhere, sweating like a martini. When Nina checked on her before sneaking out at night, Kate was often wearing it over her pajamas.

There are no clear borders to the universe. It stretches away from you infinitely, in every direction. Before Kate, this fact had pointed to the conclusion that Nina really was, as she had suspected, the center of the universe. But now, she had no idea where she was, or who. Under the surveillance of a neurotic eight-year-old, she wasn't able to move with the freedom she was used to. Until school started, Nina was stuck watching her all day. She couldn't keep doing what she was doing now: sneaking out when Kate was asleep, a note next to her pillow. The kid kept opening her eyes and sitting up just as Nina was about to fade into the dark.

How do other women balance work and family? Sunlight was antithetical to crime. The things that made Nina invisible at night—her murky hair and dark clothes—stood out in silhouette form during the day. People were less drunk, or not drunk at all. They were, um, nice. When she bumped into men, they said, "Excuse me," even when it was her fault. They smiled at her before she had time to rob them, and she lost her nerve.

The notes taped to her door from her landlord were no longer written on notebook paper. Now they were typewritten on pink carbon paper and looked official. Nina threw them in the garbage without reading them, but Kate always noticed. "What's that?"

"Love letter."

"Who loves *you*?"

Nobody, Nina thought until Kate added, "Besides me?"

This situation was becoming impossible to give up.

One morning while Kate was downstairs coloring, Nina tiptoed over to her desk to drop a new wallet in. She pulled the bottom drawer out and reached inside the dead space at the bottom for the familiar feel of leather.

The wallets were gone.

Nina groped, but she only felt the flat bottom of the desk. "Oh *shit*," she said. She scanned the room, but saw only Kate's few toys, books, and clothes in rumpled piles. She kicked through them, but no wallets.

Downstairs, Kate was wearing Nina's Ramones T-shirt cinched around her waist with a bungee cord she had found in a hall closet. She sat in the middle of the floor with the coloring book Nina had gotten her—Godzilla, eating Tokyo.

Nina pulled on Kate's shoulder until the little girl faced her. "Where are they?"

"Where are what?"

"The *wallets*," Nina nearly shouted into Kate's face. She softened her voice. "The wallets. Where did you put them?"

"I threw them away."

"What?" Nina ran to the garbage can and started pulling out banana peels and crumpled plastic wrap.

"I threw them outside in the dumpster," Kate said.

Nina ran out the door without stopping for shoes. Downstairs, she sprinted to the dumpster, just as she saw the garbage truck backing its way out of the alley. "Oh shit oh shit oh shit oh shit oh shit," she prayed as she thrust open the lid. But it was empty, except for the smell.

Nina took a breath before reentering her apartment, and closed the door behind her gently. Kate was waiting, her crayons all replaced in the box.

Nina kneeled next to her. "Why did you do that?"

"They're not yours anyway."

"But I really need them, Kate, one in particular. One in particular was very important. It was my insurance policy, in fact, and now I don't have it anymore." She tilted Kate's chin, searching out her eyes, which kept looking away. "You didn't perhaps save one of them? One that says Cage Callahan, with a police ID inside?"

"I threw them all away." There were tears starting in her voice.

"Crap. Kate, you have no idea what you've done." Kate started crying, and Nina drew some satisfaction from that. "How did you even reach the dumpster?"

"A man helped me. He said he was a garbageman." She sniffled, "He didn't *look* like a garbageman."

"Jesus, Kate. Stay away from strange men, okay?" Wait. "What did the garbageman look like?"

"I don't know. A man."

"A man, yes, but what kind of man?"

Kate started crying again. "I don't know. A big one?"

"We're completely fucked." Nina rubbed her eyes. "What am I going to *do*?"

Then she remembered something in a hot flash that struck her heart. She sprang up and ran to her closet. It was gone. Then she ran up to the loft and tore through Kate's clothes, half of which had been stolen from her closet. She finally found it stuffed into a basket with Kate's stuffed animals—her black skid hat.

She sat down in relief. In a fit of irony, she had pinned Cage's badge on it before she had gone out for her last wallet. Now, she pulled the silver-and-gold badge off the hat and held it in her palm like a baby bird. She traced one fingertip over the seven points of the star, the eagle on top, head turned as if averting his gaze. She pressed her thumb over Cage's badge number, hard, imprinting it into her skin. He would be back for this.

Nina carried it the living room and sat next to a dejected Kate, slumped at the foot of a chair. "So. How did you know about the—what was in the desk?"

"I snooped."

"Well. That's bad. That makes you a bad girl." Nina straightened Kate's T-shirt-dress, asking casually, "Did you tell Isaac?"

"No."

"Well, don't."

"*You* don't."

"I'm just trying to put hot dogs on the table. Listen. I want to show you something." She uncovered the badge in her palm. "See this police badge? From my hat? It's a real one."

"Is it yours?"

"Possession is nine-tenths of the law."

"Are you a policeman?" Tears clung to the eyelashes around Kate's eyes, like petals on a flower.

"No. But as long as I have this, I'm safe. You're safe. We'll be able to live together like this. But only as long as we keep this badge safe. Okay?"

"Okay."

"And that means we have to hide it. Somewhere only we know."

"Under my bed?" When Nina shook her head, Kate asked, "Where?"

Nina's gaze snagged on No-Hair, lying akimbo on the floor. She kept staring at the doll, even when Kate touched her arm.

When she raised her gaze to meet Kate's, the tears had already dried on the girl's face. Kate picked up her doll and held it in her lap.

"Will it hurt her?" Kate asked.

"No," Nina said. "She can't feel pain."

Kate looked back and forth between Nina and No-Hair.

"It's your birthday soon," Nina said. "I'll get you anything you want."

"I want two things."

"Two things, then."

Nina picked up the doll for the first time. It was surprisingly heavy for something made of plastic. No-Hair was fat, with modeled rolls on her arms and legs. The doll designer had given her tiny, bizarre breasts, and a large, round stomach. Her eyebrows looked like stitches. Her eyes were starbursts of blue, with eyelids that closed with a tap when she was horizontal. Her lips were pursed, as if she were about to say something ironic.

Nina went to the kitchen and came back with a knife. Kate sucked in her breath, but said nothing. Nina removed No-Hair's dress, and laid her on her stomach. Kate held the doll's hand as Nina sliced into her back with the tip of a paring knife. Kate winced.

The room was so solemn, Nina almost expected to see blood, but the doll was, indeed, just a doll. Nina slit No-Hair's spine down to the place where her butt began. She stuck a finger inside. The air inside the doll was cooler than the air outside it. Nina wedged the police badge inside No-Hair, realigned the edges, and then superglued them back together.

Throughout all this, Kate silently watched. Nina put two Band-Aids over the incision and sat up. She rattled the doll and listened. Nothing. That badge was snug inside.

She smiled. "We're done." She turned to Kate, whose eyes were full of tears. "Whoa. What's wrong?"

Kate wiped her eyes and picked up her doll. "She's different now," she finally said.

"Different how?"

"She has a secret."

"Secrets are good." Nina straightened Kate's shirt. "So what do you want for your birthday?"

"I want you to stop taking things."

"That's not a birthday wish. Don't you want a new doll or something?"

"You can get in trouble, and then they'll take me away. Don't you want me?"

Did she? Nina stared at the spunkless kid, buyer's remorse already well in place. She had made such a big noise about it, her rights, her blood. Now, with Isaac a thousand miles away, Kate didn't look like such a prize after all. She looked like a prematurely worried little girl with ketchup on her shirt who needed a bath. Her hair was a scribble. Crusty yellow stuff was stuck in one corner of her eye and mouth. She seemed lost in a too-big T-shirt and a strange house with nothing but a coloring book between her and the cold reality that nobody in the world loved her anymore.

Almost for the first time, Nina realized that Kate had lost her father less than a month ago. Nina lost her brother, but Kate lost her father. Father trumps brother. Which meant that, in her own grief, Nina had been ignoring the fact that Kate was grieving all alone. An unfamiliar sensation invaded Nina's chest.

But she had been silent too long. "You *don't* want me," Kate said. "Nobody wants me." Her eyes filled again immediately.

"That's not it. I do want you. It's just that we need that money."

"Why don't you marry Isaac, then? He has money."

"Isaac doesn't like me. He rejected me in advance. He prejected me." She remembered his laugh at the thought of dating her, her miserable colaugh.

"Will your dad give you money?" Kate asked.

"I think he's dead. He wouldn't help us anyway."

"Why not?"

"He used to hit."

"You hit," Kate pointed out.

"I don't hit you."

"You might hit me." Instead of fear, Kate's face showed only curiosity, the innocence of a child who's been hurt but not hit. "You promised that you'd give me what I want, and you cut up my doll."

"Jesus, Kate, I thought you were going to ask for something I could buy."

"Steal, you mean," she said, surprising Nina. Kate stamped her foot. "Can't you do something else?"

"No." Long ago, Nina's world had been converted into sharp points and dull ones. That's a value system. What can replace that?

Kate grabbed Nina's head and yelled into her ear, "Stop it! Stop it! Stop it!"

Nina tried to yank her head out of the little girl's hands, but Kate had fistfuls of her hair. Nina was shocked at the sheer amplitude of the little girl's ordinarily tiny voice. Her eardrum felt like it might burst. Nina yelled over the yelling, "Quiet! Quiet down!" but Kate kept screaming even when Nina covered her mouth with her hand. "Kate Black! Katrina…what's your middle name, anyway?"

"Mmpha." Kate stopped yelling into her palm and started licking it.

Nina took her hand off Kate's wet mouth and wiped it on her leg. "Yuck."

"Nina."

"What?"

"No. You asked my *middle* name. I'm telling you," Kate said. "Nina's my middle name. Dad named my middle name after you." She recited, "Katrina Nina Black. It rhymes."

Nina's voice came out funny. "Why would he do that?"

"Dunno. Why do we have middle names, anyway?"

"So we can tell the difference between George Foreman's children." Nina frowned. It somehow felt different, now that she knew that they shared a name. "So, what's birthday present number two?"

"I want us all to be together. You, me, and Isaac. A family."

"Can't you just ask for a pony or something?" Nina grumbled.

Kate gazed at her, Chris all over her face. Nina realized that the girl hadn't changed her clothes in two days, and her nose was running. Nina pulled the cuff of her sleeve over her hand and wiped her face. She tugged Kate's dirty dress over her head. Kate danced around, chilly, her arms crossed over her bare chest. Nina yanked her sweater from a chair and dropped it over the little girl's head. Kate flopped her arms around until the long sleeves whirled like pinwheels.

Remember this moment, Nina thought.

Her secret had hit the open air and had strengthened, as she felt herself weakening. Soft and pliable, she was bumping against the days. She had quit smoking and hadn't even noticed. She was part of something outside of the boundaries of her own skin, losing the edge she had cut her life on. The muscles in her body relaxed for the first time, and she tried to prod them into tension. They didn't respond, sleeping snakes. She was feeling better and better. And it was dangerous.

CHAPTER NINE:
ONE THING

A SQUIRREL AND A BIRD were talking about foxes.

The squirrel said, "I know fifteen ways to escape a fox. I freeze and dodge, jump, flip my tail, climb trees. Sometimes I run in zigzags..." After the squirrel finally finished, it asked the bird, "What about you?"

The bird said, "I only know how to do one thing. I fly away."

Meanwhile, a fox had been stalking them from the bushes. It now jumped out with a big commotion, tearing and biting.

The fox's jaws closed on the squirrel as it was trying to decide which of the fifteen things it should do.

The bird had already flown away.

~

NINA WAS SO NERVOUS, she woke Kate up two hours early for her first day of school. She bullied the girl into the shower, made her brush her hair and teeth, and then argued with her for fifteen minutes about why Nina's Avengers T-shirt didn't work as a first day outfit. Nina finally wrangled the kid into a plaid jumper dress from a secondhand store. Kate hated it. "It itches."

"Life itches." Nina handed Kate the lunch bag she had carefully assembled with a roast beef and provolone sandwich,

Cheetos, and an apple. She wondered if school cafeterias were still the same—scratched tables with wads of gum crouching underneath, cherry Jell-O with carrots shaved into it, the farty smell of waterlogged string beans boiled until they were yellow. She wondered if Kate would have friends, or if she'd be stuck at a table with the kids who didn't wash, the kids who chewed on their pigtails and shoelaces, the kids with nicknames that referred to fat or mucous. The thought worried her. "Come on." She pushed her out the front door. "Where's your backpack?"

"It fell in the dumpster when I threw the wallets out." Kate skipped ahead of her on the street.

"I'm not getting you another one."

"But I need somewhere to put my books and shit."

"Don't say 'shit.'" The yellow bus rumbled up next to them. "Say 'crap.'"

"Why do I have to go to school, anyway?"

"To learn things." Nina's voice wavered with nervousness. "Two halves make a whole. The major exports of Brazil. Shit—crap like that. Remember to wipe your nose today, Kate, okay?"

The boys boarding the bus looked like carjackers-in-training. The middle-aged bus driver leaned over and asked Kate, "Are you getting on or what?"

Little eyes grilled them through the bus's half-open windows. Nina couldn't believe there were so many kids. Except for Kate, she had forgotten about kids, how the world was infested with them. The littlest kids were so little, with such big heads and short arms. They looked like teddy bears.

"Get on the bus, dummy!" one of them hissed out the window, startling them.

Nina hurried to shove Kate onto the bus with all the other little criminals. If she had learned anything from *Return of the Jedi*, it was that one teddy bear is cute, but fifty pissed-off teddy bears is a revolution. "Nina," Kate said before the door closed on her, shutting Nina out. Her mouth moved, but Nina couldn't hear what she said.

Kate's face was tinted gray by the bus windows. Nina tracked her outline until she dropped out of sight into a seat. The bus vomited exhaust and pulled away. The back of Nina's throat constricted, and she blinked away quick tears. *What's wrong with me?* she thought. Kate was eight, hardly a person at all. Nobody to cry over, certainly—timid as a rodent, with occasional shrieks that made Nina want to move out.

But Nina was keeping the girl. Here's why—yesterday, Nina was about to go downstairs to get a newspaper when she felt something tugging at her finger. She looked down at Kate, holding her pinky finger with her entire fist.

She didn't know why that made her want to cry.

The Denver Human Services office was across from Rude Park. Nina got in her car and headed west on Colfax. It only took twenty minutes to get there, twenty more minutes to find the right building, ten more to find the right person, and an hour and half to wait to talk to her.

When Nina was finally admitted into the lady's office, she had to breathe through her mouth. The office was too minuscule to hold one person and all her varied smells—tuna sandwich, supermarket cologne and BO from polyester clothing and bad HVAC. The lady typed rapidly on a keyboard and didn't look up, so Nina interrupted. "I'm trying to adopt my niece."

The lady's plastic reading glasses slid down her nose, and a pen was lodged in the most spectacular afro Nina had ever seen. "Disposition of the biological parents," the lady droned, still looking at her computer.

"Um. Well, um. Sunny, I guess. But I only knew one of them."

She looked up. "Are they alive, dead, in jail, what?"

"Oh. Dead."

Meanwhile, the lady had stacked a bunch of papers together with efficient hands. She gave them to Nina and retrieved the ballpoint pen from the depths of her hair. "You need an affidavit of citizenship, a physical examination, a parenting plan—"

"What's a parenting plan?"

"Your plan for parenting." The lady tapped the papers with the pen. "Here's where you fill out the financial information. We also need three years of back taxes."

"What if I don't know where my back taxes are?"

"You don't know where they are." It wasn't a question, but still demanded an answer.

"There was a fire."

"Did they burn, or did you misplace them? Or both?"

"Both," Nina said.

The lady sighed. "How about a spouse? Does he have a job and a tax record of such?"

"He has a great job. But he's not my spouse. Or even my boyfriend," Nina said. "So that won't work at all."

"Your bank account?"

Her bank account was a sock.

"Pay stubs from your employer?"

Nina chewed her upper lip.

"Was there a fire there, too?" The lady put down her pen and massaged her stockinged foot, slipped out of its worn shoe. "These are the minimum requirements: stable employment. Stable living situation. No recent criminal activity or jail time. No recent or previous history of domestic violence or drug or alcohol abuse. No reports from a therapist about dealing with such. No history of crimes against children." She stopped rubbing her feet and clasped her foot-smelling hands on the desk. "Listen, I don't care how you do. They just want to see that you can do a better job caring for this child than the state can."

"I'm a bit short on money these days," Nina said. "But I'm in her dad's will."

"It won't matter if you're in the Old Testament. I'm just telling you how they do. Get a job, fill out the forms, do the home visits—"

"They visit my home?"

"They find out all about you. They fingerprint you and do a background check."

This made Nina even more nervous. She hadn't ever been arrested, but who knows where her fingerprints had ended up? "My niece doesn't have anyone else," she said. "Just me."

The lady said, "Then get a job, right?"

"Or?"

"If there's no other family, the child will go into a group home. What's your name?" She pulled out an index card.

"Your office smells like feet," Nina said and left.

Anyway, there was more than one way to keep a kid.

Climbing back up the fire escape to her apartment, she almost felt better, looking up at the pretty sound of a dove flapping its white wings in the wind, settling high on the branches of a tall tree. As she reached the top step, she realized that it wasn't a dove but a seagull, no, a pigeon, no, it was in fact a white plastic bag stuck up there, trying to ruffle itself free.

"Hello, Nina." The voice came from below. She bent over the railing and looked down.

Cage trudged toward her in khakis and a white dress shirt.

"Oh, you," Nina said. "I forgot about you."

Through his hair, Cage's pink scalp shone when he looked down to scrape at something invisible on his shirt. It looked like his hair was thinning, compared to the last time she had seen him. He wore his holster again, but didn't draw his gun.

"Don't you work?" she asked.

"I'm working now." His Lysol aftershave wafted up, fuerte as ever. She sneezed. His face worked as he resisted, but OCD won out: "Bless you." For fun, she fake-sneezed again, and again—"Bless you. Bless you. Shit, goddamn it," Cage muttered.

"What do you want?" she asked.

"I want to quit my job," he said. The anguish in his voice spoke to exactly what Nina had avoided her entire life—the tedium of mandated routine, having to shower, the illusion that she could be bought for a designated hourly wage. He flashed teeth. "But I can't without my badge, right?" He didn't mention his ID.

"Just say you lost it. I lose everything."

"Losing a badge would make the newspaper."

"They say even bad press is good press."

Still smiling that cold smile, he made for the stairs.

She crossed her hands into a T. "Time out."

"Time *out*? This isn't a football game." Still, he waited.

Back in the day, when Jackson took her around to other martial arts schools, Nina met certain men, usually short men, who loved to hit women. But Cage was different from those stunted men and their divorces, their lesbian girlfriends, their on-again-off-again erections. No, with Cage, Nina felt like she was staring into a distorted mirror, angled slightly away to a place she'd seen but didn't understand. Big and red, he had a sex appeal that comes naturally in boxers, swimmers, and anyone who habitually works out with no shirt on. He looked nice in his dress clothes, so ironed and clean. "Love," he had said. She let his gaze trace her body, but knew any kind of sex with him would either be anticlimactic, or one of them would end up dead.

Cage said, "So, let's go. You and me. I'm ready now."

Nina wasn't sure exactly what he was ready for. "The thing is, I have a houseguest."

"What, Mr. Dinner Slacks? Yeah, I saw him."

"No, not him. Wait—how did you see him? Never mind. He's gone." She muttered, "Gone, gone, gone. Anyway, I should probably stop fighting and…other stuff. Get a job."

Cage said, "That's not you."

"It could be me."

"It could never be you." He clapped his hands together and rubbed them, as if that matter were all settled. "So. I figured out why we keep meeting up."

"I thought that was because you're stalking me."

"Ha! No. It's because we're inverses. You understand what that means?"

"Yes," she lied.

"No, you don't, because I made it up." He inhaled through his nose in a self-satisfied way. "You and I, we're on this invisible seesaw together. Like, if you're up, I'm down, and vice versa. You're happy, I'm sad." His eyebrows were very thin. He pulled a tissue from his pocket and scrubbed dirt from his shoe.

"It's a possibility," she said. Maybe they were inverses, or maybe they were just different manifestations of the same parallel destiny. Or maybe they were just two stupid people in the same alley.

"It's a fact. To be remedied." His cheeks stained red. "So why don't you fetch my little badge, and come on down here?"

It was tempting. Nina imagined herself sliding down the railing into his arms, or maybe kicking him in the head. She played the fight forward in her mind. It could be the kind of win that would carry her through many a bad night of waiting in the dark for nothing.

But she knew that if she started fighting Cage, she'd keep going far beyond the scope of their twisted relationship, just because once she started, time would stop, and she could forget that her brother was dead. She could forget that Isaac left her alone, a criminal and single mother with no tax returns. If she took one step down this road, it would never end, because the way she felt right now, at this second, she'd keep fighting Cage until she killed him, and the truth was, Nina kind of liked Cage.

So, even though she knew it would sound fake with a still-blue sky overhead and the smell of hot garbage ripening below, she said, "My twin brother just died."

One corner of Cage's mouth floated halfway up, but that was it. "So that guy isn't your brother."

"Isaac? No. He's a friend."

"Isaac." Cage looked at the smoggy sky, and Nina saw it was the same color as his eyes. "Your brother's daughter is yours now?"

"How do you know about her?"

He tapped his head. "It's not just a hat rack."

Nina started to sweat. "She's visiting. She's going to live with my, my sister. In Cleveland. That's where we're from, Cleveland, Ohio." For a second she panicked, thinking that Cleveland was actually in Michigan. But Cage was still consulting with the sky on some grave affair.

"Do you keep a journal?" he asked.

"A what? No." Nina didn't know if she owned a pencil.

"That friend of yours coming back?"

"Yeah. But not to see me."

"Okay. Later, then." He waved a meaty hand and started to walk away.

"Wait. What—why are you—" but he disappeared behind the gun shop and was gone.

Something had just happened there, but she didn't understand what. Why had he walked away? Now that Cage was gone, she kind of missed him, the way she missed a cigarette after she stubbed it out. Inverse or no, being his girlfriend would mean a life at the bottom of their seesaw—black eyes with occasional hot sex. In other words, it would be like her life now, except someone would actually love her, even if he hated her, too. Wasn't that what she deserved? She fingered the bills in her pocket.

Nina's last score had been the night before, at a hotel bar next to the mall. A European soccer game had been playing on the television, and the jukebox was on high to simulate bar noise. The only promising prospects were four men talking loudly with wide gestures. Actually, just one was loud—a lunky, balding man named Pete.

He had an enormous torso, and his thin, vestigial legs hung from the tall barstool. He looked like a rodent on a stick. Nina sat next to him and he smirked at her. He put his hand on her thigh. He couldn't pronounce "rendezvous." He said, "I'd fuck me."

As all the chess pieces lined up, Nina wondered what Isaac would think of the way Pete laughed at her while eyeing her thighs, the tip of his tongue dabbing his upper lip. Her mind flashed forward to Kate, older, sitting in this chair or one like it, next to this man or one like him. Kate dressed in black, eyeing the bulge in the man's back pocket, letting him grope her leg.

Sensing that he was losing her, Pete pulled out his wallet. He started stacking money on the bar, balancing the bills on their sides. "How much for a night?" he asked Nina as his friends snickered. "One hundred? Two hundred?" The money fell flat, Benjamin Franklins felled by lightning. Then the bills changed. "Two ten? Two fifteen? Two seventeen?" Pete's pallid face flushed under his eyes. He was high off his own nerve. He jingled the change in his pocket.

As Nina was figuring out how to scoop up the money and hit him at the same time, a chair scraped loudly across the wood floor.

A businessman stood up from his briefs at a nearby table. He was tall, and dressed in a black suit, his hair combed back like early Johnny Cash. He walked over, nodded at Nina: "Ma'am." If he had worn a cowboy hat, he would have tipped it. He kicked his briefcase under the bar.

Then a smile spread across his face like a slow sunrise as he punched Pete in the nose. Pete banged into a barstool, and then fell over with a whump.

The bar fell quiet. With a quick flick, the businessman swept the stack of bills into his hand. He presented the neat package to Nina with a little bow. "For your trouble," he said. He reached under the bar for his briefcase and exited through the back door.

Nina left through the front door for once in her life, squinting at the streetlight in her face. She looked at the folds of money in her hand, two hundred and seventeen dollars. Was she worth more than that? Kate thought so. So did her cowboy avenger. Maybe they were right. Maybe it was time for a change.

~

NINA WAS DRESSED IN her most conservative clothes: a gray blazer, beige pencil skirt, and PVC boots from a swanky secondhand store. Her hair was parted in the middle, dividing her face into two careful sections. She wore lip liner. She wore nylons. But it didn't matter, because the only thing looking at her at the temp agency was a computer.

Nina had seen computers before, many times, but she had never put her hands on one. She had never actually typed. She knew the bullet-shaped thing was called a mouse. It didn't look like a mouse. She wiggled it. An arrow jagged back and forth on the screen. In front of her stomach was a keyboard. Why weren't the letters in alphabetical order? The box on the screen asked her to italicize the word "Parrot" in the sentence below. Nina scanned the keyboard. Nothing said italicize. She pressed the closest button, Insert. The box on the screen said she had the wrong answer.

Fine, Nina thought. *But can you break a man's arm?*

The box told her to insert a bulleted list.

I can break a man's arm, she thought.

She took a Microsoft Word test and a typing test, and then ate three of the agency's stale jelly donuts while she waited in the pearl-gray lounge.

It felt strange to do these computer things: such small motions, sitting still, using muscles that had atrophied or maybe never existed. She tapped her boots on the carpet. The place smelled like dust and window cleaner, reheated food and boredom. It reminded her of school, like a kind of dress-up school. She wondered how Kate was doing. Nina would have to steal her some more school clothes. No, *buy* her clothes. Buy, buy. The heater blew directly down on her, and she started to sweat in her suit. She looked down. Chris would love her in *this* getup. She wondered if he could see her now. She wondered if she was going to start crying again. She wondered if they would notice if she ate another jelly donut.

This wasn't Nina's first attempt at gainful employment. She never had been able to hold a job down. Instead, they held *her* down. Nina had been everything (except queen) for a day: ticket taker, inventory stocker, plant waterer, haunted corn maze ghost, waitress, mall Christmas tree decorator, and phone psychic. Elevator girl. For three weeks she had worked as an employee of Gorilla Mattress Supply during a springtime heat wave. They made her dress in a moldy gorilla suit and wave all day at passing cars on the highway. She got heatstroke and passed out next to the company sign. They didn't believe that she had fainted, and fired her for napping.

But this would be different. She inhaled the carpet shampoo residue. Work could save her. Money and legitimacy. She could join the women she saw each day, the ones with high hair who clicked to work, dressed meticulously for their wage-slave jobs. Maybe she would grow to like work in the way that prison inmates grow to like lockdown at night. She'd answer phone calls for other people, wash dirty coffee cups, and file pieces of paper nobody would ever look for. Gravity would push her into the great American work mechanism. She would be a cog in the wheel. Wheels need cogs. She would be needed.

It's just that the thought fit her the way an argyle sweater did—not at all, and it itched like hell. Until she had fainted, the Gorilla job had been her favorite because that's how she felt, like a Gorilla in a mattress store, or an extraterrestrial in a supermarket: the wrong thing at the wrong time. It might have been different if she had been good at any of it. But she was only good at one thing.

A woman with glasses and a long brown braid called her name from an inner doorway. The lady was about fifty and wore a lemon-colored dress with a gold belt buckle and puffy sleeves. "I'm Priscilla."

Her handshake was soft. Nina kept gripping harder and harder, trying to get a handhold. "Hi. I just wanted to say—"

"Ouch."

"—oh, sorry, I wanted to say thanks for the interview, because I need a job really fast, something high-paying with benefits."

Priscilla held a sheet of paper by the edges as if it were infested, before dropping it on her wood veneer desk. "I have your test results here." In her grip, her pencil snapped in half. "Do you know how employment agencies work, Nina?"

"Yeah. You get me a job."

"I don't know if we're going to be able to help you. We do mostly clerical work. We don't have many jobs in, um, manual labor."

"But I *want* clerical work. I already do, um, manual labor."

Priscilla's eyelid twitched from a potassium deficiency. "Have you considered going back to school? Maybe a secretarial school, for basic business skills?"

Nina wondered what basic business skills were. "Don't you have anything for me?"

Priscilla tapped on her computer for an uncomfortable minute. "I have a receptionist position for minimum wage."

Nina rubbed her eyes, remembering her mascara too late. "How can I support a kid with that?"

"There's room for advancement," Priscilla said.

"There's certainly no room for retreat." Nina leaned over to peer at Priscilla's computer screen. "That's all you've got?"

Turning her squeaky monitor away, Priscilla glanced at Nina's wrinkled shirt, her blurred lipstick. "Without a college degree or a high school diploma, you're looking at minimum wage, maybe a dollar over. In this economy, anyway."

Nina felt tears begin in her stomach.

"Listen," Priscilla sighed. "If you want a job, you really have to sell yourself, usually for less than you're worth." Her thin nostrils flattened. "I'm just trying to help."

And she was; that was the worst part. Nina looked at her broken pencil and puffy consignment dress. "I'll think about the receptionist thing."

Outside the office building, Nina bought a *Denver Post* and leaned against the dispenser, scanning the classifieds. So many jobs! Why hadn't she tried the paper first? She licked a finger and turned the pages:

"Do you have a smile in your voice?"

"Trial lawyer needed."

"Exciting employment opportunity. Send full body shot in bathing suit."

"Ice cream scooper. Must have college degree."

Nina didn't have a smile in her voice. She didn't have a bathing suit. People hustled by, clutching briefcases or messenger bags. They all had jobs. When had she become the only jobless freak in the world?

"Corrections officer, top pay."

"Great opportunities for loving nurses."

"Do you want to be a model?"

One word stood out from Nina's newspaper in bold type: "Security." *That would be good,* she thought—*security.* The ad was for an armored car company, searching for drivers and guards. They were fourteen blocks east of the agency. Nina felt too twitchy to take a bus, so she ran toward her destiny, feeling lighter at every step. Nina, driver. Nina, guard. The sun was out, and she sweated inside her gray blazer. By the time she entered the glass doors, she felt wet and slippery.

A fat ex-football player type (weak knees) faced Nina in a swivel chair. His face was puffy and jaundiced. He picked at the skin of his thumb with his forefinger. A smoker, but he couldn't in here. Listening to the phone, he looked her up and down, his gaze snagging on her breasts. He hung up without saying anything at all and smirked, "I hope to God you're looking for me."

"I'd like the job," she said. "The security job."

His body contracted in a grunt. "Prior experience?"

"Plenty," she said, faking it 'til she made it.

"Clean record? Written references?" When she bit her lip, he said, "No references, no job."

"I can do this job."

"Sure you can. But we don't just hand out firearms to anyone who wanders in off the street."

"Firearms? Oh. No. I don't believe in guns. I mean, I believe they exist, clearly, but I don't want to, myself, you know..." She pulled an imaginary finger-trigger, inadvertently shooting the man in the face. He frowned. She realized that she was already on her way to getting fired again.

"We guard trucks with a lot of money in them. What if someone shot at you?" His eyebrows skipped. "All our security guards are armed. That's the job, sugar." His chair squealed in pain.

"I don't want to kill anyone," she said.

"We're not asking you to kill anyone."

"Then why carry a gun?"

He opened his mouth, shut it, opened it again. "The person we hire has to carry a weapon, and we don't consider anyone without experience, references, a social security card, a driver's license, and a clean criminal record. Goodbye."

Nina rubbed her eyes. It was all so complicated. Maybe she could carry the gun, just as long as she wasn't expected to use it. She started to explain this, but it was sweaty in that office, and when she gestured, her arm made a loud scudding, farting sound in her armpit.

She froze. His chair creaking, the fat man leaned away from her.

She whispered, "That was my arm. Not…the other thing."

"I think we're done here."

"I didn't—"

"Out, before I have to put on a gas mask."

Outside the building, Nina shed her suit jacket, letting her body cool. That was her armpit. She did *not* fart in that man's office.

She looked up at the blank sun and remembered the desert she had grown up in. That parched wind had blown her from there to here. She didn't belong in either place, the way that dust doesn't belong in the wind, but it's there anyway. She threw the want ads in the nearest garbage can. After all.

She only did one thing.

~

"SCREECH LIKE A MONKEY! Screech like a monkey! Dickson? Aw, shit." The director yelled "Cut," and sighed. "What the hell?"

Isaac tried to let his arms drop but couldn't, as he was encased in a giant yogurt tub. "Chaz, I'm playing a yogurt. Why do I have to sound like a monkey?"

"Because there's a giant monkey graphic on the tub, holding a banana. You're banana yogurt." The director pointed at Isaac's chest area. "See? Monkey."

"Why aren't I in a monkey suit, then?" *At least I could hide my face*, Isaac thought.

"No. You're not a monkey. You're banana yogurt. Monkeys like bananas." Chaz sighed. "It's not literal. It's not high symbolism. It's just a commercial."

Isaac waved his oversized plastic banana prop at the other actors. "I don't see boysenberry or mango having to sound like zoo animals."

"Strawberry has to sound like a hooker, and blueberry sounds like my grandmother on crack. Which one you want to switch with?"

"I'm just saying, maybe you should rethink your vision."

Raspberry hissed, "Oh, for fuck's sake."

Chaz looked at his watch. "Okay, time for a break. Everyone grab a sandwich and we'll start again at three. Can you be ready with your one line then? Isaac?" He stalked away, muttering, "Fucking divo," pinching the space between his eyes.

This was the second of four commercials with Chaz he had lined up in LA over the next month. The guy was a major asshole, but Isaac knew for a fact that he'd be directing for thirteen associated products in the future, one of which was to be a series—a five-commercial story about a fictional family Isaac hoped to be part of.

The problem was, Isaac didn't feel qualified to act like he had a family. Instead, he had that weird feeling you get in dreams, that you're in the wrong place at the wrong time. As if his purpose in life wasn't selling the world on exercise equipment, or gum, or yogurt.

He squeezed his eyes shut and tried to get in the right headspace. He had done his usual routine to pump himself up for this job: slapping his cheeks in the bathroom, going through his vocal exercises ("Ma meh mi mo mu! Fa feh fi fo fu!"), only to stand mute at his cue. A newspaper lay on a table next to him. In those pages, there was war. There was genocide. There was corruption in high office. These things meant something. Maybe art could transcend devastation, but this was not art. Nina was right.

He wondered what she was doing now.

The other actors in tubs of yogurt drifted toward the schwag table offering (you guessed it) yogurt donated by the client. Isaac felt a strange unease at the cannibalism before him, big yogurt containers consuming miniature versions of themselves. He slumped lower at his card table in the corner, sitting at a slant so he didn't have to wrestle his costume off.

The lady who played Blueberry stepped in front of him and waved her hand back and forth in front of his face. "You okay?" She was the only one who had bothered to climb out of her costume, and he looked at her with envy. He didn't feel like parading around in his yellow spandex bodysuit, thinner than paint, but a bodysuit looked entirely different on a woman. Her eyes matched the blue of her makeup, the blue of the walls. She adjusted her blue wig and nodded in Chaz's direction. "He's a prick, you know that."

Chaz was gesturing wildly while yelling into his cell phone. Isaac said, "Yeah. I know. Thanks."

"Well?" When he didn't say anything, an outraged blast of air shot through the woman's teeth. "You don't recognize me, do you? Jesus, Isaac, you've been inside me." She pulled off her blue wig like a top hat.

Marcy. His ex-girlfriend. He jumped up to kiss her blue cheek, trying not to bump her with his costume. "I'm sorry. It's the makeup." They had dated for a year and it had ended badly. That was over four years ago—maybe she forgave him. He forgave himself. "So, are you seeing anyone?"

"God, you don't waste time." She tucked her hair back into her wig.

"I didn't ask that to—to—"

"I am seeing someone, for your information. I'm happy now."

"I'm happy you're happy. Everybody's happy."

"My boyfriend is great. *He* knows what he wants."

The contortions we go through, he thought, *just to be together. And maybe I knew what I wanted. Maybe it was just that I didn't want you.*

Marcy unwrapped her sandwich and blinked a few times. "Good to know you're still the same, Isaac."

"No, I'm actually not."

"Yes, you are. How's your 'friend?'"

"Chris? He was my friend, not my 'friend.' And he died."

"I'm so sorry." Marcy's hand covered her mouth. "I'm so, so sorry. Death is so final, so, so…" Her napkin was still in her hand, as if she were too sorry to do such a mundane thing as drop it. "When you lose someone close to you, it's just—"

Why does everyone have to comment on death? Isaac wondered. *It's as common as life, yet everyone struggles to say that one new thing that'll finally put it all together into something that makes the slightest bit of—*

"So that's what you mean. When you say that you're not the same." Marcy's face had softened into prettiness. She had always been pretty. Isaac tried to remember exactly why they had broken up, but it had seemed like any other relationship— fabulously sexy in the beginning, followed by criticisms, ending with phone calls spiked with long silences. During one of them, Isaac had fallen asleep.

"Marcy, can I ask you a question?"

"You just did."

"Yeah. Right. So, what if I were to, you know," he fired off his fingers like they were six-shooters, "get back out there." She winced. "Like, even you and me. I mean, if you weren't seeing this great guy who knows what he wants. How might I, you know, do things better next time?"

"Okay. For starters, don't propose to the girl on the second date." She arched a blue eyebrow.

"I didn't do that. Did I do that?"

"You said, 'You're the kind of girl I could marry.' Right before we not-so-coincidentally slept together for the first time."

"Yeah, but that's not—did you think—" He rubbed his forehead. Yellow greasepaint came off in his hand. "That's not a proposal. A proposal is a direct question. Anyway, you can't take the first month of a relationship seriously. The first few dates, nobody's ever really being themselves. They're just representing themselves. You know, 'I'm a Democrat, I eat meat, I love the Patriots,' like that."

"I was being myself."

"Okay. You're perfect. So whatever, tell me all my mistakes. Call it catharsis."

Marcy's face screwed up. "I don't need catharsis. I mean, Christ, Isaac." She dropped her sandwich onto the table. "I really did love you, you asshole. Then, after two months of leaving messages on your *machine*, all I got from you was a stupid Christmas card with penguins on it. You put me in therapy. I lost all my confidence. My friends told me to forget you, but yours was the name in my head." Under the makeup, the arteries in her temples pounded.

"God, Marcy. I had no idea. I'm sorry." He wondered if his not-so-subtle rejection had put Nina in therapy, but immediately dismissed it. Nina would never pay to talk.

Marcy shrugged. "It doesn't matter now. It shouldn't have mattered then. I mean, you're kind of nobody. Eraserface."

Isaac hated her.

Marcy tapped her lip with a blue index finger. "But I always defended you. I called you my desert island guy."

Just as swiftly, he unhated her. She did look nice, even blue, with her wig swept across her forehead and one tendril pointing down toward her lunch. "Desert island guy?"

"Yeah. If I were ever stuck on a desert island with someone I'd eventually be forced to kill and eat, I would want it to be you," she said.

Hate? Unhate? Isaac closed his eyes, and, finding no refuge blind, opened them again. He stood. "Well, Marcy, I'd love to stay and chat more, but you're a bitch."

"Ready in two minutes," Chaz shouted.

Isaac lined up with the other actors, sleepy from the food, grateful they were in tubs so they didn't have to suck in their stomachs. Marcy hustled into her yogurt container, her blueberry face turned sour.

Isaac stood still for the makeup powder puffer, the light meter man, all the fast-moving people brimming with haughty importance, the voices inside them hollering, "I'm more than this! This is just what I do for money!" Everyone else was, at least internally, something noble—a Shakespeare actor, a novelist, a painter, a guru, a deer hunter—except for Isaac. This was the best of him.

So it was pathetic that, even when the director yelled "Action" and the camera was rolling, he couldn't unlock his frozen face. He tried to relax, breathe, be one with his lines. But at his cue (Strawberry: "I don't know, why don't we ask Banana?"), instead of jumping up and down and "ooh-ooh-ooh-aah-aah-aaah-aiiiiyaiii"-ing, scratching the tub in the vicinity of his ribs, waving his plastic banana and pooching out his lips like a chimpanzee, plastic tub incongruously rattling on his shoulders, zooming his face into the camera, pretending that the TV audience was an understanding friend, a little drunk and a little stupid, who always loved you for who you were, regardless of how ridiculous you acted—he just stared, his face in rigor mortis.

The cast waited.

The director waited.

Then, "Dickson? Christ. Cut. What the hell is wrong with you today?"

Isaac mumbled.

"Come on. You're Eraserface. This isn't you."

"It isn't?"

"No! To suddenly have trouble with my fucking vision? Like you have an opinion or something? Why did I hire you?"

"Why?"

"Because you're nobody."

There it was again.

"You're the product, goddamn it. You're a billboard. You're an arrow." Chaz projected his voice and gestured around the room as if he were talking to an audience of thousands, instead of a stripped camera crew and six sweating actors encased in oversized Tupperware. He leaned in until Isaac could smell the garlic on his breath. "Listen, Eraserface. Here's a little secret between you and me and all these fuckers. I don't have a vision. I have a legally binding contract, with you, for a commercial. This commercial."

"Don't call me Eraserface."

"Zip it. Next thing out of your mouth better not be words. I want you to stop speaking English, and start speaking monkey."

"I—"

Chaz stuck his fingers in his ears. "I don't understand you. I only understand monkey."

Dissension was growing among the other fruits. They shot Isaac mean looks, dabbing their foreheads and calling the frantic makeup girl to come over with powder. Isaac stood up straighter inside his costume, but nobody could see it. "I said, don't *talk* to me like that."

"Oh, Jesus," Marcy hissed.

Chaz stepped one foot up on his chair and leaned on his knee. "You know, I just don't understand you people. You're paid inordinate sums to play a simple part, that of an animated inanimate object. You're a cartoon. But you come here and expect it to be something that will justify your entire existence." Chaz's eyebrows arched. "It will not. This commercial will not mean anything in the scheme of your life. It will not make up for that thing you have not got, nor will it get rid of the thing you do not want. It is nothing, going into airspace, which is also nothing, to be ignored by people while they wait to watch the TV show that they really want to see. Which is also nothing." Chaz was now speaking with a faux British accent, perhaps to demonstrate that he, too, had gone to theater school. "It's not Shakespeare." Arm flourish. "There are no great tragedies here." Flourish with the other arm, so both were raised like a ballerina's. "There is no death, no rebirth." He let both arms drop. "Just yogurt. You are a tub of yogurt. You are not Hamlet. You are not Willy Loman." When he saw Isaac climbing out of his costume, Chaz said in his normal voice, "Hey, what are you doing?"

"Quitting."

"What?"

Isaac was having trouble with a latch.

"You're walking out on *this* job? Jesus Christ, Eraserface." When he saw Isaac had pried himself out, he said, "Okay. Dickson. You made your point. Keep your tights on. No screeching. We'll write you a different line, okay? Just get back in your tub."

But Isaac was already out.

It felt exhilarating to throw his yellow wig on the floor with an arm flourish of his own. He was free of plastic, free of nicknames. He was only himself, whatever that meant. He rotated his shoulders in relief.

Chaz tried on a reasonable voice, like he was talking to a high-functioning mental patient. "Isaac, Isaac. What did you expect? A soliloquy? A three-act play? We have two more jobs scheduled after this. Nobody's angry. Just relax. Everyone's on the same side, here." Chaz made patting gestures in the air.

Everyone silently watched the two of them, even the caterer. Isaac thought, *Maybe I am being a baby.* His costume didn't seem so threatening, now that he was out of it. *Maybe I should just finish the job and get it over with*, he thought. *This is LA. This is what we do.*

Chaz's air patting got softer and softer. Just as Isaac was about to give in, Chaz's voice took on a dull, mean edge. "Now get back in your fucking tub and screech like a monkey."

Isaac regarded his director. Chaz had been good looking once. Now, his skin was bloated, and his nose blushed from an undiagnosed drinking problem. One shoulder slumped lower than the other. Like Nina used to say, you can't surf a tidal wave. Within five years Chaz would be finished, and like a sucking drain, he'd take everyone he could down with him.

"You don't understand actors," Isaac said.

"I understand *you*," Chaz sneered.

"No, you don't." Fluffed and powdered, the other actors were definitely staring now. "For an actor, the big question isn't 'To be or not to be.' It's *what* to be or not to be." Isaac turned and said to Marcy, "I am a nobody," then he turned back to Chaz. "But I'm also Willy Loman. And I'm Othello. I'm

Hamlet, Vladimir, *and* Estragon, hell, I'm even Norma fucking Desmond if I want to be." He pointed at his tub costume. "I'm just not that. Not anymore."

Isaac grabbed his clothes and climbed up the stairs out of the set. He paused at the top. The other actors turned up their purple, red, pink, orange, and blue faces at him. Chaz and Marcy looked up with wonder and hatred. He had just given his best performance yet.

Areté, motherfuckers, Isaac thought.

CHAPTER TEN:
CONGRATULATIONS

N THE EARLY 1800S, Bushi Matsumura Sokon was the most feared fighter in Okinawa, a kingdom known for its deadly fighters. He was undefeated, even after he was ordered to fight the king's bull empty-handed. When it was time to marry, he chose Yonamine Chiru, who came from a long-standing martial arts family and was no slouch herself.

Okinawa is a small, gossipy island. People began to talk. Who was the better fighter, Matsumura or his wife? Given a challenge, who would beat whom?

It bothered Matsumura. Chiru quietly filled his rice bowl, washed his clothes, and cleaned their house. Every now and then, she did something unexpected—lifted a fifty-pound bag of rice with one hand while wiping the table beneath it with the other, or pushed down a dead tree in front of their house with her hands. Matsumura stared at her through the long evenings.

One day, they were at a festival and things got rowdy, so Matsumura sent Chiru home alone. On the path to their house, she was confronted by three shabby, dirty bandits. "Leave me alone, or I'll have to teach you a lesson," she said. They laughed.

They stopped laughing when this dainty lady's face turned into a banshee's, whatever a banshee looks like, and she charged them. Kicking their throats, faces, and knees, she quickly dropped two of the men. The third man ran. She chased him down and beat him up, too.

She dragged all three barely conscious men to a tree and tied them there with her obi, her silk belt. After that was done, she went home and finished her chores.

By early morning, the men were crying for help. Matsumura, stumbling home from the festival, recognized his wife's obi. He untied the men and they staggered away. Matsumura held the fabric in his hand.

At the door of his home, he held out the obi. "I think this belongs to you."

He hoped she'd say, "No, I've never seen that obi before," or "I gave that old thing away years ago." Anything, no matter the lie. Instead, she took it from his hand and quietly resumed her cleaning.

What did he have, there in his own house? Who was she, this wife? Matsumura slunk around, peering at Chiru. What the hell was going on?

He had to know. One night while his wife was out visiting, he dressed like a poor farmer and rubbed soot on his face. He walked down the trail leading to his house and hid among the Ryukyu pines. When he spotted her small figure on the trail, he let out a wrenching yell and charged her.

He just wanted to catch her. He just wanted to catch her in his hands, and see who she was. If he held her, could he then have her?

He snatched and grabbed, but missed. His little wife turned into a hellion, a spitting cat, a lunging dragon. She flew at him, everything snapping. Matsumura had no time to think. He had no time to fight back. Chiru knocked down her disguised husband, and tied him to a tree.

Near dawn, a horseman encountered Bushi Matsumura and untied him. Matsumura walked home, in the worst depression of his life. Not only was he defeated, but he was defeated by a woman. His woman. No longer a man, he decided to seek counsel with his teacher.

His teacher said, "Next time, hit her in the breasts. For women, it's like getting kicked in the groin. Hurts a lot."

The next night, Matsumura pled ill when his wife got dressed for a social call. She offered to stay home and tend to him, but he urged, "No, you go." The minute she left, he disguised himself as a fisherman. He rubbed himself with oil and his wife's rouge to look like a sunburned peasant.

Matsumura crept outside and hid next to the path. His heart pounding, he waited for his wife with more excitement, more anxiety than he had on their wedding night. What was this feeling in him? Could it be hate? Could it be love?

After an hour, there she was, Chiru. She was so beautiful in her kimono, her sweet hands in front of her. She walked lightly, humming a song, so happy there without him. She was a mystery, this woman before him, and he fell in love with her for what might have been the first time.

Matsumura sprang from the brush and yelled. This time, he kept his distance as his wife dropped into a low stance and circled him. He charged and struck her hard in the breast, like his teacher had instructed.

Chiru fell down. Matsumura wondered how badly she was injured. He wondered if he should help her up, or finish her off. She struggled to her feet, and he dashed away.

Once home, he quickly washed, changed clothes, and pretended he was drinking.

Chiru limped into their house a few minutes later, put down her things, and began to make tea. She had dirt and pine needles in her hair. Matsumura hid his shaking hands under the table.

She turned to him. There was no anger or remorse, nothing but the consequence of natural events. She said, "Omedetou."

Congratulations.

~

It was three o' clock, almost time to pick up Kate from the bus stop. Nina hurried down the fire escape, still in job interview clothes. Work attire was perfect for shoplifting. Just that afternoon, she had shoplifted a slinky black dress that fit so perfectly under her beige pencil skirt and blue blouse, she still wore both, double dressing like Clark Kent.

She had needed a pick-me-up, after another botched interview and eviction notice posted on her door. Nina imagined Kate's sleeping bag thrown on the pavement, No-Hair stuffed in a trash bag. Had Kate gotten trapped in Nina's bad karma? Were we all caught in the web of each other's fates, hurting and saving each other over and over until the universe explodes and we start all over? Had Nina lost her last chance at redemption, when all she ever wanted was—

"Payback." Cage stepped out of a nook in the brick. He wore his holster, but other than that, he was dressed like a young Marlon Brando: a brilliantly clean wife beater, ironed dress pants, and polished black leather shoes. He raised his eyebrows, plucked almost to extinction. "You look ridiculous," he said pleasantly.

Nina looked down at her outfit. "They're work clothes."

"Who employed you?"

"Nobody yet. I'm looking. There's a job answering phones. I don't know. I might do it. I mean, these clothes fit and everything." Nina had worked dull, flat jobs before. The minutes passed slowly, but they also passed slowly when she was depressed or injured and she hurt too much to make it to the video store and hadn't vacuumed in weeks. Wasn't life always dull and flat between the wildest moments?

Each bristly hair on Cage's head stood up and gleamed white, but his arms were bare. "Did you shave your arms?" Nina asked.

He glanced at his forearms. "Plucked them." He shrugged. "I'm having a hair issue."

A hair issue. "Wait a second." She checked the outline of his nipples through his wife-beater. Sure enough, they drooped. A hint of back acne showed around the edges. "Are you on *steroids*?"

"Don't play Pollyanna. Has your friend arrived yet?"

"What friend?"

"Doesn't matter." Cage squared up and tugged the air with his fists. "Let's go."

"Come on, Cage. Can't we just forget it?"

"I'd have to kill you to forget you."

It felt strangely good to say, "Then kill me."

"This first." His eyes turned pale in the sunlight.

"Why on earth would I fight you for a badge I already have?"

"Because you want to." He gave her a grin, a real one. "And I'm all you got."

Kate, she thought. *I have Kate and Isaac. Not you.*

She smelled fall's beginnings—dying leaves, a wisp of smoke from somewhere, someone cooking something with cinnamon in it. "Okay," she said, almost before she realized she had said it.

"No sucker punches?"

"We'll do it your way." She shucked off her shoes and kicked them under the fire escape. The pavement warmed her feet. "But let's make it quick. My niece's school bus is coming."

Cage danced from foot to foot. He crowded Nina forward and she stepped back, clumsy. He was light on his toes, picking his way back and forth, ducking his head and weaving a little. A light sheen of sweat coated his tattoo, and the tiger rippled in and out of view.

Nina was beginning to feel embarrassed, her mitts around her face, slowly waltzing her way down the alley. She was a counter-puncher, and Cage wasn't throwing anything. She never struck first. *Am I supposed to do something?* she wondered. Out of confusion, she stuck an experimental jab in his face. Cage slipped it and sent a powerful undercut to her chin.

Nina blocked it, but her arm vibrated at the force and she caught the tip of the blow. *Oh no*, she thought.

Cage went into a flurry. He pelted her with a barrage of hot punches and kicks. His mechanics were smooth and forceful. His follow-through sent vibrations through her body as she blocked and parried.

There was joy in the flash of his teeth, the ripple of air through the tips of his short hair. That joy was supposed to be hers, but she was too busy to feel anything.

Nina backed up, on her heels. She tried to remember her tricks, or his. She tried to kick him, but her skirt cinched her at the knees. Her clothes were wrong. The rhythm was wrong. She was wrong. The sun bounced into her eyes. It was too much. *I can't beat this guy*, she realized. *This is a different guy.*

She caught a cross to the jaw.

It's okay, it's okay, she thought until a fast roundhouse blindsided her.

Now she couldn't see anything but black pinpricks in half the universe, floating fireworks of pain in the other half. *Two halves make a whole*, she thought. A low-grade panic attack began in her chest and radiated outward. Still, she was doing okay until she caught a sucker hook on the ear followed by a clean liver shot.

Her body caved. The pavement was hot against her cheek, her bare arm. She tried to bring her eyes forward, but they had floated up behind her eyelids.

Shoes scraped against asphalt. One foot nudged her onto her back. Something metal brushed her hair from her face. It pressed against her temple, a cool circle.

She couldn't see the gun, but Cage's face was beginning to sharpen into view. It shifted, haggard, the way a man's does when he's having sex with you but it's not you. The barrel of the gun vibrated as he tapped his finger against the trigger. His voice was soothing. "Where's the badge, Nina?"

She shrugged, punch-drunk. She didn't mind the gun to her head. It felt nice. Cage dragged the barrel down her face and neck until it came to rest, pressing against her heart. *Whoa,* she thought. *No.* She tried to grab the gun, but her arms didn't move. She tried to speak, but her mouth wouldn't move.

The metal vibrated against her chest. Cage's hand was trembling. Then he muttered savagely, "Not yet. Not yet. Not yet."

Cage shoved the gun back in his holster and pulled something else out of his pocket. Nina heard a click and felt the icy slice across her ribs, quickly warmed by what must be her blood. It was quick but careful, whatever he was carving into the flesh in her side. She tried to roll over, kick him, but only rocked gently on the ground. *My new dress*, she thought stupidly. Her side was wet.

As she heard the switchblade close in his hand, she thought, *Lucky*.

Then he just had to kick her in the stomach a few times, and twice in the kidneys.

She lay on the pavement, drifting on just this side of consciousness. *So this is losing*, she thought. Jackson had never told her about this. He had never lost. She tasted asphalt. A car alarm somewhere sang its one song.

Cage said, "Oh, yeah. One more thing." She opened her eyes in time to see his foot arc back. As he soccer-kicked her temple in a dark, iron blow, he said, "Hii-ya."

~

ISAAC FACED NINA'S APARTMENT door, a bulging suitcase hanging from each hand. He flashed a few different kinds of smiles and checked for bad breath against his hand, which never worked, but you have to try. He knocked and waited.

Isaac was happy to be back in Denver. Denver, inventor of the cheeseburger, the only city in history to turn down the Olympics. He felt sane in Denver, quiet, the kind of person who might answer a question with two words instead of gesturing and drawling on like he did in Los Angeles. Colorado felt like home. The sky's so blue, it's purple. He felt his shoulders loosen and his jaw unclench. There was change here, seasons here. It made life worth living to start every day from baseline as the world warmed itself and cooled, warmed itself and cooled.

He had already stopped by the bank Nina worked at, but they said that she didn't work there, had never worked there. He dragged his suitcase up and down the block, but that was the only bank. Had he gotten it wrong, or was she, in fact, unemployed?

He tried on emotions—mad, congenial, disappointed. He decided on understanding.

He raked his fingers through his shorn hair, rough at the ends from a new haircut, and knocked again. He checked his watch and waited for the pad of female feet across carpet, the brief tension as Nina looked through the peephole and released the lock.

None of which happened. He knocked a third time, and then tried the doorknob, surprised when the door just opened in his hand. *That is just not safe,* he thought, and made a mental note to yell at Nina about it.

"Hello?" Inside, he took a deep breath. That aged apartment smell had now become part of the walls themselves—a combination of cooked canned vegetables, candle wax, and old shoes—but the place was mostly clean. Someone had vacuumed, and the heat registers had been recently dusted. Nina had also hung more pictures, garage sale stuff: framed posters of wine bottles with cheese, stylized cats sleeping on rugs, European cities she'd clearly never visited. Still, they had both grown up with these clichés of class, and he felt strangely comfortable here. This was exactly where he wanted to be.

"Nina. Kate." Isaac wandered into the kitchen and checked out the refrigerator, recently cleaned. Inside, he found Nina's weird food—fancy condiments and cuts of expensive red meat. Nonvegetable vegetables, like pickled artichokes and enoki mushrooms. He opened a plastic drawer. Nina had bought package upon package of hot dogs for Kate. He shook his head. Did she have to be so literal?

Nobody was home. Might as well snoop.

He drifted into Nina's room. He breathed in her menagerie of smells, spicy and clean, and felt his shoulders unlock. He sniffed her pillow. It stank of cheap shampoo. He smelled the truer smells of her sheets—lit paper, grass, pepper. He got an erection. He opened her chest of drawers and immediately found exactly what he was looking for—her underwear. He plunged his hand into the scattered panties and unearthed a pair, instantly disappointed. Pale blue cotton, scrunched up like a face. He tried again. Much better—wine-colored satin, with black lace stuff around the edges. He wondered whom she had bought these for, and got instantly jealous.

"Not wallets," he mumbled and marched up to the hot loft.

Kate's green sleeping bag housed a little community of secondhand stuffed animals. The floors were clean. He approached the little desk. No-Hair stared up at him as he opened the top drawers.

Just papers, stamps, expired coupons, and pencils. He pawed through them and then opened the drawer beneath it. More papers, bills, reminder notes—"Call landlord. Get carrots. Try Harry's Saloon." A fossilized pack of gum, an expired condom. No pay stubs.

He opened the empty bottom drawer, the deep one, and reached into the empty space inside it.

He laughed. All that he felt was a skin of dust. It was completely empty.

He had made up this entire story in his head. Kate had been telling the truth. Nothing was in that drawer. Not wallets, anyway.

He heard a knock on the door. Without pausing to wonder why Nina and Kate would knock on their own door, he plastered down his cowlick and headed downstairs to welcome home the only two people in the world that he had left.

But instead of Nina at the door, it was a large man holding out a cardboard box. "For you," the man said.

~

NINA WOKE UP IN a dumpster.

She didn't immediately know it was a dumpster. She just knew she couldn't see anything. The interior air was musty and damp, clotted with rot and bacteria. Whatever she was lying in was wet and cold and smelled like decaying raw chicken.

She gagged and tried to sit up, but everything hurt too much. She kicked one foot out and recoiled at the clank and impact of the hard metal wall. She tried to maneuver through the morass of plastic and garbage juice, but she kept tipping over. She cut a finger on the jagged edge of a tin can coated with something that was either vomit, brains, or menudo.

She touched her head, still intact. So it wasn't *her* brains, although she had a giant bruise-egg on the back of her head, filled with fluid. Her mind clanging and kidneys sore, she groped along the edge until she found where the lid gave above her fingers. It took all her remaining strength to heave it up. She blinked.

She was in her own alley. She was in her own dumpster. It was night. The street outside was quiet except for a low hum. Nobody was there.

She counted to three then pulled herself up and over the rim, moaning. She landed on the concrete.

The pain was so intense it had to be a trick. Nina found her feet still attached to her ankles. Clinging to the side of the dumpster like its drunk date, she dragged herself up.

A banana peel was adhered to her thigh, and her blouse and pencil skirt were soaked in something. She probed her side and felt a cut in some kind of a shape, more for effect than murder. She couldn't see it clearly, from the blood.

She slowly shucked off her blazer, blouse, and skirt. She tried to adjust the black cocktail dress she had sneaked out of the store underneath her clothes. She was glad it was black, but even so, the bloodstain showed through like she had spilled something. The side was shredded. She had garbage in her hair. She smelled spent fear on her own skin. Her kidneys felt mutilated. She had wounds on her knees and a huge bump on her head. Her nose was busted, her jaw was offset, and her lip was split.

She might have to put off that receptionist job for a while longer.

Kate, she thought. She looked up at the night sky. She was definitely late for the bus stop.

Somehow she made it upstairs, down the hall, and inside her muggy apartment. It took forever; it took one second. She shut the door behind her and stood with her back pressed against it. "Hello," she said.

"Hello," Kate said. She was sitting on the floor. She had been crying and needed to blow her nose.

Isaac stepped forward from the kitchen.

"You're here," Nina said before realizing that he already knew that. "Why are you here? You're here."

"I was going to surprise you." His lip hardened. "You're late. And drunk."

"I'm not drunk," she slurred.

"Right." He pronounced the T.

"I'm so glad you're here." She was also glad that she never replaced the light bulb in her hallway. Cage had been a righty, so she kept her left side in shadow.

Kate's suitcase waited by the door on its little wheels. "Are we going somewhere?" Nina asked.

"No, *we* are not going somewhere. *We* are going somewhere." Isaac stuck out his thumb and pinky and jabbed them between himself and Kate. "It's ten o' clock at night. You never picked Kate up from the bus stop. She searched the streets *by herself*, looking for you. That was over six hours ago. An eight-year-old."

"Almost nine," Kate whispered.

Isaac was breathing rapidly through his nose. "If I hadn't been here when she came back, she would have been alone, all this time. But that's not even what I'm most mad about."

"It's not?"

Isaac pointed at a cardboard box on the floor. "A man named Cage brought this box to your doorstep this afternoon. He said he was the garbage man."

"He never looks like a garbage man," Kate said.

"He said that this had come from your trash, and he had me inspect the contents, in case there was something missing." Isaac kicked the box over to Nina. "What's that smell?"

Like an old lady, Nina kneeled down on one cut knee and then the other. Between the dimness and the blood loss, she couldn't see very well. She reached blindly inside the box with one hand. First she saw Kate's backpack, with her name Sharpied in Isaac's big print. "Hey," she said. "It's your backpack."

Kate looked up at Isaac.

Nina reached back inside the box, and froze at the familiar touch of leather.

"There must be a hundred men's wallets in there," Isaac said. "Stuffed inside Kate's backpack."

"Ninety-eight." But Cage had probably reclaimed his own wallet. "Ninety-seven."

Isaac brushed her hands aside and grabbed a few. "Maxwell Fargas? Dirk Ashfield? Alejandro Conway?" He flipped open another wallet. "Rhett Sanders? How did you get all these? Forget it. I know how you got them." The contempt in his voice hurt more than the rest of it. "So you *don't* work in a bank."

"Doesn't look like it," she said.

He was staring at her like she had morphed into something repulsive. He pulled on the cuffs of his jacket. He was wearing a yellow tie. He looked so wholesome she wanted to catch him in her hands like a butterfly. "You look nice," she said.

"Is that dirt on your face?"

She pretended to rest her face in her hand.

"There is no excuse for this."

"Self-defense."

"It's theft," he said.

"You say potato."

"What *are* you?"

Nina knew that there was some magical thing to say that would fix everything. Isaac was waiting for it, his weight on his left foot like he was about to take a step. Nina looked at her blank ceiling, her filthy floor. She didn't know what she was.

But Isaac did. "You're a worthless thief. You fooled me. Me and Kate."

"No. Kate knew."

Isaac whirled on her. "You *knew*?" Kate shrank from him, but he grabbed her arm. "Don't follow us," he told Nina.

"You can't take her."

"Right. Come on, Kate."

"But—the will says—the custody—"

The danger in his eyes made her stagger back. "Do you really want to go to court with me, Nina? Because I'm sure someone, somewhere is dying to know exactly who's been terrorizing all these poor people." He nodded at the blank custody forms on the table by the door. "You never even applied, did you?"

She shook her head.

"Then this will be easy." Isaac yanked the door open, and shoved the suitcases into the hallway.

They both reached for Kate's hand at the same time. Kate stood in the middle, whimpering. For a second, Nina wondered if they were going to play tug-of-war with Kate's body. Then Isaac snatched Kate's hand out of Nina's and pulled her out of the apartment.

"Listen. Listen." Nina shrank from the harsh hall light, but Isaac didn't even turn around. He picked Kate up in a fireman's hold, grabbed both suitcase handles with the other hand, and headed down the stairs. Kate cried down his back, mouth open with the weight of the implosion, the grief of the ages drawn upon her small face.

Nina limped hard to catch up. By the time she made it out the front door, Isaac was already ducking into the driver's seat of his rental, his neck rigid. Kate banged on the window. A tear dripped from her chin. The car peeled out of its parking space, almost ramming into a green SUV.

"I just want an ordinary life," Nina shouted.

Their rental car gunned down the longest street in America, away from her. Nina stood on the corner, a black gash in space.

She waited for the car to come back with Isaac and Kate in it, so she could explain, so she could apologize, so she could lay down her broken self while they told her it was okay, that they loved her anyway. The wind kicked up. Her lacerations felt like ice burns. She wheezed from a cracked rib. Her knees buckled beneath her over and over again.

A skate rat offered to sell her heroin.

A Jesuit asked her if Jesus Christ was her personal savior.

A homeless man asked her for some money. Then, peering closer, he offered to give her some.

She didn't know how long she stood there before an elderly black man shuffled over and stood next to her, his shoulder touching hers. He smelled like cat urine and cigarettes. He veered his head, looking down the street with Nina.

After a little while, he said, "Whoever he is, honey, he ain't coming back." He shuffled off, the sound of his slippers scraping against the sidewalk with each step until it, too, was gone, and Nina was alone in the black street.

"Goodbye," she said to the night and empty air. Although nothing was good about it, goodbye. She still didn't know the words, the right words for something that hurts you quite like that.

PART THREE

CHAPTER ELEVEN:
THE MARTIAL FOREST

I T USED TO BE called the "martial forest," the loose diaspora of martial artists around China. They took work as courtyard sentries, bodyguards, and temple warriors. It gave them time and opportunity to practice. Many of them formed secret societies with names like the League of Hard Bellies, the Carnation Eyebrows, the Vegetarians, the Boxers. The Triads. The martial forest was a rogue collective of compatriots, a family that transcended blood.

But that didn't stop them from fighting each other.

In the 1960s, Xie Peiqi was five-foot-three and only 140 pounds at his heaviest, but he was the most feared fighter in Beijing. He went undefeated his entire life. He fought people twice his size—Japanese karateka, Mongolian wrestlers, the mafia scoundrels of Beijing. During the Cultural Revolution, the police sometimes woke him up in the middle of the night to arrest criminals they were too afraid to contend with.

Liu Shichang was also a renowned fighter, a champion wrestler. He was six-and-a-half feet tall, and famous for lifting railroad ties by himself. When he met Xie, Liu Shichang looked him up and down. "You're the famous Xie Peiqi? What a waste! Throwing you is like throwing a pillow."

They crossed hands. Liu Shichang ended up on the ground without knowing exactly how he got there. They crossed hands again. Twice more, little Xie threw him down.

Liu Shichang was angry. He was a famous wrestling champion, getting tossed by a tiny runt five years older than him! He was losing face. Liu Shichang let out a yell and attacked Xie one last time.

Xie hit him hard. Liu Shichang passed out and started drooling.

A few minutes later, Liu Shichang opened his eyes. The little man named Xie stood over him. Liu Shichang didn't apologize. He didn't ask to become a disciple. Instead, punch-drunk, he blurted, "Daddy!"

~

NINA WOKE UP IN a strange house.

The first thing she saw was an unfamiliar ceiling. The water stains on the chipped asbestos tiles came into slow focus. The house was silent, except for traffic noises seeping through the seams of the walls.

Nina groped at the thin mattress, the rusty bar poking her in the back. She was lying on a cot next to an immaculate kitchen. The smell of steaming rice clotted the air. On the wall was a tattered scroll of a lotus rising from the muck, and a set of dog tags dangled on a nail by her head. She knew whose house she was in now.

She peeled back the fusty wool blanket. She was wearing pajamas with locomotives on them. The tops didn't match the bottoms, which were instead printed with mallard ducks in various stages of flight. She didn't recall putting them on. She wasn't wearing underwear.

She tried to remember how she got here, but her brain was a soup of blurry material. Her mouth tasted like a toilet. She touched a spongy bump on the back of her head. Like a button, it triggered one quick memory after another—Kate, Isaac, Cage, losing.

Nina had forgotten how much shame hurts, somewhere right behind the eyebrows, spreading backward toward the ears. It hurts worse than regular pain, because it's trapped inside the mind, where nothing ever escapes until the relief of old age. Twisting away from her thoughts, a kind of wildfire spread across her ribs. She yanked up her locomotive jammies. A bandage the size of half a diaper swathed her abdomen, secured with athletic tape. She peeled away a corner.

Well, remind her to teach Jackson to sew, if she ever learned how. He had given her ragged stitches with what looked like ordinary thread. He had also covered the stitches with an orangey paste of something closely resembling baby crap. "Why do you call them Chinese herbs?" she used to tease him. "Herbs are parsley, sage, rosemary, and thyme. Not rattlesnakes, cockroaches, and fungus off the heads of diseased silkworms." She pawed at the mealy mess, scraping away the salve. The cuts were pink where the flesh joined, zigzagged with awkward stitches. The design was strange. Nina looked closer, as far as her body would let her, and read an upside-down "ID," inside a jagged heart.

It would scar that way. Cage had branded her, like a cow. All this for a fucking ID. But the heart was confusing. Did he still love her, with a love that was sick but true?

Something hard and cold was pressing against her leg. She pulled it from underneath the blankets. "Well, hello there," she said. No-Hair blinked at her.

Nina was unprepared for how relieved she felt to see a familiar face, even a plastic one. No-Hair looked like a blue-eyed chemo patient who had seen just about everything. "No wonder Kate likes you," Nina said. "What's it like being dead?" No-Hair appeared to think about it.

The front door opened. Nina threw the covers over her head.

Air leaked out as the blanket drifted down over her legs. There was the sound of shoes shucking off, and slow barefoot steps. A hand yanked the blanket away.

Nina blinked at the old man's face in her face. She kept looking, and looking, and didn't understand because no matter how long she looked, the face on the other side didn't morph, didn't alter, it was still Jackson there but so *old*.

His characteristic fine wrinkles had multiplied until they took over his entire face. Frown lines divided his eyes from each other. The outline of his skull showed through his black hair, which was sparse and fine as coal dust. He was using a cheap brand of hair dye, black-hole-black. The pores in his nose had deepened, darkened. She remembered doing somersaults for this man in his backyard. She wanted to lock him in a humidor. She wanted to keep him in a box, like a cricket she'd feed with tweezers and never let out.

"Jackson," Nina said.

"Nina," Jackson said in his old guttural singsong.

"Jackson?"

"Nina." Then, "Get up. It's noon."

She tried to roll away from him, but the stitches in her side didn't let her. He poked her shoulder. "You have to eat something."

"I'm not hungry." How was that possible? She was always hungry. She ate constantly: chunks of meat seared in sesame oil, dripping mangoes slurped over the sink, crunchy raw red peppers, toasted bagels dripping butter. Yuck.

"You're just feeling sorry for yourself," he said. A beagle snuffled at Jackson's bare feet. Jackson's toes were spread wide, like fingers. Nina remembered that when he kicked the air, his foot always looked like a hand waving hello.

"You look old," she said.

"You don't look so hot, either."

Her face felt greasy, and her stiff hair stayed where she pushed it. "How long have I been asleep?"

"Two and a half days."

"What? That's impossible." She looked at the clock on the wall, but it only told her the time.

"You went to the bathroom a few times."

She didn't remember that. She didn't even know where the bathroom was.

"I changed the sheets. And you," he said.

Nina groaned and dug her bruised face into the pillow.

Jackson said, "It's not your fault. Blood was in your urine. You had a fever of a hundred and four and open infections when I found you. Oh, and I also drugged you with leftover Oxycodone from my root canal, but I got the dose wrong and gave you triple. So don't feel bad about it."

"You drugged me?"

"For the stitches."

"Thanks, that."

"No problem, no problem." Jackson sat on a stool and tugged up her pajama top. "Excuse me." He dislodged a corner of the bandage and poked the sludgy cut with one finger. He reattached the bandage with a grunt. "Good. The pus and swelling are down. Very hot, this cut. I thought maybe I should take you to the hospital, but I figured you probably didn't have insurance." He headed into the kitchen. Something clattered, and an electric can opener whined. "What's ID stand for?" he yelled, a little too loudly. Was he losing his hearing, too?

"ID, like identification," Nina said. "The guy…lost it."

"What guy?"

"Cage Callahan."

"Is that a real name?"

"Yeah."

Jackson popped his head out of the kitchen for a stare. "That's the guy who hit you? You're sure?"

"I was there," she said, and he disappeared again.

"And the heart?" he yelled.

It took Nina a second to realize Jackson meant the cut in her side. "It's not what you think."

"You don't know what I think." Jackson came back with two bowls.

Nina smelled it before she saw it—sardines and rice, which worried her. One, it meant a long talk. Two, it meant she'd have to eat sardines. Jackson handed her a bowl and sat on a stool next to the cot. "Now, then. What's the last day you remember?" he asked.

"I don't know. Friday night? What day is today?"

"Tuesday." Jackson shoved rice in his mouth. "I found you on Sunday morning. You were pretty out of it. You had garbage stink, and melted makeup all over your face. I thought you were dead, except you wouldn't let go of that weird doll." He stopped eating. "Someone trashed your apartment. Broken glass and wallets were everywhere. Blood. What happened?"

Nina picked around her sardines, mining for unpolluted rice. "I don't know." She had a vague memory of Cage there, upturning everything, but it could have been a hallucination. It could have just as easily been her.

"What happened?" Jackson asked again, as if he hadn't asked the first time.

"The butterfly effect." At his face, Nina said, "It was a stupid fight. Over nothing."

Jackson's tongue groped for his missing tooth, and Nina felt her own hardened gums against her tongue. She had underestimated him again. Jackson knew that no fight is over nothing.

"Why did you come to my apartment?" she asked.

"That man, the one with the little girl. He called me."

"Girl—you mean Kate? Isaac? What did he say?"

"Don't get excited. He just gave me an address and said you were there. Then he hung up."

Nina picked up her chopsticks and set them down again. "I wanted to call you. I always wanted to call you."

"I'm in the phone book."

"The phone book." Impossible that it would have Jackson's name in it. His missing tooth flashed black in his mouth as he ate. "You never had your tooth fixed," she said.

"Are you training?" he asked.

"Not really training. Just this."

"Butterfly effects."

"Yeah." Nina straightened her arm, grabbed the skin over her elbow and pinched it hard, like she used to as a kid. It didn't hurt at all. It was odd skin—bendy and crosshatched. Even when he was younger, Jackson's face had always looked like it was covered in elbow skin. She used to wonder if he felt pain.

Her gaze snagged on a snapshot tucked inside a painting of a fisherman gathering up his nets. "Can I see that?" she asked.

Jackson plucked the photo from the frame and handed it to her. He bent over to pick up some rice she had spilled.

The woman in the photo was her mother. She wore an electric blue skirt Nina didn't remember, in a city she didn't recognize. Her mother's smile was crooked, sick, also happy. Nina tapped the photo against her thigh. "When did you get this?"

"About six months after she left. It was forwarded here. Had Japanese stamps. She didn't write again."

Nina stared at the photograph until she memorized it. This was her mother—the same nose, scarred chin, sloping shoulders—after she was no longer her mother. "She's dead, isn't she?"

"I don't know."

He did know, just like she knew. He just didn't know how he knew.

"What happened with that girl, that man? Ivan," Jackson said. "What's his last name?"

"It's Isaac, not Ivan. I was supposed to take care of Kate, the little girl. My brother died, and she was his." She could think about Kate if she avoided picturing her face. "I'm her only family left. But I blew it."

"You're relieved," Jackson said into his rice bowl.

"No!" But underneath the depression and ideas of suicide, she was the slightest bit, well, absolutely relieved. "I'm not parent material."

Jackson cleared his teeth with a finger. "Neither am I, but I took you on."

Nina gestured at her atrophied legs, her bruised face. "You must be so proud."

"One door closes, another door opens. And here you are."

"On your army cot, with homemade stitches in my side."

"You're alive," he pointed out, canned fish in his chopsticks.

Nina didn't know if this was a good thing or a bad thing. "Are *you* training?" she asked.

"Nope." He shook his head vigorously. "Gave it up."

Nina couldn't believe it. "When?"

"About two years after I knocked your tooth out. I renovated the basement into a dojo and trained in it alone for a while. Waited for you to come. Then I quit. It just wasn't fun anymore."

"It was never fun. It's not supposed to be fun."

Jackson shrugged.

Nina was unprepared for the rage that inflamed her. "For fuck's sake, Jackson. It was just a fucking tooth."

"You are what you do," he said. "And I didn't want to be that anymore."

"Nobody *wants* to be like that. We just *are*." Nina had spent every afternoon on this man's dead lawn, running around his trailer and punching the air. She had learned to fight the way a starving person eats. She could just open herself like a hand. The relief.

Jackson's eyebrows furrowed until the wrinkles threatened to engulf all his other features. Nina thought it was the sardines until he said, "Maybe we could—" then he shook his head. His Hawaiian singsong came back. "Maybe we should train together again."

The shyness on Jackson's face was the only thing that kept Nina from laughing. "No offense, Jackson. But you already taught me everything I know."

"Yeah. But I didn't teach you everything *I* know." He wiped his mouth with his hand. "I taught you how to fight. I forgot to teach you when."

"I keep my own counsel," she said.

"You need help."

"I'm not your little girl anymore. I've already grown up. You missed it."

"Okay," Jackson said in the voice he used to shut her up. When he spoke again, his voice was as smooth as paper. "You can stay here. You can heal here. We will train here, together." Nina opened her mouth to protest, but Jackson said, "Then you will return to the girl who has nowhere to go."

In the quiet of the room, the wind pressed against the window screens. The clear breeze washed over the roof before passing on to somewhere else, sinking into lakes, mirrors, wherever it came from. It was almost fall.

Nina stared out the window. "Remember the time when you sent me out for groceries one night? I was sixteen. You hid in that tree in your front yard, that cottonwood. When I came up the walk to your trailer, you jumped down with a big yell and hit me behind my neck."

Jackson's voice was faint with memory. "You dropped the bag. You broke the eggs."

"Then you tapped me here," she found her sternum, "so hard, it felt like I was hollow inside." She did it now, and they both listened to the knocking sound. "You said, 'To fight and win, you must have a vicious heart.'"

He nodded.

"I have one now," she said.

Jackson's eyes sparked, light against dark. "Good," he said.

She blinked.

He said, "Give it to the girl."

~

NINA SAT ON JACKSON's sofa in the ripening twilight, icing her wound, and pursuing the elusive nothing. The mystery of the day dissolved into other things—pain in her side, noise from the television, stale smells from the kitchen. Jackson had turned on a *Murder She Wrote* rerun. Hank slept curled at Nina's feet, occasionally wagging his tail until it hit him in the face and woke him up.

Nina breathed in the smell of old lead paint, stared at the water stains on the ceiling. They were in the shape of a large monkey, or maybe a complicated gun. It wasn't a bad life. Being with Jackson was like being alone. His skin flickered and faded in the light from the television. Birds slept in the swaying trees. The wind roamed around, looking for a soft place to land, or something to tangle into. Hank snored himself awake. It wasn't boring. Grief means the end of boredom.

"Hungry?" Jackson asked. Nina shook her head, but Jackson retreated to the kitchen anyway. She repositioned the baggie of ice over her wound. Commercials erupted from Jackson's ten-inch television: some guy with a butt-chin trying to sell the world on can crushers, or magical ShamWow chamois that can absorb a bucket of water. Nina realized, *That can be my life. I can just be a loser.* She was already a loser—she had lost. Now she just needed to buy a ShamWow and a can crusher, start drinking, get leggings and blue mascara, laugh too hard at jokes or not at all, and maybe collect some kind of domesticated animal made out of plastic. She could buy a sequined hat and stick metal buttons all over it that said things like, "Visualize whirled peas." She could frequent the same dirty bar every night, mooching drinks from drunk strangers, emptying bowl after bowl of free peanuts, trying to pick up the same married bartender who wasn't that hot to begin with.

Or maybe she had already been born a loser. Maybe her life had started on its distorted path at birth. Before that, even, when she was just a parasitic fetus, feeding off her mother's body. Give me your oxygen. Give me your food. Give me your blood.

Give me your money. What's the difference?

Suddenly, Nina's breath left her body. Isaac's face, the nonangry version, filled Jackson's TV, as surely as if Nina had conjured it. He was looking with love at a woman who wore her shining golden hair in a French twist. He pecked her cheek and packed the trunk of a car. They were vacationing in Cleveland.

"Let's go!" Isaac said, and his voice echoed in Nina's body. The woman gave him a sexy smile. Their TV kids looked so much like the two of them, for a second Nina believed it. By the time she realized that Isaac hadn't had nearly enough time to marry someone and have two adorable children since he slammed out of her apartment last week, the commercial was over, leaving Nina with a potent longing for Isaac and, strangely, Cleveland.

"Stop feeling sorry for yourself," Jackson called from the kitchen.

Nina looked back at the TV, but Isaac was gone. In his place, Angela Lansbury frowned, jutted her head, ascertained a clue. Jackson returned from the kitchen with two bowls of ramen and bonito flakes with a dab of soy sauce, chili, and sesame oil. He handed her a bowl.

"Jackson. You're a white guy."

"I'm more Asian than you are. At least *I* lived over there." He pulled the baggie of ice from her hand. "Ice is for dead people," he said. He emptied the ice cubes into a flowerpot and turned off the TV. "Now, then. Explain this butterfly effect to me."

"Oh. Well, a butterfly flaps its wings in Africa, and it turns into—"

"Tell me about that girl. That man."

Nina shook her head.

"Okay, tell me what you've been doing for the last twelve years."

"I thought we went into that."

"Nope." When she didn't say anything, Jackson said, "We didn't."

Wind brushed through leaves.

Jackson said, "Nina, 'mysterious' is not the same thing as 'interesting.'"

She opened her mouth to lie to this man who fed her like a father. What came out was, "I steal."

"Steal what?"

She hiked one shoulder. "Money. Wallets, mostly. From men in bars. Sometimes stuff from stores." It felt good to say this out loud. She scanned Jackson's face, but she could read nothing there.

"No drugs?" he asked.

"I don't do *drugs*, Jackson."

"So, that's what this was about." He gestured around his eyes. She spotted the beginning of a cataract in one corner of his eye, like a soft, cumulous cloud. Then she realized that he meant the yellow bruises orbiting her own eyes.

"Sort of. Thanks for the soup, Jackson."

"No problem, no problem." Jackson asked, chin tucked into his bowl, "So you like to steal? It's fun for you?"

"It was money. I needed it."

He pounded the coffee table, and soup splashed out of her bowl. "I would have given you money!"

"You gave it all to my mother!"

"That's true." He resumed eating.

"It wasn't just money." Money was only a concept to be traded for food and shelter, worthless in itself—an emperor without any clothes. "We fought for it."

"That's not fighting."

"It was definitely fighting."

"Were you ever scared?" A drop of soup shone on Jackson's chin.

"A little. No."

"Then it wasn't fighting. Anyway, aren't you worried about your karma?" Throughout her childhood, Jackson used to talk about past lives, future lives, how you have to be good or you'll come back as a worm or a gym teacher or whatever. But Nina wasn't afraid of suffering.

"I'm not afraid of suffering," she said.

"That's the future. What about fixing your past lives?"

"I don't think I had any. I think I'm new."

Jackson swallowed some noodles without chewing them. "I also did what you did, starting out."

"You stole wallets?"

"Wallets, Nina? Jesus. No, I picked fights in bars."

"Why?"

"I needed a reputation. I'd choose a table of guys and beat them up. Sometimes I went to another dojo and challenged the teacher. Then I'd beat him up in front of his students."

"Did it work?"

"It got me a bunch of hotheads wanting to learn the mystical art of karate." He rippled his fingers in the air. "Paper tigers asking stupid questions. 'What if a guy comes at you with a moped? How do you fight a spatula?' That's why I quit teaching. Except for you." He looked at the short ceiling. "You were always an exception to everything."

Tell me what to do, she begged him in her mind. *You survived a war.* But Jackson just picked his teeth with a thumbnail and burped into his fist.

Nina thought, *He's no guru. No family. He's a worn out vet with no war. He was just grabbing at straws, and I was the shortest one. We're both fumbling toward our deaths, alone in this together.*

"I bought something for you. It's a surprise," Jackson said.

His surprises were usually violent, but this time he just tapped something on the coffee table. Nina picked up a VCR tape, and Jackson grabbed it.

"So what are we watching? *Bambi*?" Nina asked.

"We're going to do a little recon." He read the box aloud: "Mixed Martial Arts."

"I didn't know you knew about that stuff."

"I don't live in a cave." Jackson fiddled with the VCR, jamming the tape into the slot harder and harder. Nina pulled the tape from his hand, turned it around and pushed it in.

As the tape activated, heavy metal music rebounded against Jackson's antique furniture, and the television flashed to a stadium in Canada filled with fat people. Jackson sat back down and leaned forward, elbows on his knees and hands clasped together in the age-old pose of a man watching sports. Nina was amused until a fight photo of Cage Callahan covered Jackson's tiny television. She gasped.

Cage was younger, with a better haircut. They had Photoshopped the pink out of his face, so his skin looked smooth and shadowy. The tiger on his shoulder snarled at the camera.

Nina gazed at her teacher in wonder. "How did you find this?"

Jackson grunted with pleasure and rubbed his hands together. "He loses in this one."

"No," Nina said. "He's undefeated."

"Cage lost to this guy, and then he killed him in the rematch. They don't sell the tape where the guy dies," Jackson said.

"Really dies?"

"Really dies, on TV. Your guy gave him too many blows to the occipital lobe." He mimed a punch to his own head, and even the fake punch swished the air audibly. "They ruled it accidental, but the commission didn't give your guy any more fights."

Nina didn't know how she felt about that. "He's not 'my guy,' anyway."

Jackson read Cage's stats—six-foot-one, fighting at 200, three wins, zero losses, twenty-eight years old then. "What's he like now?"

"Older. Heavier. Dreaming about a comeback."

"He's getting one," Jackson said.

"What?"

"They gave him a twenty-four-hour-notice fight in Las Vegas a couple of days ago. He won it, so they're looking at him again. It's on the Internet. They call him 'Bad Cop' now, Cage 'Bad Cop' Callahan. I guess he's on probation at work for excessive force or something. Anyway, they're hungry for heavyweights, and he only has one loss on his record. Every fight sport is desperate for heavyweights. He's scheduled for two more fights. If he wins, he'll get a title shot."

"So soon? But he's a killer."

Jackson shrugged.

You're a killer, Nina thought. Jackson bit a hangnail, spit it out.

"If you beat him now, as a heavyweight contender, that would really be Areté," Jackson said.

"Christ. Still with that?"

A commentator was saying, "Cage Callahan is easily, pound-for-pound the best newcomer in the division right now."

The color commentator said, "You know, Cage is his legal name. When he was little, his parents kept him locked in an actual dog cage. They fed him out of a dog dish. Nobody knew his real name when they found him, so they called him Cage where he grew up, in a boy's home. Now he's a police officer when he's not training."

"Fitting end to a tragic story."

Next were the interviews with Cage and his opponent, each sitting in front of a black background. "This is where they try to get them to talk trash about each other," Jackson said.

Cage's hulking opponent, Frankie Louis, said he was going to take Cage down, smash his bleeping head in, knock him bleeping unconscious, send him home, tuck him into bleeping bed, and make him a bleeping grilled cheese sandwich. Then he just swore so much, all you could hear were the bleeps interspersed with "the" and "and."

When they cut to Cage, however, his voice was soft. "My opponents are the best, and that makes me the best fighter I can be. I have nothing against Frank. I like the guy." Cage half-smiled. "He's just in my way. I'm looking past him."

"He *sounds* all right," Jackson said.

They flashed to the arena. Cage jogged down through the crowd to tinned heavy metal music, all treble. He lifted his face like he was receiving communion as the cut man coated his nose and cheeks in Vaseline. Cage flashed his mouth guard, knocked his cup with a fist, and climbed into the cage. He jogged around it, slapping his face and hopping up and down. His pectoral muscles undulated inside his skin.

They announced his opponent, Frankie "Cannonball" Louis. Frankie was a steroidal, puffy-looking man. "I never trust men with two first names," Jackson said.

"You have two last names," Nina pointed out.

"Exactly."

Frankie pushed up to Cage, chest first. Cage was taller, and ducked for the stare-down while the referee recited the rules. Their faces were so close it looked like they were going to kiss. When the ref instructed them to touch gloves, they didn't.

This is kind of cool, Nina thought. *I mean, I know this guy. So what if he did knife me and throw me in a dumpster? He's on TV.*

When the fighters broke and returned to their corners, Nina found herself hoping that Cage would win. The bell rang, they touched gloves again and sussed each other out, lobbing jabs and misfired leg kicks.

"Louis is a powerhouse," the commentator blared. "All muscle and aggression. But Cage Callahan is the one to watch for. He's a sleeper. A *very* patient fighter. He'll look like he's losing, but then you find out that he's been winning little by little the whole time."

"I wish I could have watched my opponents on TV first." Jackson jabbed his finger at Cage's head. "See how he drops his right hand when he fires his roundhouses? You could counter-strike then. You could wait for that." Cage threw a barrage of punches, but only one of them landed. "Ha! Not so accurate."

"Jackson. This guy is a professional fighter. He's fighting another professional."

"You fight the tiger, not his stripes. Oh, wow." Cage shot in, lifted Frankie by the legs, and slammed him on his back. On top now, Cage held the mount and began delivering elbows. Frankie writhed, escaped, and stood up.

"Not so good on the ground," Jackson said. "But still, we'd better practice that when you're healed." Jackson had been an Olympic alternate for judo and a freestyle wrestler, and he had taught Nina enough judo and Brazilian jiu-jitsu to fight comfortably from her back. But that was no place for a

115-pound woman. Anyway, with her speed, even Jackson used to have trouble throwing her.

Cage hopped up, a tinge of disgust mixing with the sweat on his face. He looked like he had eaten something rotten. His corner man gave him a towel, and Cage scrubbed at his skin like he was trying to sand it off his bones.

"Why is he doing that?" Jackson asked.

"He probably didn't like the other guy's sweat, or being on the mat." She explained, "He doesn't like dirty things. He has to take a pill for it."

"Then why does he fight?"

"Because..." but Nina didn't know how to answer. A samurai of the old school, Cage would always fight when pushed. He'd always think he was pushed. "You know it's over with him and me, right?"

"He hits women. With men like that, it's never over," Jackson said.

They both thought about Nina's father in the quiet, separate cavities of their minds.

It's over for me, Nina thought.

Cage was in his corner, guzzling water in a chair. His corner man said, "You won that round. Just keep doing what you're doing," rubbing all over his shiny arms and chest.

The camera cut to the other corner, where Frankie said, "He's covered in Vaseline. There's Vaseline all over him." His corner man said, "We'll take it up with the Commission. Keep your mind in the fight."

"What's wrong with Vaseline?" Nina asked.

"It's only allowed on the face. It's cheating."

"Oh."

"He cheats," Jackson said.

In round two, Cage shot in for another takedown, but it was too low and his opponent sprawled out of it. Frankie Louis reversed him with a sweep, and Cage landed in the bottom of the mount position this time.

Frankie shoved his knees forward into Cage's armpits. Cage's elbows floated to defend himself as his rhinoceros of an opponent delivered hammer strikes to his face. Cage started punching from the bottom, bucking high in the air over and over. Frankie Louis rode him. Every time Cage came back down, it was with an elbow in the teeth. Cage's forehead split open, and blood streamed into his eye and ear. *Where's the ref?* Nina wondered. *He's getting killed.*

The referee finally woke up and stopped the fight. Frankie Louis jumped up with his arms raised. He skipped around the ring, blowing kisses to the crowd.

But Cage didn't know. Punch-drunk and blind, he grabbed the referee around the legs and dragged him down. With more will than strength, Cage punched the man, knocking him out before realizing that it was only the referee, that the fight was over, that he lost.

Then he leaned back. He pressed his gloves against his face. Blood ran down his wrists. His shoulders heaved and shook. Cage rolled onto his knees, back bent against the burden of everything unjust that had ever happened to him. He cried into his gloves, his broken heart disintegrating in a pool of media, money, and blood.

Jackson switched off the television. "Now you know that about him," he said.

I was lucky, Nina thought. *Even the last time, the bad time. I am lucky.*

"You're the only person alive who's ever beaten him," Jackson said. "Be careful."

CHAPTER TWELVE:
EMPTY YOUR CUP

A PROFESSOR VISITED NAN-IN TO ask him about Zen. As Nan-in prepared tea, the professor talked. He knew a lot, and talked a lot. Nan-in began to pour tea into his cup until it was full. Even after that, he kept pouring. The tea spilled from the cup to the table and dripped off the edges toward the professor's lap.

The professor stood and exclaimed, "Stop! What are you doing? The cup is full! No more will go in!"

Nan-in told him, "Just like you. How can you learn anything unless you first empty your cup?"

~

THE NEXT MORNING, SOMETHING dropped onto Nina's cot with a thud. "What's this?" she asked, knowing exactly what it was. She unfolded the old karate *gi*, stiff at the seams, pilled at the cuffs. "Is this yours?"

"It was your mother's," Jackson said. "Get dressed."

"But I'm an invalid."

"You're A-O-K." Jackson thumped her shoulder with each syllable. "Just whiny. You have a talent for healing. You need exercise."

"We can't train in the rain." The wind blew drops against the windowpanes for emphasis.

"I have the basement," he said, and went into the kitchen. Nina heard the crack of eggshells against a metal bowl, the quick beating of a fork, the crash of eggs in oil.

She didn't want to do this. She didn't ever want to leave Jackson's army cot. She had spent more than half her childhood nights on this cot, especially when her father was on a tear. She felt like the same angry little kid right now, except stupider and full of scar tissue. When Jackson came back with a steaming plate, she said, "You can't make me do anything."

He passed her the plate and waited. She held it on her lap, untouched.

"What now?"

"I lost," she said.

"Lost what?"

She lifted her top to show her scar.

"Oh. That. I thought you meant the little girl. That young man." He bobbed his head. "Sometimes you're the hammer, sometimes you're the nail."

"The nail sucks."

"Yeah, well, get used to it. You're living here, we're training. So eat your breakfast, you ingrate." Jackson clipped Hank to a leash and walked to the door, Hank trailing behind. Jackson was the only person in Colorado who used an umbrella. The outside air radiated through the open door, warm and soggy. "Be dressed when I come back. You have five minutes. Longer if he poops." The door was a wet slam behind him.

The walls creaked and shifted into stillness, except for the fingernail sound of rain on the roof. Nina let the plate slide slowly down her legs. It hit the floor and the eggs spilled out.

The gi lay on the army cot, like a deflated person. Nina would have to wear it. Besides Jackson's vast selection of polyester pajamas and V-neck undershirts, it was the only clothing he had offered her.

It hurt to be upright. The ceiling hovered. Her legs shuddered on her feet, and her side ached. She slid the pants over her hips and the gi top carefully over her undershirt, the left side crossed over the right. It felt like an old Halloween costume that still fit. She couldn't think of the last time she had worn white. Jackson had left her a pristine white belt so new, it hung in starchy folds. She tied it around her waist, held it by the tips, and whipped the knot tight. She lined it up—perfectly even. Strange how you never forget some things.

Jackson soon returned with Hank, who ran over to sniff Nina's bare toes as if she were a new person he had never met before. Jackson wiped his feet on the mat. "Looks good," he said. "It fits."

She blurted, "This is a white belt." When he didn't say anything, she said, "You gave me my black belt fourteen years ago. It was your own black belt." *Remember?* she almost said.

"So where is it, then?" he asked.

"I didn't know I could get demoted," she grumbled.

Jackson was snipping a pair of scissors in the air. "Time for your stitches to come out." He opened her gi and pulled at her shirt.

There was dried soy sauce on the scissors. "Shouldn't we at least attempt sterility?"

"Hold still." He slid the tip under the thread.

It was a teeth-gritting, nails-on-chalkboard feeling when each stitch snagged on the scab. After he was done, Jackson probed the cut. "Not bad."

The laddered wound was in the shape of a crooked heart. It felt better without the stitches, but loose in an uncomfortable way. "Will it hold?"

"Maybe. Let's go."

Nina followed him out the door in the rain, to a trapdoor entrance to the basement. The house was lined with the same old makiwara she remembered, sticking out of the ground like short, weird trees. Jackson spun the combination to the lock, opened the trap doors, and disappeared inside. She hesitated at the entrance. It was the perfect setup for a murder. The rain landed gently on her head. She touched the stucco of the outside wall, crumbled in the shapes of fists. She wiped her bare feet on her pant legs one by one before climbing down the stairs into the cool basement, and closing the trap door behind her.

Jackson pulled on a string, and the basement was dimly illuminated. There was no other light. The basement was an uncommonly deep one. A cracked mat curled against the ground. It smelled like dust, and every movement seemed to create a current of stale air. The cement walls were dirty, mostly naked except for masonry hooks holding weapons at odd angles, like the wooden farm implements they were derived from: *tonfa*, *nunchaku*, *bo*, *kama*, *eku*, *kuwa*, and Nina's favorite, the three-pronged metal *sai*. She remembered it in her hand—cold cast iron, perfectly weighted as she flipped it forward and backward. She reached for it, but Jackson said, "Later."

A few pictures hung in cheap frames—Jackson's teacher, his teacher, his teacher, his teacher, and then his teacher, the originator of the style he learned in Hawaii. Nina looked closer at the picture of Jackson's teacher, her own grandfather. She had never met him. He looked like her mother, and he looked like nobody she knew.

Jackson still hadn't moved. He stood with his lips parted, hands folded behind his back. "What's wrong?" Nina asked.

He cleared his throat. "I haven't been down here in ten years."

"Not at all? Not even to walk around?"

"No."

Jackson picked up a push broom from the corner and began poking at the cobwebs on the tall ceilings. Nina kicked dead spiders off the mat. The whole floor was coated with a carpet of dust.

"It's no use," he said. "We have to mop."

Nina went back upstairs for a bucket, detergent, and a couple of mops. When she came back, Jackson was pushing dirt into a pile. She began swishing the mop around, scrubbing the basement patch by patch, emptying bucket after bucket of filthy water while Jackson mopped the walls. It took them more than an hour before the air cleared and the edges of things looked sharp again.

"There," Jackson said.

The room smelled clean in the way that mud smells clean. Jackson seemed nervous. He smacked a fist into a palm. "Should we warm up?"

They began swinging their limbs in the proscribed ways. It was painful to do the old exercises, but Nina felt her torso loosen as her endorphins revved.

"What have you been doing for training?" Jackson asked. "Besides preying on people."

"Mostly strength and speed stuff. Wind sprints, resistance, stuff like that. For skills, heavy bag and drills. I get books from the bookstore on strategy and techniques."

"And you practiced them on...?"

"People."

"Ah. Any *kata*?"

"Some," she lied.

"We'll start there," he said. "I want to see how you've deteriorated."

Jackson called out the names of the old forms. "Seipai." "Kururunfa." Nina did her best. She hadn't practiced them in years, but was amazed to remember the order of the moves: blocking, punching, kicking the air, obscure throws. She realized how much she had used these very combinations in fights— against the guy with the switchblade, against the guy with the goatee, against the guy who carried his money in a plastic bag. They evoked summers before that, on Jackson's dead lawn, the thousands of times she had repeated these combinations, and she found her new body conforming to the old motions. Doing them was like being a small child, lying on her back, staring at her hands and feet as they made shapes of their own for the first time.

"Wrong!" Jackson finally shouted. "All wrong! You didn't practice!" Then, "Your side okay?" Without waiting for an answer he said, "Now, defense." He waved a floppy hand at her bruised face. "Clearly, you need defense. I'll hit you."

"You're kidding."

"Fix your stance," he said.

Her left foot was forward. "This is how people fight now," she said.

"I don't care what people do. I care what you do."

She sighed and switched her feet. Jackson started throwing punches at her head and torso. She blocked them. There was rust on the old man, but his movements quickly went from jagged to smooth as his fist found its invisible track. It was hard to tell that he hadn't practiced in ten years. His face rippled with each strike, even the slow ones. In each punch, Nina could see the hundreds of thousands that had come before.

But he wasn't what he used to be, and Nina was much more than she used to be. It was easier to paw his punches aside now, even injured. She thought of the last time their fists met, when his soft, old skin and bone gave way under her knuckles with a clacking noise, right before he uprooted her budding wisdom tooth and split her chin.

"Pretty good for an old man, huh?" he said. "Pretty good after twelve years, huh?"

But something was wrong. He was swinging high, elbows up and chest out, belly exposed—all the things he had taught her not to do. Before she could stop herself, she landed a punch square in his abdomen. She shook her core upon impact to deliver the shock, the way he had taught her.

Jackson bent over, hands on knees, his diaphragm straining against the vacuum of his lungs.

Nina gasped, hands pressed against her mouth. She had hit a senior citizen. She patted his back. She wondered if she should call an ambulance. "Why didn't you—You always used to block everything," she blurted. *Shut up*, she told herself.

Finally, Jackson hacked into his hands a few times. His flat eyes glazed over with involuntary tears as he straightened up. "Again."

"We should quit," she said.

"Okay. Take a few minutes."

"No. I mean we should *quit*." She hung her aching hands on her hips. "This is ridiculous. I need a job. Not this." She waved her hands at the basement dojo, the walls, the air, and the darkness. The thought of quitting felt odd, like a free fall into a hole with no bottom. Would it feel like flying, or dying?

"You want a job? Then let's go into business together," he said. Nina had an odd vision of the two of them going door to door selling candy bars until Jackson said, "Get some students and teach."

She laughed, rage behind her teeth.

Jackson looked at her with such focus, she sweated in her gi. "Okay," he said. "Just say what you want to say to me."

"I don't want to say anything to you."

He stood with his arms crossed.

"Oh, so we're doing this now? After all this time, you really want to talk about it?" she asked.

Only his eyes tracked her as she paced back and forth in front of him.

"You left me. You *left* me, you son of a bitch. I was seventeen, Jackson. I had nobody to trust but you. Then you left me there, with my father. Just like *she* did. You coward. Coward!" Nina sidestepped to catch Jackson's drifting gaze in hers. "And now you judge my choices? I have no choices! I have nothing but these." She shoved her two scarred fists in his face. "That's all there is between us. We're not family. This isn't a reunion, not some second chance. You're talking about our future like we have one. We're over."

"Then why are you crying?"

"Damn it." She wiped her face on the collar of Jackson's undershirt, and then just gave up and cried into her hands.

After a while, she dried her face and blew her nose into her shirt. She couldn't look at Jackson, who sat motionless the whole time. She had never talked that much in her life. No matter what had happened, she had never cried in front of him.

He said, "I want to fix it."

Her nose was stuffed up, so she sounded like a child when she said, "You can't."

"Let me train you."

She scoffed, "I'm better than you now. Don't you realize that I could kill you anytime I wanted to?"

"You're killing me now, Nina." Jackson fitted his fingertips together and pressed them to his lips, as if in prayer. A well of love rose in Nina's chest, but she didn't care anymore.

She climbed up the ladder and opened the trap door to the rain and glaring light. Jackson looked up at her like she was Rapunzel. Nina just stared back from the top of the ladder, stone-faced. That's what her people were good at. She didn't let down her hair. She didn't give him anything.

~

LATE THAT NIGHT, ONCE Jackson's soft snoring beat time in the next room, Nina slid the thin blanket from her legs. She dressed in the dark. The laces of her shoes sawed against the rivets, and she tied them without seeing her fingers. There was no moon, no stars through the clouds. Nina opened the door as gently as she could, wincing when it shuddered on its frame. The night opened, too, and she stepped into it.

She jogged to Five Points and slowed down. She had never tried this neighborhood. Of course not—it wasn't her clientele. The Financial District was just a few streets over, but there wasn't much money here. A few people strolled outside, people without air conditioning, people looking for relief from the heat. Nina smelled microwaved food, urine, cat sex, puddles, and pot. She stood next to a street light, across from a package store. It only took twenty minutes.

"Hey," a youngish man said. He crossed the street, over to her, carrying a bottle in a paper bag. He had affected a limp, but Nina could see his leg was fine. "You lost?" He gestured at his friends slumping against a wall, and they nudged themselves upright. They leaned their bodies in her direction, and let their legs follow.

There were four of them. Nina shivered.

The man asked, "You cold, baby?" His friends laughed. Laughter isn't a nice sound. It's a scary sound, scarier than crying. People don't cry when they're going to do something horrible. The men surrounded her, one at each compass point.

"We'll warm you up," another man said. He hesitated, and then just grabbed her.

His hand kneaded her bra-less breast. "Come on, baby. I'll fuck you good, baby, I'll fuck you like a rough little bitch until you scream for it, like uhn, like uhn and uhn and uhn," and more like that, and she didn't move, so now all four of them were grabbing her and saying things.

So softly, so gently but unmistakably, they pushed her backward into the neck of an alley, behind a building, against a wall, as one of them tried to find an opening in her pants. "No zipper," he said, looking up to the leader, who was grabbing Nina's crotch and twisting it like a doorknob for some reason. They both tried to yank her mother's cinched karate pants over her hips with sharp movements that buckled her knees. The other two men were grabbing flesh wherever it would give, looking for handholds, something to take.

Nina closed her eyes.

The leader laughed. "We got a live one," he said, which was confusing because Nina wasn't moving at all. Then, "Marcus, what's the holdup with these pants?"

Marcus was wrestling with the double knot in the drawstring, tied in darkness. "It's some kind of string."

The men were so close, it was hard to breathe. All Nina's oxygen was gone. One of them was kissing her, forcing his tongue between her teeth. She heard a quick zipper, and felt two hands on the top of her head. They were pushing hard, trying to push her to her knees. Her legs buckled.

Wake up.

Nina closed her eyes more tightly. This was the end, and she wanted the end. She wanted it, but there was too much white noise and strange, rubbing flesh. There was bad breath and whispers and screaming above it, that voice saying wake up wake up wake up wake up.

Nina opened her eyes.

Her body moved without her permission. Before she had registered it, she pivoted to break apart the hands pushing on her head, grabbed one arm, turned her back, and launched the man off her hip. He fell into his friend, who was struggling with his own zipper, and they tumbled to the ground with an "oof."

His pants open, the one called Marcus tackled her football-style, but Nina sprawled out of it. No amateur could take her down. She gripped Marcus by his exposed testicles and his neck, hot and wet with sweat. She twisted and threw him into the wriggling pile of men as they strained to get up.

Which left Nina with the leader, who had already landed two untrained punches on her cheek and kicked her thigh. She smiled. *She* laughed, now. Fear crossed the leader's lean face, and his gaze flitted before latching onto her fists, which were already en route to his face.

They landed, one-two, and two more. Nina kicked at his friends as they got up, and stepped backward down the alley. When fighting in groups, Jackson had taught her to cut the angles and back up until they're all in a line, *your* line. Nina fought in three directions, which winnowed into one as the men packed together. They grunted, swore, head-butted each other in their rush to get at her. Kick them into each other, Jackson had said. Punch their eyes and noses, so they can't see you. She heard her fists swish through the air, and barely felt the bodies as she hit them.

The men swung and crunched, knuckle against cartilage. They were just pieces to Nina now—bone, skin, blood. She caught their errant fists and unschooled kicks, simple bruises. She responded with strikes to their cores, relishing the shock in their eyes. *I'm not who you thought I was. Ha.* She made sure each one tasted her, what she could give, until one by one they fell away with a mouthful of blood. One man began to hobble down the street, cradling a rib, and then another, and the third, limping for real this time and holding his dick with his hand.

"What the fuck?" sputtered the leader after his friends. He scrambled up from the ground again. He turned back to Nina, alone now, a crack splitting his face below his eye. "Listen. It's—I thought that's what you wanted."

This was usually when Nina relieved the man of his wallet. But this time, she stepped closer, asking in a smooth voice, "Why would I want that?"

"I don't know," he stammered, backing up.

"Nobody wants that."

The leader looked after his retreating friends as they turned a corner.

It felt wild, that first solo punch, like a whip on a chain. Nina released it at his chin, and his head snapped back. Amazing how easy it was to hit first, to start something from nothing.

Her next fist found that fresh blood under his eye. She delivered a generous elbow to his ear, and then a knee and another knee to his gut, with his grunting, sweating head in her grip and the smell of his scalp and she was gone, gone, gone in the darkness and the taste of it all, his sweat and hers and the tang of fear and the streetlight blinking out from above them so everything was fair. Nothing hurt. She was fighting loose and slippery now, every limb whipping and free. She took him apart piece by piece—cheekbones, nose, jaw, chin, teeth, ears, eye orbital, solar plexus, floating ribs, hips, thighs, knees, shins, feet, toes, neglecting nothing on this man in this alley on this night. The leader of them all was on the ground and Nina was on top of him, ramming her elbow into his teeth until they broke out like windowpanes. He was screaming under his haggard breath, and Nina knew that everything she had ever done until now was academic because she was done with his skin and his bones and most of his organs and she had never felt so alive and she was going to kill this man now just because that was next.

The leader's half-conscious face was pulpy and misshapen, his pupils drifting forward and backward under swollen lids. Nina decided to crack his windpipe and let him suffocate. His busted chin blocked his throat. She sat beside him, pulled his head onto her thigh like he was a child, yanking his head back, exposing his dark neck. She opened her stiff hand for the old "karate chop" Jackson had taught her, the *shuto*, the knifehand strike she hadn't used in twelve years.

"You're done," she said, and the man fainted in her lap.

Nina took a deep breath, channeling every disappointment, fear, and loss in her life. In the dark theater of her mind, she saw every man she had ever fought, her raging father, her cowering brother. Isaac.

Kate.

Again, that voice in her ear, begging now: wake up.

"No," she said. The man was still unconscious in her lap, but Nina's rage was ebbing away fast, like water. She grasped after it, winding up for the blow, the one she intended. She had to do it. It was the culmination of everything she had ever learned.

But her fingers loosened. She pushed off the man, ran toward a wall, and vomited.

When she had finished, the man on the ground was still alive. His eyes were closed, but his chest was heaving, legs akimbo. He moaned softly.

Nina staggered from behind the building and tripped into a broken run until she found a pay phone outside a convenience store. She called 911, whispered instructions, and hung up.

She threw up again, once more next to the pay phone, but nothing came out. She was empty now. It was over. Slow words began to form in the mud of her mind:

I. Am. Broken.

She hung onto the cradle of the phone. The ambulance came. The police came. The ambulance left, lights on. So did the cops, lights off.

Nina didn't know how long she hung on there before something began to leak in, pooling into that empty space left inside her. It was as faint as a rumor, no more than a scent, beneath the traces those men had left on her skin: liquor, sex, sweat, methamphetamines, and something new growing among all that. Something green.

CHAPTER THIRTEEN:
NOT THE WIND, NOT THE FLAG

TWO ZEN MONKS SAT outside, watching a flag snap in the wind.

One monk said, "The flag is moving."

The other said, "The wind is moving."

The sixth patriarch was walking by. He said, "Not the wind. Not the flag. The mind is moving."

~

THE NEXT MORNING, NINA rose before Jackson began his series of rustlings and snuffles from his bedroom. She dressed in her mother's clothes and went outside.

The sun was still beyond sight, and Nina shivered in her gi. She felt raw. Her groin still hurt from where the men had grabbed her, and her jaw ached. She had contusions that kept surprising her. The wound in her side ached.

In the predawn light, she swished through the dying grass to the makiwaras and leaned against the dented stucco. She ran her fingers over the makiwaras, planted in the ground like weird, stunted trees. She shivered again.

The front door slammed, and Jackson was out in the yard, no shoes. A shaft of sun made its first appearance of the day.

246 ⌒ Erika Krouse

"Morning," he said, more an observation than a greeting. Then, "You went out last night."

They hadn't spoken since their fight yesterday, and Nina couldn't look at him. "How do you know?"

"There's blood on your pants."

She looked down. In the dark it had looked like dirt, but in the scant sunlight, it now showed rust-red.

"Where did you go?" he asked.

"Somewhere I don't want to go again."

Not gently, he turned her bruised chin so she had to look at him.

It was impossible to say it, but she did anyway. She cleared the gravel from her throat. "I need your help."

He nodded. He kept nodding and nodding, like an old man, which he was. "You know that you choose, right? You choose who you are by what you do. You're not your father. And I did love your mother. But you're not her, either."

What am I, then, she silently asked.

"Let's get to work," Jackson said.

He pointed at a mangy makiwara. The wood was bleached gray. It had a long crack in it. The sun was now fully out and humidity rose from the ground, thinning by the time it reached their faces. Jackson rested his gnarled fist on the top of the post. "Now, then. Hit this for a few weeks."

"Weeks?"

"You have to punch the meanness out of you."

"*Weeks*?"

"It's not a quick job. You're pretty mean." He leaned against the makiwara with his whole body. When he stepped away, it sprang back in place.

"I don't know if this is the kind of help I need."

"I do."

Nina surveyed the piece of wood. Karate is about defeating your opponent with a single blow. *Ikken hissatsu*—one strike, one kill. To train for this, you use the makiwara, a long striking post planted in the ground. You can make it out of a four-by-four beam. You cut it so that the post is thin at the top and thick at the bottom. You plant the thick bottom end, and pad the thin end with soft leather or a towel, to protect your hands. Then you punch it over and over and over, like it's a stubborn weed in your garden that has outgrown you.

It's not for hitting hard, like a heavy bag—at least, not at first. It helps you condition your body for hard blows, for fighting. Without it, your own force can bounce back like karma, and you end up hurting yourself as much as you hurt your opponent. When you hit a makiwara, it vibrates with a deep thwack that rebounds at your fist. The spring of the impact travels down your arm and back, down your rear heel and into the ground, if you hit it right. Hit it wrong and it just hurts.

First, your hand bruises. Then, the skin over your knuckles splits. It scabs. Weeks later, it hardens. Scar tissue forms on the outside of your knuckles, and then on the inside. The blisters flatten, hard as burns. The aim is to exceed human limits, to turn your body into an object that feels no pain and cannot break. In high school, Nina punched the makiwara until she couldn't write her name.

Jackson rubbed his hands together, as if to warm them. "You either fight for your life, or you don't fight at all. That's what it's all about."

"Now you're quoting the Hokey-Pokey."

"It's not a joke. This is the real thing. You know enough to be dangerous, and not enough to be safe." He glared. "In a true self-defense situation, you have to hit hard enough to end someone bigger than yourself—Cage, for example—without it killing you, too. You have to learn to absorb an uncommon amount of shock, both from him and from yourself."

"So that's your plan for self-defense? Learn to hit harder than the other guy?"

"Yes."

"You do remember that I'm a girl, right?"

"Yes."

He couldn't be that stupid. "I can't actually stand toe-to-toe with anyone," she said. "I only ever won against those guys because I surprised them."

"What happened when you couldn't surprise Cage?"

I lost, she thought.

"I never lost," Jackson said. "A runt like me. Want to know a secret?"

"Of course I want to know a secret."

He leaned forward, as if there were spies hiding behind the waving aspens on his front lawn. "Whenever I got into a fight, I told myself, 'I just committed suicide.' That way, it's absolute. You think clearly, feel clearly." He tapped Nina's skull so hard, it hurt. "You don't leave anything out. Every fight is the fight of your life. Not showing off and stealing wallets."

Nina turned to the makiwara and studied it. They're harder than people. The first time she ever punched a makiwara, she sprained her wrist. She made a face and punched the leather pad. The wood barely moved. She hit it again, harder. Her already-sore knuckles ached at the impact.

"You're not focusing." Jackson pulled Nina's retracted fist and examined it. He traced over her raw skin. "Try opening your hand." He demonstrated the shuto, the classic karate chop.

"Step to the side and strike, like this. Imagine here—striking under the chin, right here." He slid his open hand under Nina's chin, pinky-side first, the protrusion at the joint bumping her esophagus. "To the neck. With the fleshy side of your hand, here, like a knife."

Last night flashed into Nina's mind. Did he know? Either way, there was no way she was doing that now. "I remember how to shuto. What do you think I am, stupid?"

"Show me."

"I need to work on my ground game. And so do you." Despite his judo and wrestling background, there was an ocean of new Brazilian knowledge neither of them had.

"That's ridiculous. Stay on your feet. If he takes you down, find a way to stand up. Don't get fancy."

"Fancy, like karate chops?"

"You saw the video. Cage tucks his chin too much for you to punch him. It's impossible to get your whole fist in there. But this," Jackson sliced his own shuto into the makiwara, "this could work. Step to the side, angle it upward, and he's dead."

"I don't want him to be dead."

"I don't want *you* to be dead."

Her skin itched, tight. The sun burned her hair. "I'm not doing any kill shots."

"So you'll grift people, but you won't learn self-defense."

"That's right," she said. "I don't have that in me. I don't want it in me."

"You think you never hurt anyone when you were stealing their wallets?"

"I was careful."

"Nobody can be that careful," he said. "You just don't know your own consequences."

"I want to change."

"From what? To what? You don't even know what you are right now." He shaded his eyes from the sun behind her.

"Still. I'm not doing *that*," she said and pointed at his open hand.

Jackson shrugged and pointed at the house. "Go on, then. Get." When she didn't move, he shouted, "Go!"

Nina walked into the house, looking back once, but Jackson was ignoring her, hitting the makiwara himself. She was confused. Was she supposed to leave? Pack up? She didn't own anything anymore, so she made up his army cot, picked up No-Hair, and went back outside to the makiwaras.

Jackson was gone. "Jackson?" The sun was hot. She scanned the yard, but he wasn't anywhere.

She studied the makiwara again. She fitted the side of her hand against an indentation in the leather. The wind rose. She wanted at least to say goodbye, to thank him, for once.

She sighed and leaned against a large aspen tree's smooth trunk. She stroked it, warm against her hand. She could almost feel the thin sap running, the sensation of growth and slipping time. The tree hummed as it curved at the waist. Aspen trees aren't individuals—they grow in colonies. The smooth white trunks are connected by an underground network, the root systems sometimes living for thousands of years. When you see an aspen tree, it's just one shoot of many, like a blade of grass. It's a manifestation: never alone, no matter how alone it looks.

Something in the branches above shaded her. She looked up.

A heavy mass dropped down on her.

Nina absorbed the blow behind her head. A human monkey was stuck to her back. He was heavier than she was, and she couldn't shake him off.

His arm snaked around her neck in a choke, and his heels hooked into her hips. She grabbed his arm, but it was cinching tighter around her neck. She twisted her head. She couldn't see anything as the blood was cut off from her brain.

With a groan, she launched herself backward. The two of them crashed into the tree trunk, and the impact shuddered through the man's torso to hers. He grunted.

His hold loosened on her neck. He let go and slid off. She back-kicked him as he hit the ground, and just before she connected with his stomach, she looked back and saw that it was Jackson.

It was too late to pull the kick, if she had wanted to. He crumpled like a wadded piece of paper.

Her adrenaline washed away, replaced by a steady river of shame. As Jackson struggled for breath, his freckled bald spot turned pale and then flushed pink. He looked up and hacked.

"Oh, Jackson," she said. "Not again."

He rubbed his stomach, grinned, and managed to gasp, "Exactly like old times."

Relief sucked out what was left of her breath.

Jackson's grin turned to a grimace. He dragged himself to his feet and let his sandpapery voice absorb the residual pain. "You never learn."

~

NINA HAD ONCE READ about a fish that lives in the bottom of the deepest ocean floor. The human body could never dive to where this fish lived without imploding. The reverse was true for the fish. When scientists brought the fish up to the surface to study it, it disintegrated under the lack of stress, the lightness of an easier life.

Nina was that fish. Under the rigors of Jackson's training, Nina felt herself able to move freely once again, without the feeling that she would disintegrate in every direction. Jackson made her do daily wind sprints with an army mask over her face. He had coated the visor with black paint. "Good for the panic reflex," he said. She couldn't see a single thing. Her breath boomeranged back at her. "Now," he'd say, and she'd run wildly in an unknown direction, rebreathing carbon dioxide. "Stop," he'd shout, tell her to turn, and they'd do it again and again until she thought she'd faint. But she didn't.

He made Nina carry huge rocks from one place in the yard to another. Once they were exactly where he wanted them, he made her move them back again.

He had gotten a paintball gun from who knows where, and stood on his roof, aiming at her while she tried to dash out of his sites. "Fun for both of us, ha!" he laughed.

By the time Nina knew him in her youth, Jackson had already killed twelve men with his hands, rescued ten POWs behind enemy lines, lost his mind twice, and was blown up once. So it would be silly to complain when he woke her up at three a.m. and said, "Do pushups until I'm done eating this bowl of peas." After what felt like forever, she looked up, her arms quaking. He was eating them one by one with a toothpick.

He dumped a bucket of ice water over her cot while she was sleeping.

He soaked his garden until it was mud, planted Nina there like a shrub, and made her defend punches without hitting back. He freed her and hosed off her feet, tied her hands behind her back, and then kicked her for fifteen minutes while she tried to fend him off with her feet.

Nina acclimated to all this, like a boiled frog. She could have said no to any of it, but she wasn't sure he'd let her stay.

Jackson force-fed her weird meats and changed her dressings, pasting more tarry goop over the letters carved into her skin. Lines of new skin were beginning to shine underneath the ragged tissue—a pink, glistening heart. He made her soak her hands in bruise wine until they were stained a permanent orange. He made her drink mottled mud that tasted like osha root, bile and sand, but her urine was clear and clean. Her jaw wasn't sore anymore on both sides, just the one, and her constant black eyes had faded overnight to a urine-stain yellow.

"I'm never leaving here," she said.

"Oh yes, you are," he said.

He made her stand with her feet in a bucket of ice.

He made her punch trees.

He made her eat five habanero peppers in fifteen minutes.

He made her punch the makiwara until her hands split, and then some more.

Jackson was clearly crazy. But this—the thud of the makiwara in the crisp purple of early autumn, an aspen tree quaking in the breeze, sudden stinging pain on her fists in the dry, dry air, a bald doll sitting on the grass, staring her down— was the antidote to her life. It was better than therapy with fabric sofas and bookshelves and herbal teas. It was a language she understood, and spoke. Maybe she could just hit something all day for the rest of her life, and then collapse every night with the kind of exhaustion that made sleep redundant. Her scar tissue broke and reknitted itself. The tiny nerves between her vertebrae stretched and rebuilt themselves, as the leaves rustled above her. She was falling in love with the rhythm of it. Every time she hit the makiwara, it bounced back again with an equal and opposite reaction, forever and forever. She was doing the same thing over and over, trying for different results, which was the definition of insanity. And hope.

CHAPTER FOURTEEN:
HEAVEN AND HELL

ASAMURAI APPROACHED THE MONK Hakuin and asked, "Is there really a heaven and a hell?"

"Stupid question," Hakuin scoffed. He called the samurai names and insulted his sword.

The price for touching or taunting a samurai's sword was death. Everyone knew that. The samurai drew his insulted sword. Just as he was about to drive the blade down onto the monk's neck, Hakuin said, "Here open the gates of hell."

The samurai froze.

He sheathed his sword.

"Here open the gates of heaven," said Hakuin.

~

ISAAC WAS SCREWED. KATE was no longer the compliant kid he had grown to love. She routinely pushed her RavioliOs in circles around her plate, saying, "Nina makes these better than you do." Or she chanted, "Nina, Nina, Nina, Nina," an endless song with no chorus. Or she'd catapult into the occasional rage, complete with flung food. Isaac had gotten good at ducking. He chewed his way through it all, cringing on the high notes, and avoided her except at mealtimes.

Kate's new shrink said that she just needed to adjust, before Isaac dragged her back to LA and made her adjust again. Maybe they should have left Denver immediately, but Dr. Simon and Isaac agreed that it would be better to let her finish out the semester. Kate hated Dr. Simon, a fat man who gave her flat, broken lollipops that she wiggled politely in their cellophane like loose teeth. She sat silent, each expensive hour. Dr. Simon said that it was posttraumatic stress, but Kate was no fool. She must have known that Dr. Simon was no more than a chubby spy.

Dr. Simon said that Kate needed closure, and that Isaac did, too. Isaac had no idea what that meant. He didn't need closure. He needed a night with a woman. He thought of his poor, unused penis, shrunken in his boxer shorts. He needed about a quart jar of Valium. He needed a helmet. One thing to be said for Nina: in their short time together, she had transformed Kate from a timid whiner into a miniature bully.

Kate appeared in the doorway. Isaac pushed down the Pavlovian dread response that now popped up at her presence. "Eggs?" he asked, frying pan in hand.

Kate swung wide and punched him hard, in the side. "I'm not moving back to LA."

"Ow. Yes, we are, just as soon as I clear a few things up."

"No, I'm not."

"We discussed this." He handed her a plate. "We're going back to a real city, with pollution, and bad weather, and traffic noise, and everything. Eat your breakfast."

She threw the plate at the wall, and it bounced (plastic. This wasn't Isaac's first rodeo). She shouted "No!" and pushed a small ceramic lamp off the counter.

The lamp broke into shards on the tile. Kate trembled at her own violence. Isaac's mind vacillated. *Nature? Nurture?*

"That's not our lamp. It's rented. Now I'll have to pay for it when we move."

"We're not moving." But she bent down to pick up the ceramic pieces.

"Leave them. They're sharp."

"If we really were going to LA, we would have left already. You want to be near Nina. That's why you kept us here in Denver. That's why you rented this stupid apartment for us."

"It's for school."

"I don't need school. I can spell anything."

"How about 'trepidation.'"

"That's not a real word."

Isaac's power of attorney had expired, so he had gone to see a local lawyer soon after repossessing Kate. The plan had been to find out if it would be easier to get custody in Colorado or California.

But the lawyer had pressed her lips together until her mouth looked like an equal sign. "I don't want to say it's impossible," she had said. "But for an unrelated single man to try to adopt a young girl, especially when there is an eligible and willing female relative in the picture...let's just say that everyone will question your motives. Especially if you cross state lines. You're risking a Class 2 felony for Second Degree Kidnapping."

Isaac could tell that the lawyer herself was questioning his motives. "What if the female relative is unsuitable? I mean, she's a thief. She's violent."

"But she doesn't have a record, right?"

"I don't think so."

The lady's eyebrows told Isaac what she thought of him. "If there's nobody else, Kate would go into the system. But she won't go to you. My legal recommendation is that you relinquish her immediately to the State, and let them decide."

There was no way he was letting Kate go into the system. "I'm like family to Kate," he said.

"Like family," she said. "But not family."

She was right. He wasn't her father. He wasn't her legal guardian, even. He was just some guy now, a man with a stolen kid. A kidnapper, according to some, including the FBI if he left Colorado. He hadn't done anything wrong, but Isaac knew better than anything that perception is reality.

He just had to figure it out. Isaac now sighed and handed Kate his own breakfast. "Eat your eggs and then get ready for school."

"I hate eggs. I hate school."

He said, "Like it or lump it," then paused, stunned. Who was he, anymore?

"What does 'lump it' mean?" Kate asked.

"I don't know. It's something my dad used to say. It's a stupid thing to say. An old man thing to say."

"So do I still have to eat the eggs?"

"Yes."

"Nina wouldn't make me." Kate toyed with the ID bracelet on her wrist. Isaac made her wear it, since she refused to memorize their new address. "I miss No-Hair." It was a grave error, leaving Kate's doll like that. Kate knocked hard on the laminate countertop. "I miss *Nina*." She whirled on one heel and left the kitchen.

It was a relief to cook his replacement breakfast in peace, without being blasted with declarative statements he could do nothing about. He sighed again. He was turning into his father, sighing and sighing. Soon he'd be cursing at his remote control and talking about how he was born before the internet.

The door slammed.

"Kate?" Isaac strode into the living room. "Katie?"

The living room was empty. The bathroom was empty. Kate's room was empty. And his room was always empty.

"Crappity crap-crap-crap." He slapped the spatula to his forehead, remembering too late that there was food on it. He jammed on his shoes and ran out into the apartment hallway. Empty. He ran down the stairwell into the street. Shading his eyes, he scanned the asphalt, white in the light. He ran down the block one way, and then the other, checking intersections.

She was gone again.

Isaac ran for his rental car, then skidded to a stop.

A very large man leaned against the hood, arms folded. When he saw Isaac, his pale eyebrows jumped. Scar tissue shone underneath them. He was enormous, a bristle-top blond. His muscles undulated through his skin like ocean waves. Isaac's muscles didn't do that.

Isaac held his key before him like a sword, indicating use, indicating ownership. The man squared up, and Isaac realized he wasn't going to get past him. He looked familiar. Isaac mentally calculated the amount of money in his wallet. He cursed himself for leaving his cell phone in his car. "What do you want?"

The man gave him a cheery smile that didn't fool Isaac. "Just Nina."

"You know Nina?" Once the stupidity of this question had fully saturated the air, Isaac followed up with, "I have to use my car. It's an emergency," as if only an emergency could justify the use of his own car.

Still smiling, the man somehow made Isaac's heart pause a second. "So, hey. Bring Nina to me?"

First Jackson, and now some goon in a tank top. As if Isaac had the power to bring Nina to anyone, even himself. He held his hands up in the surrender position. "I don't know where she is. But if I did, I don't think I'd bring her to you."

"You will, though. Right now I'm just asking nicely." He smiled again. Arms still folded, the man's bicep spasmed. The giant tiger tattoo on it writhed, like it was stretching after a nap.

"I know you," Isaac said. "You're the garbageman." This was the man who had delivered the box with the wallets inside. He had been wearing coveralls then. Now, despite his hairless body, the man's sex appeal was undeniable, even to Isaac, a confirmed and tested heterosexual. The garbageman was raw, like something unfinished or unfiltered. The hairs on Isaac's arms rose. Was this what Nina was into, gigantic shaved blond garbagemen with tattoos? More than treadmill actors with wry senses of humor?

But she loves me, he thought.

"Was that Kate I saw go by?" he asked.

"She—how do you know Kate?" Isaac asked, feeling sick. "Where did she go?"

"Have you gone before probate yet?" the garbageman asked pleasantly. "Or are you still milking that expired power of attorney?"

Isaac had almost forgotten what it was like to be scared. It was very different from acting scared. "Who are you, exactly?"

"I'm your competition." The man shoved off the car and advanced with rigid eyes, neck jutted. "Tell Nina to bring me what I want, Dinner Slacks."

"What do you want?"

But the garbageman was doing something weird. He looked down and started rapidly smacking at the backs of his jeans. He rubbed the denim so hard, Isaac wondered if his hand hurt. When the garbageman finally looked up, his face was reproachful. "You didn't wash your car."

"It's a rental," Isaac said.

"It messed up my pants."

"I really am in a hurry, here." Fear of one kind battled with another. Kate could be anywhere.

"Right." The man's whole face squinted, suddenly friendly-looking. "Don't forget what I said."

Isaac nodded. He had forgotten already.

The man took a step away, whirled back and faked a punch at Isaac. It wasn't a punch, exactly. It was just that his eyes hardened and his bare shoulder twitched forward an inch. But it was enough to make Isaac stagger backward, one arm out to protect his face.

The garbageman relaxed. His gaze traced Isaac's entire body. That's exactly what Isaac felt like right then—a traced form, blank inside. The man's lip curled before he turned and sauntered off, slower than he needed to.

Isaac jumped into his car, hands shaking. He locked all the doors. It took two tries to start the ignition, and then he pulled out, glancing at the big man slouching away in the opposite direction.

I'll call in an Amber Alert, Isaac thought, *even if I lose Kate over it*. But he couldn't afford to lose her. Kate couldn't afford to be lost. A kid like that was more likely to be struck by lightning than to exit the system sane, once she entered it.

He drove to Nina's apartment, scanning the streets.

Isaac took the stairs two at a time, sprinted to Nina's door and knocked, rapid-fire. The door's surface was littered with eviction notices, deadline tomorrow. Isaac brushed them aside to knock louder. He yelled through the door crack. "Kate? Nina, open up." He kicked the door and it shuddered on its frame. Then he turned the knob, and the door opened.

Well, that was a smell he hadn't experienced since college. The place looked like it had been smashed in by a giant fist. A dragon tail of garbage wound around the apartment, culminating at the empty can. Wallets were everywhere—strewn across the floor, one next to a broken lamp, another two on a counter laced with shattered drinking glasses. A chair was hacked to pieces. Isaac almost stepped in a dried pile of vomit with corn in it.

"Kate?" he shouted.

He followed a swampy smell to the coffeepot. The goldfish inside was finally dead. Someone had thrown in the whole jar of fish food, including the plastic container. A wallet drowned in a quagmire of bonito. The decomposing goldfish floated in the middle, belly up and staring like he didn't understand how God could do this to him.

Breathing through his mouth, Isaac waded through the detritus to the living room and the bedroom, past the painting of a cat Nina had bought at a yard sale, her plastic cactus, her crumpled Parliament T-shirt and the ukulele she had never learned to play. In the bedroom, he flipped a light switch, but the power was off.

On the unmade bed, a small rat posed on the rumpled bed before jumping down and racing into a closet.

Isaac jumped back and made a high-pitched sound of some sort. He then cleared his throat in the most manly way he could muster, flicked aside a tissue, and looked closer. There was a smear on the bed, dried to a dank, dark brown. The rat had been chewing on the stain of someone's blood. Nina's.

~

ISAAC BANGED ON JACKSON's hot front door until his fist hurt. The door swung wide and Jackson poked his head out. Upon seeing Isaac, he started to slam the door, but Isaac stuck his foot in the gap and shouldered past the old man into the house.

There was Kate, with Nina. Both were flushed, sitting on the carpet. Isaac was so relieved at the sight of the two females, both alive and whispering, he almost wept, almost smacked them, almost sagged to the floor himself and begged their forgiveness.

Nina's arm encircled Kate's waist. Their fine hair combined, two shades of the same substance, light brown and black. They relaxed in each other's arms as if they were reattaching their own limbs to their rightful places. It was an embrace made of relief. It erased everything else.

Isaac didn't like being erased. "Kate, you scared the shit out of me. How did you even remember where this house was?"

Kate leaned into Nina. Nina buried her nose into Kate's shoulder and inhaled.

"Take your shoes off, please," Jackson told him.

Isaac didn't see how he could bend over and untie his laces without losing some kind of competitive advantage, so he ignored the old man. It felt good to be this rude. It was humid inside and he was already sweating, the way he did when he was angry, and when he was wrong. He told Kate. "You just can't run away like that. There are assholes everywhere."

"There's one in my house right now," Jackson mumbled.

"Please," Nina said to Jackson, who sputtered. Then she said to Isaac, "Kate wants to stay."

"You—" he pointed at her, "—don't have a say in this. What the hell happened in your apartment? There was blood on your bed?"

Kate looked wildly back and forth between them. Nina said nothing, as usual.

Isaac fake-strangled the air. "Kate, are you going to come, or do I have to carry you out?"

The sun reflected through the window into Kate's brown eyes, so they shone golden. "If you touch me, I'll scream," she said.

Go ahead, he almost told her. But he stopped himself in time. If Kate screamed and a neighbor came, Isaac could go to jail. Kate would go to a foster home. Or to Nina.

"Your boyfriend showed up," Isaac said. "He wants his drugs."

"What?"

Isaac flicked an ant off the wall. "Big guy, blond. He almost punched me."

Fear sprang to Nina's face. "What did he say?"

"He said, 'Tell her to bring me what I want.' Shit, Nina. What are you involved in?"

"He doesn't want drugs." Nina glanced at Kate and lowered her voice, inadequately. "He's a cop."

"A cop." That's the last thing he needed. "Why couldn't you just get a fucking job?"

"I want to live honestly." A line of sweaty soot clung to the bottom of her jaw.

"What's honest about beating people up and stealing their money?"

"I've stopped. And I'm sorry."

She really did look sorry, but nothing's that easy. "You never should have done it in the first place. I swear, you're your own evil twin."

Nina pointed with a jabby finger. "This isn't about morality. It's about the fact that I fucked up your fantasy about me."

"Why would I fantasize about you?"

Her face flushed to a pastel color that looked ironic on her. "Because you love me."

"I don't," he said. "I actually hate you." But that wasn't it, wasn't it at all.

Tears collected instantly in Nina's eyes. Her hands found each other. She didn't see him reach for her—couldn't, as she spun around. She ran out the door and slammed it behind her.

"Nina!" Kate shouted and tried to run after her, but Isaac caught her slim arm. She whirled on him. "She *said* she was sorry!"

"You're so stupid," Jackson said. He was leaning against a door jamb. He waved toward the kitchen. "Come on. I'm making soup."

"Soup?" Isaac dredged his voice in as much sarcasm as even he could stand.

"I will not get angry at you," Jackson said.

With one sour look at Isaac, Kate marched to the kitchen behind the old man. Isaac followed behind, like a flat punch line.

In the kitchen, Jackson chopped scallions, making sure each slice was thin and even, as if this was a vegetable deserving respect and attention. A drop of sweat fell into the pile of food. Isaac found himself getting jealous. Jealous of an onion.

"Your shoes are still on," Jackson said.

Isaac sighed and shed his shoes, one heel against another. In his sock feet, he felt a little silly, especially since one of his socks was blue and the other was brown. How had that happened? He really was losing it.

He flung a hand in the direction of the army cot in the living room, made up with military corners. "How long has Nina been staying here?"

"Since you called me with her address. I went and got her."

"Well, I kept my promise. I brought her to you. Or you to her, at least."

Jackson picked up a wooden spoon. "Did you know she had knife wounds?"

Isaac didn't know that.

Kate's head snapped on her neck. "What? Knife what?"

"She's okay." Jackson patted her shoulder. "Much better. You saw her. Very healthy." Hunched and clucking, he showed her how to peel a ginger root with a bowl of warm water and the hard edge of a metal spoon, scraping the thin skin until the root was as naked as a heart. "Peel it on the sofa in the living room," he said, guiding her out of the kitchen.

Isaac said, "And if you try to run away again, we're leaving for LA tonight." But he knew this was unnecessary. Kate was exactly where she wanted to be.

When he and Jackson were alone, Isaac asked, "What happened?"

The wrinkles on Jackson's face deepened in the shadow of the overhead light. "I don't know. Someone cut her up. Right here." Jackson pretended to slice his own ribs with a carrot.

"Who?"

Jackson was looking at him hard. "At first I thought it was you."

"Me?" Isaac flushed, and slumped against a wall. "I mean, I'm mad at her and everything, but I could never do that to her. Or anyone."

Jackson started to peel a potato with what Isaac could tell was a very dull peeler. He worried that the old man would cut himself until Jackson said, "She has custody, Ivan."

"It's Isaac. She's a thief." Yellow leaves detached from an oak tree outside the window and drifted down. "She just takes everything she wants."

"Then you're the perfect pair. You seem to take everything you don't want."

They were quiet during the chopping of the potatoes.

Isaac suddenly remembered a story Chris had told him a long time ago. Their mother, Miko, was standing on a cliff in

Okinawa. She was pregnant with the twins, contemplating her upcoming move to America with her marine sergeant husband. She saw an American by the cliff. He was walking toward the edge. He swayed on his feet, like he was sleepwalking. It worried her. His eyes were drifting shut, his face a shell of pain. He leaned forward into the wind, into the fall. So she grabbed at him, just catching his pinky finger. She pulled on it, bending it hard so his legs buckled right there at the rim. He staggered backward, away from the cliff's edge. She said, "Wake up," and Jackson's eyes focused on her for the first time. "He imprinted on her like a baby bird," Chris had said. "He'll forgive her anything."

"You think I'm wrong," Isaac said. "You think she deserves forgiveness."

"I'm the one to blame." Jackson threw a bowl of something into a frying pan, and spices attacked the air.

"You taught her how to steal wallets?"

"You ever hear of Plato's cave?"

"Don't you believe in segues?"

"Shut up and listen. So, everyone is a prisoner in a cave, right? Watching shadows, making shadows on the cave wall. So then some unlucky bastard prisoner finds himself unshackled for a second. Now, then, what does he do? He sees a little light, and heads up toward the sun."

"That's you? The enlightened one?"

"Nobody gets enlightened. The sun is too bright, and it blinds you. Hurts you." Jackson's voice had slowed, blurred, until Isaac felt hypnotized. "The sun isn't good. It's not benevolent. It's just the sun, and it doesn't care about you. So if you're irresponsible enough to lead someone else out of the cave with you, you can't just leave her in that burning sun. You can't abandon her. And yet, you do. You leave her alone, blind and hurting. Because you're blind yourself."

Jackson spun his knife on the counter. It pivoted in a whir so tight, Isaac couldn't tell the handle from the blade.

"Do I deserve forgiveness?" Jackson asked.

~

As the sun set, Nina ran past stunted trees in the early autumn heat, sweating to avoid crying. So, Isaac hated her. So, Cage was talking to Isaac. Talking wasn't bad. What was she thinking—talking was terrible. No good ever came from talking. What did Cage want with Isaac? Her life was poisoning itself, the bad elements infecting the good until everything was toxic. Nina ran faster.

And something was happening to Kate. Nina could recognize it just in the few minutes they had together. One month ago, Kate was like an oily rainbow puddle in a parking lot, full of wavy lines and potential. She wore Nina's leather and torn T-shirts as dresses, but she was as soft as dirty water.

Now, she was clean and dressed in a little flowered jumper dress with frogs on the pocket. Her ponytail had been secured by an elastic with two giant green marbles on it that perfectly matched the color of her shoes. She was organized into clean lines, but inside the clothes that smelled of fabric softener, Nina could see that the girl was hardening.

The habit of waiting was vitrifying into anger. Kate's hands had locked themselves into fists. Her gaze scissored everything she looked at. It's easier to know than to wait, and this anger would dissolve into its own vacuum. Nina knew where Kate was headed, and it was somewhere she didn't belong.

So. Isaac didn't have custody. He only had insinuations. All Nina needed was money, and then she could adopt Kate and leave all her messes behind. She had taken a train here and she could take a train out. It was a free-ish country, and she could begin her honest life in any old boring place.

But first, she needed some dishonest cash.

As she ran toward downtown, the buildings thickened, the air graying around her. A group of sweating men emerged from a sports bar to her right, shouting about a football game. Nina stopped at the bar's entrance, Efrain's, and slipped inside before even she had realized it.

She breathed in the bar scent—spilled beer, Windex, cologne, and sweat. It had been a while. She felt her cells sharpen at the familiarity of this new place. The requisite neon signs gleamed against the oak tables and wooden bar. Even on a hot afternoon, it's always night inside a bar. That's what you pay a bar to be.

Nina scanned the sparse crowd of happy hour alcoholics. Nobody looked at her. She climbed onto a stool and caught her reflection in the bar mirror: shiny face, no makeup, hair in two haphazard pigtails. The only thing she had going for herself was that she wasn't wearing a bra.

"What'll you have?" the bartender asked. He didn't even leer at her, not even for a tip.

"I'll have a, um." She didn't own a cent. She slid off the barstool. "I'll just hit the bathroom first." The bartender worked his rag away from her. Nina slunk to a dark corner, leaned against a wall, and scoped.

There was a man with a puckered ear. The bill of his leather cap was either suede or covered in finger grease. There was a man shaped like a carpenter's pencil. A man with double-jointed elbows. A man eating corn.

A man playing a phone video game that made bowling sounds. A man wearing parachute pants. A man with his legs crossed. Overgrown frat boys watching MMA on TV.

She approached a good option, a thick man in a tailored shirt and expensive haircut. He was sitting alone in a half-circle booth. His toast-colored hair stuck out at the sides. It could be fashion or it could be laziness. A folded newspaper lay in front of him. Despite the wealth in his shirt, it was wrinkled. Maybe he had slept in his clothes. Maybe his wife kicked him out. Hope rang in Nina's chest. "Can I join you?"

He glanced at her sneakers, her old-man workout whites. He shook his head no, but she had already slid in next to him.

"What's your name? Where are you from?" She reached for his beer, but he stayed the mug with his hand. He raised his eyebrows and flicked a corner of his newspaper.

"Is your girlfriend here?"

He held up his hand with a wedding ring on it, and blew a smoke ring in her face.

She broke it with her palm. "If you're so married, where is she?"

"Dead."

"I'm sorry," she said, brightening. "What did she die of?"

"Cancer."

"What kind?"

"A cancer only Austrians get." He was muscular, but cigarettes, alcohol, and drugs had blurred his edges. He looked puffy and irritable, unpredictable.

"How long were you married?"

"Still am."

"But if she's dead, you're not still married."

"I never missed a year," he said.

Another muscular man slouched up to the table, much younger. He was wearing a tank top, even with the overly aggressive air conditioning. "Hey Mr. Spina. Great card last night. You got anything for me?"

"Not if you're hanging out in bars," the man, Spina, said. Nina used this distraction as an opportunity to finally drink from his beer.

"Just here to watch the replays," grinned the man sheepishly. "Keep me in mind." He slouched away.

"Your name is Spina?" Nina asked.

"It's Antonio Ricardo Ricardito Gino Joseppe Irving Spina."

"Can I call you Tony?"

"You can call me Antonio Ricardo Ricardito Gino Joseppe Irving Spina. Now shut up. I want to watch this." He reclaimed his beer from Nina's hand.

Nina leaned back on the creaking Naugahyde and decided to wait it out. The bar was dark and cool, and it was nice to sit next to a man who wasn't thirty-five years older than her and spitting into a coffee can. But the name was familiar. Nina worried that she had hit this man before. She played his name back in her head.

Awareness descended like rain. *Holy fuck*, Nina thought. There couldn't be two. This was that guy Cage was talking about, VP of something talent. The biggest matchmaker in the sport of mixed martial arts. Nina stared at his slightly bloated face, next to her. *This is a miracle*, she thought. *This is money.*

"We've met," she said.

He looked at her, and looked again.

"I knocked out your boy," she said.

It took Antonio a minute to translate her words into memory. His face unlined. He turned his back to the TV screen and looked her over. He shook his head and said, "You were lucky."

"It's not luck if it's repeatable."

Antonio flicked a finger, like he was waving off a refill of a bad drink. But Nina was still sitting in his booth.

"Give me a chance," she said.

Antonio sighed to show her that he abhorred wasting information on women. "Not my type."

"I don't want to be your girlfriend," she said. "I want to fight your men."

He laughed into his own breath.

The old excitement was generating in her limbs, feet, hands. She said, "Try me out. Use me on any man. Any crappy contract, any fighter you want to get rid of. One chance on the undercard. Believe me, you'll hire me for real after that." There must be rude fighters, stupid fighters, boring fighters who won anyway. "You'd make gate. And pay-per-view." This was confusing for Nina, never having owned a television herself, but she was faking it 'til she made it. "Women would come to see it."

Antonio stilled at the mention of this barely-tapped market, fifty-one percent of the population. His fingers found his money clip on the table, stroked it once. Then the blinds closed in his face. "Time for you to go, sweetie."

"But—"

"This was fun. But you're boring me. Hey," he called for a bouncer, but the bouncer was flirting with a blonde.

Nina stood. She spoke low, so her desperation wouldn't leak out. "Okay. I'm used to people not believing in me. You didn't invent that. And I know I'm not much to look at, or in the best condition, or a well-rounded fighter. I'm not even that talented."

Antonio grunted.

"But you've seen, yourself, that it doesn't make a shit of a difference, Antonio Ricardo Ricardito Gino Joseppe Irving Spina," she said. "I knock them out anyway."

He looked up at her through his eyebrows.

"I could knock you out, too," she said.

Had she overstepped? Maybe, but a smile fought the corners of his mouth.

Nina said, "I'm telling you your fucking fortune. Cage is flesh plus steroids. But there's nobody like me. My name is Nina Black." She stabbed his table with one finger. "*I'm* the contender."

Antonio was watching TV again. Any possibility of getting Kate back was slipping away with his attention. Then, because she couldn't think of anything better to do, Nina whirled her insides up tight and smacked the table hard with both hands.

It made a big sound, and the standup beer menu jumped a couple of inches. The bouncer glanced over, and then back to his blonde. Antonio's eyelashes didn't flicker.

Nina was achingly disappointed in herself. As she walked away, she watched Antonio through the wall-mounted mirrors. He didn't even register her absence. It was as if she had never happened. He took a sip of beer. He gazed at a commercial for a video game. He wiped his mouth. He lowered his beer to the table. The bottle grazed its surface.

The table broke in his lap.

The gleaming plank slid to the floor with a barking, hollow clatter. Antonio's bottle broke on the tiles, sounding surprised. The bar fell silent. Even the TV announcer stopped talking. Nina walked to the door and smiled to herself.

He was watching her now.

CHAPTER FIFTEEN:
HOW TO BE A HUMAN BEING

BODHIDHARMA. YOU FORGOT ABOUT him, didn't you? So lost and dispensable, fighters who do not fight. This onetime contender sitting in a cave, armless, legless, eyelid-less, alone—no legend ever ended like that.

It had been nine long years of meditation. Nobody believed that Bodhidharma would ever leave his cave alive until one day, a man named Hui Ke stood at the entrance in the snow, begging for instruction.

Everyone knew that Bodhidharma was finished with people, as fickle, flawed, and fragile as we are. We don't commit, don't love, don't learn until we do, and then it's usually too late. Nothing good would come of the human race.

Bodhidharma told Hui Ke that he wasn't dedicated enough to learn how to be a human being. Nobody was. He should give up, go home, and leave Bodhidharma to die alone.

Hui Ke went home and chopped off his left arm at the elbow.

When the bleeding stopped, Hui Ke carried his severed arm back to Bodhidharma's cave, laid it at the entrance, and waited for an answer.

Bodhidharma was, needless to say, impressed.

~

OUT IN THE FRONT yard, Nina smelled Jackson before she saw him. He smelled the way the inside of a mouth tastes. She wondered if he were there to throw her out, or to beat her up. But he just watched her strike the makiwara.

The night before, Nina had found the coffee can in Jackson's freezer, opened it, and removed all the money. She peeled off three hundreds and put them back in the can, and took the rest without counting it. The money was in her underwear now, the only place on her body Jackson would avoid.

"You're thinking about the wrong things," he now said. He was picking his teeth with a skinned twig.

"How do you know?"

"You're bleeding."

The makiwara was streaked with her blood. He must not know about the money, or she wouldn't still be standing. Nina tried to empty her mind as she hit the wooden post. Then she thought about how nothing becomes something when you try not to think about it, like trying not to think about a pink elephant and *boom!* There's a pink elephant with a pink trunk and a little pink bowler hat and he's juggling mice and *shut up shut up shut up.*

"That's not it, either," Jackson said.

"Critic." Nina looked at her split knuckles, and sucked on a fist. She picked up No-Hair from the ground. Kate had left her behind again, but not before tying her blue ID bracelet around No-Hair's leg like a garter. Their address was written on the bracelet, in Isaac's handwriting. Nina tapped it with a finger. "I know where they live. I'm going over there today to get Kate. We're leaving town."

Jackson studied the ID band. "You think you should run away?"

"Cage has a vendetta against me. He could take Kate away. He could put me in jail, once he finds me." *He could hurt you,* she thought.

Jackson snorted. "That guy? He'd kill you before he'd arrest you. Best to lay low."

"And hit a post all day?" She hit the makiwara as hard as she could, rotating her core behind the punch the way he had shown her. Her hand hurt, and a crack sounded as the gray wood splintered down the middle. She had broken it.

"I'm sorry," she said, but thought, *Ha.*

"It was old," Jackson said. "I've broken them before. That one was no big deal. My oldest one. Cheap. Cracked already. Been out in the rain and snow for decades. You hit it behind my trailer in Junction, way back. Why didn't you break it, then? And your technique was bad." He pointed at the makiwara he had made Nina install herself last week. "Try the new one." She uncovered it and ran her hand over it—pale blond wood, perfectly sanded, and planted into concrete. Jackson punched it once himself and the thin, hollow sound reverberated through Nina's chest. It sprang back. That's all it knew how to do.

"Anyway, running away isn't your answer," he said.

She punched the makiwara twice. New, it hurt. Jackson kicked the brown grass.

"Courage isn't hope," he said. "You practice it. It's a skill, like any skill. You do it badly, until you do it well."

"Stop quoting yourself. And this isn't about courage."

"Then why won't you stay and give it your best?"

"This is my best. It just isn't very good." But she suspected that this wasn't true, that her best had never arrived.

Jackson brushed sweat from his eyes with a knuckle, the better to glare at her. "I mean it. He could kill you."

Nina wondered what it was like to kill someone. She wondered what it had been like for Jackson to kill men so far from his home. She wondered what it would be like to kill Jackson, to hold his weathered heart in her hands and then let it go.

Nina reached into her underwear and pulled out his money, fastened tight with the rubber band on it. "I'm sorry I took it," she said. "I was going to pay you back when I got settled somewhere."

He didn't seem surprised. "Keep it."

She grabbed his hand, forced the money into it. "I'll find another way."

Jackson turned from her.

She said to his back, "I love you, old man."

He leaned over in the grass and picked something up. Was he crying? She hoped so. That would serve him right for the toothpick peas.

Jackson turned around and opened his hand. Nina's long-thrown tooth rolled in the center of his palm, roots still intact. He patted her hand open, and dropped the tooth in it. "If you're going to go, go," he said quietly. "But show me that shuto first."

She pocketed the tooth.

A shuto is a strange thing. It's very different from a punch. A punch relies on Newton's Third Law—every action has its equal and opposite reaction. Your fist shoots out, the opposite hip and shoulder move back to counterbalance. You rotate on an axis—half your body moves forward, the other half moves backward. Hips, shoulders, core pivoting—all this gives your punch power, weight. A power punch knocks people in the other direction.

A shuto has a different source, and a different aftertaste. The source is centrifugal, beginning with a coiling compression in the gut. It's almost like a mood. You think it, and your body does it. Your lower body drills down while the circle spirals upward, growing bigger—your ribs, your shoulder, your elbow rotates, and your hand whips around as the inevitable result. It's the karate chop—the knife hand. It's made for necks, not noses. Done right, it doesn't move a person. It severs him.

But it's still outdated, odd, demanding precision and positioning. It takes a little longer to create a small hurricane inside yourself, while a punch meanwhile demands an immediate answer in kind. *Get away,* your body says, so we punch and kick and push and drag people to the ground. If someone broke into your house, would you first reach for the baseball bat by your side, or turn your back to grab an antique sword?

Jackson stamped his foot. "Stop stalling."

She stepped to the left and struck the makiwara with her best shuto. The edge of her hand glanced off the makiwara, which buzzed slightly, but that was it.

"That dog won't hunt," Jackson said. "You have to commit. And straight to the side is too far away to counterstrike. Rotate around him, like hands on a clock."

"I told you, I'm not fighting him."

Jackson pointed to a patch in the ground at a forty-five degree angle from where she stood. "Here. Remember how he drops his guard for those big bombs? Rotate away from his roundhouse, but close enough for him to still hit you. He'll overreach, exposing his neck a little. You'll catch the punch, but not in the sweet spot, and you can sneak in through the gap under his elbow. See? Step *here*. Now do it again. And again."

So she abandoned herself to the feel of the leather against her hand, the pain of the splitting skin, and the bruising underneath.

She felt the whip of the stroke, the tuck of her elbow, the length of her spine as the impact shuddered down her side and out her feet. Her callouses swished against the grass as she stepped left, right, left, right, slicing at the makiwara with the opposite hand each time. The sun burned her neck. Air flowed in and out of her lungs like they were bellows. New sweat lined her forehead for just seconds before the thirsty air claimed it. A bee buzzed by her head. She could hear the sun fall on the grass.

Then colors inverted like the negative of a photograph, over-saturated. Green turned red, and darkened to gray. Jackson stood on the grass next to her, sharp as acid. Her mind wound through murky alleys. A hand clapped on her wrist, twisting, the streetlights ticking, the ground shaking under her feet as she navigated the web of acrid smells, black sounds, dirty people.

"No. Not that. Like you're looking for something you lost," Jackson said.

She closed her eyes, striking and striking. The makiwara shuddered each time. She felt it without seeing it. There was her mother, tense in a doorway. Isaac, suitcase handles in his hand. Her brother, huddled in a corner of a gas station. Cage, fists up. The glint of a knife, eyes closing in Kate's pale face. The flash of teeth, an orange tail. Black stripes, and white, and light. She was sinking. She was disappearing. She shouted and opened her eyes.

Her hand was covered in blood. The top of the makiwara broke off and fell like a heart.

She turned to Jackson, panting.

"My girl," he said.

~

RUNNING DOWN THE STAIRS from his audition, Isaac pumped his fist in the air. The director had offered him the lead on the spot for *iHamlet: the App*. Director Carlos Soto was famous for deconstructed Shakespeare plays, like *King Lear and Zombies* and *Romeo and Juliet for Dummies*, as well as other satires such as *Jihad: the Musical* and his *One-Man Pygmalion*, in which Henry Higgins turns out to be (of course) transgender. Soto was an up-and-comer, exiled to Denver with his ironic mustache until his sick parents passed away, and Isaac would reap the benefits by playing his Hamlet (or Applet, as he would be called).

Wait until he told Kate. He looked at his watch; the theater was only half a block away from her bus stop. Finally, Isaac would be recognized as something other than a chimpanzee selling car insurance or an elf selling bathroom cleaner. He would get to be himself, in the shape of Hamlet/Applet. In the lobby, Isaac clicked his heels together and shouted, "To be, or not to be," which made an old lady turn from the elevator and stare. Who cared? Isaac felt so utterly fantastic that he didn't realize that he had been punched in the face until he was on his back.

His head smacked against the marble tile. A man jumped on top of him and straddled his torso, delivering punches to his face that would have been staggering if Isaac had been upright and able to stagger. They defined pain.

Isaac tried to push the monster away, but it didn't work. He was blind. His eyes were running. Something crunched loudly, something attached to his face. His arms were empty of all strength, so he just tried to cover his head with them. He couldn't see anything but a flurry of flesh, white teeth, and the flash of an orange tail on a bicep. Strong antiseptic and aftershave seared his newly-busted nose. His mind bounced against the walls of his skull. *Nina,* Isaac thought with each punch. *Nina. Nina.* He hadn't realized that he had spoken her name aloud until the man hissed in his ear, "Nina's mine."

How could that be? Hers was the name in his head. He tried to say, "No."

"Yes," the strangely clean maniac said in a patient voice, like he was talking to a crying child as he beat him. Each punch hurt on both ends—the delivery end, and the end where his head smacked back against the floor. Through the glass doors, Isaac caught a glimpse of the sky, which was sunny on this, his last day, and he thought, *At least there's that.*

It took a few seconds to realize that the man had stopped hitting him. Isaac opened his eyes.

The man sitting on his hips was the garbageman-cop, the one who wanted drugs. He leaned back, evaluating Isaac's face. He then looked down at his hands, which were covered with rubber gloves, which were themselves covered with blood from Isaac's face.

"That ought to do it," the garbageman-cop said.

He stripped the gloves carefully from his hands, turning them inside out. Then he placed the gloves in a plastic baggie and slid his thumb and finger along the edge to seal it.

Such fine movements were confusing to Isaac. The garbageman-cop still sat on him, but let him roll over onto his side, hacking into his fists, the air clouded with pain. Toothpaste breath flooded Isaac as the man leaned over him and said in a strangely conversational tone, "You know, I've had trouble locating Nina. Where is that girl?"

Isaac shook his head, coughing.

"Well. Just tell her that it's time to end this. The badge or the girl." The friendliness of his voice was surreal. Then his weight lifted, leaving a sudden emptiness in the space he left behind.

After a minute, a female voice quavered, "Are you okay?" Isaac realized that he wasn't okay but he was alive which was in itself okay, definitely okay with him. He managed to focus his eyes on an old lady with puffed-out hair. She was the same lady as before, and it was just the two of them again in the lobby, as if nothing had happened. "I called the police with my cellular phone," she said and held out her cane for him to grab.

Isaac pulled himself to sitting. His blood was smeared across the pink marble tile.

"You're the gentleman in that cereal commercial," the old lady said. She dropped a lacy handkerchief into his hand and pressed one painted fingernail against it. "I tatted that myself."

Isaac wiped his mouth with the handkerchief, staining it red. He heard the faint sound of sirens. He was supposed to avoid the police, for some reason.

He pulled himself to his feet. They wobbled underneath him. The sirens grew nearer, but something was pushing his feet forward. *Kate,* he thought. "Excuse me," the old lady called after him, but he stumbled out the revolving door, stolen handkerchief in hand.

In the brightness of the street, light drowned out everything at first. Then he saw her, Kate. She stood alone at the bus stop, turning her head in all directions. Nobody that young and skinny should be alone on concrete. He willed his legs to move faster, but his feet slogged behind them. "Kate," he said, as loudly as he could without fainting.

She didn't seem to recognize him at first, then she stared until saliva collected in her bottom lip. Her skin looked transparent. "Why is your face like that?"

"Why is *your* face like that?" he tried to joke, but gave up halfway. He slung an arm around her warm shoulder. "Someone punched me about five hundred times. I don't feel so hot."

"Who did that? Nina?"

"No. Although she probably should have." He sniffed and wiped his nose. It stayed where he pushed it. "Is my nose broken?"

Kate peered into his face. "It's not broken *off*."

Blood leaked onto his upper lip. He tried to find a dry place on the old lady's handkerchief.

"Don't blow it," Kate said. "It gives you black eyes."

"How do you know that?"

"Nina told me. Shouldn't you go to the doctor?"

"A doctor." He hadn't considered it.

"Your face might stick like that."

"I'm tired of my face." He realized this was true. "Maybe it looks better this way."

"No," Kate said. "It doesn't."

A police car and an ambulance pulled up next to the studio behind him. "Home," he said.

"But isn't that ambulance for you?"

"I don't think so." He lowered her pointing arm with a flat hand. He had trouble walking, so he leaned on Kate a little more than he wanted to. She staggered under his weight, but they kept moving.

Isaac felt better inside the elevator of his apartment building. He forgot which floor they lived on, so Kate pushed the button. Suddenly, she smiled at him. He was stricken by the radiance of it, of a smile rarely given. She tugged on his shoulders until he crouched down. She gave him a kiss on a battered cheek. When she pulled away, there was blood on her lips.

Isaac thumbed her mouth clean. "What, you like me now that I'm a broken mess?"

He suddenly realized this was true. He looked at the kid, almost his kid now, with her love for broken messes. Which meant that she would probably turn out okay, despite her past, and despite his own fuckups and best intentions. If you love the mess you're in, that's enlightenment, right?

Kate said, "You're a good dad."

Shock pushed tears into his throat.

The elevator door opened to Nina, trying to pick the lock to his apartment.

Nina stood upright and stilled at the sight of the two of them. "Oh no," she said. Her gaze examined each piece of Kate before returning to Isaac, this time with the beginning of tears. "What happened?"

"I love you," Isaac said.

It was easier to say it than it was not to say it. When Nina didn't say anything, he said it again: "I love you."

"Since when?" she finally asked.

"Since you were in Garanimals."

"That's a long time."

"Well. I was asleep for most of it." A sudden lightness made him want to sit down. But he kept standing, a battered man in love.

Kate shrugged him off and ran to Nina. She blushed and dropped to a knee. She hugged Kate, smelled her hair, and avoided Isaac's gaze. "I'm so confused," she murmured into Kate's shoulder.

Isaac gave Kate his keys, but Nina had already picked the lock open. "Kate, go inside and get some ice." After another brilliant smile, to Nina this time, Kate whipped inside, leaving them alone.

Nina said, "You're a disaster."

"Do you love me?" he asked.

"Of course."

His face stopped hurting. He leaned forward to kiss her, but she drew back. "Your nose is broken," she said.

He grabbed her anyway. Her kiss was the only soft part of her, and he pulled her tighter and tighter until he was sure that some piece of him had edged inside some piece of her.

They broke apart when Kate came back out. She paused, the toes of one foot resting on the ankle of the other, like a potbellied ballerina. She pointed at Nina's face. "He got blood on you." She opened her hand. In her palm was one ice cube.

Isaac stared at it, trying to remember why it was wrong. "No. Ice in a baggie."

"How many?"

His brain hurt. "I don't know." Kate sighed and left again, the ice cube in her fingers. "Eight," he called after her.

Nina's fingertips grazed Isaac's cheek, and he shivered. "What the hell?" she asked.

"Oh, that. I got into a fight. I think I have a little concussion."

"A fight."

"Like you!" He tried to smile, and his lip split. "Except it wasn't really a fight. Just, some guy hit me. Then he hit me again, and hit me again." Isaac snuffled through his broken nose, but the air didn't go anywhere. "It just went on like that. I won't bore you."

"Who?" she demanded, but seemed to already know. He wanted to hold her again, but she had started to pace in front of him like a Labrador. "Cage?"

"No. We were in a building."

"What's his *name?*"

"You know, it never came up."

"Tiger tattoo? Big?"

"Yeah. Blonde buzz-cut. Your boyfriend, or whatever. We met before. I don't think we'll be friends, though."

Kate returned with a baggie of ice. Isaac pressed the baggie against his nose. The edges of the cubes hurt. "Peas would have been better," he told her.

"We don't eat peas," Kate said.

"Why not?"

Nina's hand was trembling when she pointed at Kate. "Get her inside. You, too. Now."

But the hallway felt fine to Isaac, like his new home. He would live out here, he decided. He would drag the sofa into the hallway and finally meet the other rent-a-neighbors when they returned from their temporary jobs in the evening. "It's okay," he said. "Don't be scared." He wasn't. In fact, there was a kind of courage from getting beaten up. He had avoided it for so long— dodging eye contact in streets, ignoring barroom shoulder shoves, ducking and driving away when he accidentally cut someone off. But after all, what was there to be scared of? Yes, it hurt. And, yes, he would no longer be able to play the role of Handsome Cubicle Worker for his last remaining commercial job. But for all the mess on his outside, his insides were clearer than ever. He was seeing Nina for the first time—the microscopic vertical lines on her forehead, the glow of her blood beneath the surface of her skin, her fingers twisting in each other. He hurt, hurt badly. And Nina probably felt like this all the time.

"Get inside, Isaac. Lock the door. Use the deadbolt," she said.

She was on the other side of the air from him, and this made him jealous. "Tell me. Are you involved with that guy?"

She shook her head. "Not the way you mean."

"Stay away from him." He enjoyed the feel of telling her what to do without saying please, like they were already lovers. "He's crazy jealous. Actually, maybe we shouldn't live in the hallway. Don't be scared. But let's move. What do you think of

Hawaii? Maybe I should buy a Taser. Is that the same thing as a stun gun?"

"What did he say to you?"

"He said—" His thoughts bounced against each other. "Shit, my head is like a maraca. Why do you like fighting, anyway? Because my first time pretty much sucked."

"Isaac."

He searched his slippery mind. "He said, 'It's time to end this.' Which is a good idea, even if you're just friends. He's an abusive person." He wondered if he should keep the rest to himself, but his mouth spilled the words out. "Something about a badge. The badge or the girl."

Nina seemed to stop breathing altogether.

"What girl?" Kate asked. "Me?"

"Let's go inside after all," Isaac said. "That's a good idea."

He staggered to his feet, but Nina didn't move. She kept staring at Kate, who stared back. Their dark eyes glimmered at a depth he could never reach. Nina said in a thin voice, "I have to go take care of this."

"No. You have to take care of *me*." When she didn't answer, Isaac said, "Okay. I admit, I'm not crazy about the stealing. But getting punched in the head really puts your priorities in order. So, the first priority is all of us being together. And the second is, is, I need help with my face."

Kate nodded, hypnotized by Nina's gaze. "He really does," she murmured.

For the first time, Isaac noticed the trash bag in Nina's hand. "What's in there?"

Nina's gaze broke away from Kate's. She reached inside the trash bag and pulled out No-Hair. Then she pulled up the doll's dress and split a hole in her back with her fingertips. She dug into the doll's inside and pulled out a police badge.

"Oh," Isaac said.

Nina handed the broken No-Hair to Kate. Her face was pale.

"But you'll go to jail," Kate cried. "And tomorrow's my birthday."

Nina gathered the girl into her arms. "Happy birthday," she murmured into her hair. She said to Isaac, "You don't need to move. I'll take care of it. And stop acting in those fucking commercials."

"I got a part today," he said. "Hamlet."

"Life and death," she said.

"Mostly death. They all kick it in that one." He pulled himself to his feet. "Let's go together and try to talk to this guy. After all, what more can he do to me?" He touched his face, which felt like raw hamburger. "We'll face him together."

Nina said to Kate, "I have to do this. I'm sorry."

She turned to Isaac and stroked his face once. She looked at him with love and discernment. Then she slapped him hard on the side of his neck.

When he awoke, he was lying on his back in the hallway, and Kate was poking him in the shoulder. "What happened?" he asked.

"Nina hit you and then left. Are you okay?"

"Left where?" He sat up. He was dizzy.

"She said not to follow her."

It took a few tries to pull himself to his feet. He grabbed the wall for balance and waited until the world righted itself again. He reached for her hand. "Come on."

"Where are we going?"

"I don't know." He took the first slow step, and the next. Kate stutter-stepped next to him, looking up. He was worried, too. Nina was out in this mess alone. It didn't matter—he would find her. She was everywhere he looked.

CHAPTER SIXTEEN:
LIVE FOREVER

When the time comes, even a rat becomes a tiger.
—Okinawan proverb

A real warrior does not think of victory or defeat. He plunges recklessly toward an irrational death. By doing this, you will awaken from your dreams.
—from the *Hagakure* (1716)

Come on, you sons of bitches! Do you want to live forever?
—Sergeant Dan Daly, Battle of Belleau Wood, 1918

JUST INSIDE HER ALLEY, Nina squinted. The sun was setting in front of her, and the alley wavered in the light, which poured down the corridor like it was aiming for her. Everything was stained red and orange. Traffic echoed behind the buildings, but the world here had fallen silent. Into a dumpster, she threw the trash bag that contained everything she owned in this life. The air split in two for her to pass. The alley turned its windowless back to her, like the blank slate her life was built on. Heat radiated from the pavement and crawled up her legs, which were already trembling.

She walked toward the light, nearly blinded. It reflected off her open hands, giving them shape. She turned them over and over, their outlines shifting. These were her hands, still. Her fingertips still felt the softness of Kate's hair, the contours of Isaac's swollen, fine-boned face. She touched her lips, still felt the imprint of his kiss there. For perhaps the first time in her life, she felt scared. She did not want to die. She wanted to live.

This thought was a total surprise. She had fought ninety-nine street fights, ridden a motorcycle, crossed the street with her eyes shut, eaten an inordinate amount of bacon, and driven a Ford Pinto a hundred miles per hour on a gravel road in a blizzard, wondering if this, finally, would be the time when she handed off her life to the next person waiting in line. Each time, she came out on this side of existence, breathing hard and looking around, wondering if life were real after all, or if she was dead and dreaming someone else's dream. But it was different now that she had something to lose.

What does courage mean? It's the second when one thing changes into another. It's the moment of risk and its transformation. It's when a touch turns into love, when one person's life enters yours and stays. It's what you practice in the smaller moments: first badly, then well. Courage is loss, and the moment of waiting before something rushes to fill its place. It's the space between fear and hope.

There was Cage. He was leaning against a brick wall. He hadn't seen her yet. His skin glowed red. Every visible muscle had swelled, and his clothes no longer fit. He was in the prime of artificial health. The steroids had bloated his gut, and a puffy six-pack floated on top of it. With his hands clasped in front of him, he was making his pecs jump under his wife beater in a steady rhythm. He was more than twice her size now. He could sweep her away like sandwich crumbs.

He turned his head and saw her. "Oh, hey, you." He had no eyebrows. In fact, except for some remaining eyelashes and the flattop on his head, it was hard to detect any hair on Cage at all. His arm hair, armpit hair, stubble, eyebrows—all gone. His skin was as shiny as scar tissue.

"You look like a burn victim," she said.

A smile stretched across his red face, but the connection between his mouth and eyes seemed to have been cut. He nudged himself upright with one heave of the shoulder.

Nina grabbed the badge from her pocket and tossed it to him. He caught it.

"There," she said. "You're a cop again."

"Actually, I'm off the force as of today. That's why I need this." He waggled the badge before pocketing it. "I have one hour to turn this in before they fine me and 'Lost Police Badge' hits the wire."

"You quit the police force?"

Cage shrugged with one shoulder.

"So, we're good, then?"

"Nope."

"Didn't think so."

He smiled again. "You besmirched my honor."

"I don't know what that word means."

"You called me 'flesh plus steroids.' To Antonio Ricardo Ricardito Gino Joseppe Irving Spina."

Her pulse quickened. "He mentioned me?"

"You raise what he calls 'an interesting question.'" Cage was still smiling. "I can't have that."

"I gave you the badge. That's what you wanted."

"No. I wanted to erase you." He stepped closer. "Everything you are, everything you did, everything you touched, and everyone you know."

The temperature rose one degree. Cage's Adam's apple chugged. She stared at that place on his neck, a few remaining hairs glistening in the sunlight. Somewhere, a cat screamed.

Nina punched him in the jaw.

The first one stung him, but he quickly recovered with a smirk. Nina punched and punched, hitting air as Cage pawed her aside. She panted, "Feeling any of these?"

"Nope." Then he started hitting back.

His first punch stunned her even as she blocked it with her forearm. It was solid, iron-like, and unemotional. He was a machine, with human muscles quivering under his pink surface. His second punch nicked her chin, and Nina's counterpunch connected with the sweet spot on his.

Cage's face registered shock, but his body kept moving as his spirit paused. He was a professional. Like Nina. But she had a piece of him now. She whirled and gave him a spinning back kick to the liver, followed with a back-fist that connected with his chin. He was covering up, this big man, backing up and offering nothing but a lame jab. Nina was winning! Joy crossed her body before she noticed his perfectly executed cross.

She felt the draft on her face before the fist landed, heard the crunch of her cheek before she felt it. Then she felt it.

Nobody had ever hit her like that.

The pain split her vision in two, and a line of light sliced through the left side of her brain. She clenched her teeth and braced herself for the roundhouse to the jaw, which came, an immaculate one-two-three combination. Still, she was doing okay until he kicked her so hard in the crotch her feet lifted from the ground.

Her world turned sideways. She was on the pavement. Cage kicked her again, in the side. Her kidneys. Her liver. Breathing was a problem. Cage didn't even bother to follow her to the dirty ground. As she strangled like a fish, her mouth opening and closing, she realized that in these bright, broken minutes, she was definitely going to die.

"Wait," she gasped.

Miraculously, he did wait. Cage stood above her, wearing that embarrassed smile playground bullies do, like he couldn't believe his own success, that any of this was real. *It's real to me,* Nina thought. *Which means worse.*

Her legs weren't working properly. Her palms flat against the hot asphalt, it took her four tries to stand up.

"It's just that damn seesaw," Cage said. "We can't both exist at once." He sounded almost desperate, like he might cry. Then he blinked his eyes and his face was an iron mask again. He reached into his pocket.

Not a mark on him. If they were shadow selves, Cage was the one in the sun and Nina was the grayer, darker version that couldn't hold its shape on irregular surfaces. She tried not to cough, but something was beginning to fill her lungs. Cage took something out of a baggie and put it on his hands—rubber gloves, covered with what looked like red paint. "Why are you wearing dirty gloves?" she got out.

"Because your boyfriend is going to kill you today."

"What?"

Cage rested the heel of his gloved hand on a railing and sighed. "I've been waiting a long time for this." Time seemed to wash off his shoulders, making them lighter by the second. "Okay. In a few minutes, I will kill you with these gloves on." Cage did some bloody jazz hands, and paused to let the word "kill" saturate the air. "They have your boyfriend Isaac's DNA on them, from when I hit his face. I will transfer that DNA to you as I render you dead."

"DNA?" She already knew, even as she asked, "Why?"

"*I'm* not going down for this." Cage's nonexistent eyebrows lifted. "They investigate these things, you know, even for worthless bitches like you. Didn't you wonder why I didn't kill you months ago?" Without hair, Nina could see the marionette-string muscles in Cage's face work to pull his lids and cheeks into a smile. "Your boyfriend has defense wounds and no alibi. God, I'm good."

Nina wished she had called the police at Isaac's apartment, but such a thought had never occurred to her in her life. "Maybe he's reporting you right now."

"Hardly likely, with an illegal kid." Cage nose-laughed at the flash in Nina's face. "Yeah, I know about that, too. But my favorite touch is the knife scar."

Nina didn't realize what he was talking about for a second. Then she lifted her shirt to look at her skin, the 'ID' carved inside a heart. "My scar ties me to *you*, dipshit."

Confusion crossed Cage's face for the first time. "Me? Why?"

"Because I have *your* ID." But she didn't have it anymore.

His face smoothed. "Not ID for 'identification.' ID for 'Isaac Dickson.'"

She was the stupidest person on earth.

"But he's innocent," she said. "Kate's innocent."

"Not when I'm done with her." Cage beat his chest with a fist. "I own you."

Nina kept her voice low, to prevent herself from begging. "We can leave town by tonight."

"Sweetheart. You just can't live." Cage's voice was as even as a sewing machine. "If I'm going to be a heavyweight contender, I've got to clean up my history. Which you have sullied. It's for the greater good." Something leaked through a crack in Cage's face—the hours of tweezing stinging nose hairs, ironing T-shirts until they disintegrated, scrubbing the bottoms of his shoes, shaving down a newspaper coupon layer by layer until it was a thin strip of perfectly perpendicular nothing. His over-scoured skin smelled like bathroom cleaner. Tiny, hair-thin fissures showed wisps of Cage's blood vessels, flowing dangerously close to the raw surface of him. "Enough talk. These gloves itch."

The sky darkened. Nina was wrong. She and Cage weren't inverses. They were as mutual as matter and antimatter, bound to collide and annihilate each other. Her left foot slid back. Her useless hands curled into fists and levitated on their own. This was the best of her, but he was better.

"I'll beat you," she said. "Then I'll take your job."

Cage laughed, and that puff of air traveled from his lungs to hers. He put up his own hands, as steady as mountains. "I'm going to miss you, Nina."

"Me too."

"No, you won't," he said. "You'll be dead."

Cage stepped forward and got back to work, hitting her head with mechanical efficiency. His teeth flashed white. The air behind him rippled orange and black. She could barely see, but she felt him against her fists. He grunted, and she knew she had dug a path into the man, even if it was a narrow one. She could follow it, except each of Cage's punches rattled her insides and drained the strength from her legs. The world got paler. She was bleeding inside, and nothing was feeding oxygen to her eyes, limbs, heart. She was flattening into a void.

I can't die yet, she thought. Yet she was dying. Her lungs pulled against nothing. It was all ending. She blinked, and her eyes opened again for the last time.

Then, just like Jackson had said he would, Cage dropped his left hand to finish her with a roundhouse.

The moment waited in the air. "Here," she could hear Jackson say, pointing to the ground, which she could no longer see. She stepped there. She opened her hand. Every cell in her body rushed to feed it. She couldn't spare an ounce of weight for herself—to cover up, to survive. She could only do one thing. She dropped her guard and thought, *I just committed suicide.*

Her hand sliced under Cage's tucked chin, in a perfect arc to his throat. It was as heavy as the moon.

His windpipe crunched against the side of her hand, just as his fist smashed into her face.

Time unwrapped itself.

The world didn't end right away. Nina and Cage still stood opposite each other. All sound leached from the alley. The air lost color, and a thin layer of dust covered everything.

Cage's eyelashes brushed together, butterfly wings. That tiny breeze waved across space until it brushed her cheek, tipping her balance and beginning her descent.

Cage fell first, dead.

Nina faltered on the edge of her own event horizon. She regretted nothing. She was not a cog in a wheel. She was the whole wheel, runaway, rolling downhill. *I wasn't born to be ordinary,* she thought as she fell. *None of us are.*

CHAPTER SEVENTEEN: WAKING UP

THERE ARE HUMAN BODIES inside the Great Wall of China. You've probably already heard about them from history books. During the Qin dynasty, seventy percent of China worked on the wall. Millions of workers and children collapsed from exhaustion, disease, or starvation. They literally fell through the cracks. Nobody saved them. Other slaves mortared over the unlucky, clumsy ones, piling new stones over the dead and dying bodies. The Wall is made of people.

But that's not all. There are rumors of other bodies in the Wall, inside the stones themselves.

They're like fossils, stuck in forward motion. Some believe that these bodies are more recent ones, belonging to Chinese mystics attempting to walk through the Great Wall to the other side.

Though we know from ninth grade science class that even rocks are made of moving particles, they don't feel like that. We live in a solid world. We can't walk through rock any more than we can swallow the sea.

But human beings did—at least, they did in our imaginations. They walked into a wall as thick as a road, separating one windy land from another. They left the world of air and light to walk through a darker, harsher one, all for the love of something. Someone.

~

OUTSIDE THE DOOR TO Nina's hospital room, a large man in a suit stepped in front of Isaac. "Excuse me," he said.

Isaac swept Kate behind him, but she raced through the door and was gone. Isaac glanced at the man's suit, his white shirt open at the neck. "I already talked to the police, just now," Isaac said. "I told them everything I know. Excuse me, I need to go in there."

"No, no. I'm not the police." The man's hands were behind his back, with Italian-American courtesy. "This is all regrettable. A tragedy."

"You are...?"

"I worked with Cage Callahan, the assailant, in his capacity as a professional fighter." The man cleared his throat. "He and I had a conversation yesterday, about him and Ms. Black. It was heated. I am sad to say I might have escalated matters by insinuating that, if a woman could beat him up, perhaps he wasn't much of a fighter after all. In so many words. I was trying to save a little money on his contract, you see." He smiled apologetically, but didn't look sorry. "At that point, Cage mentioned a desire to kill her."

Rage flashed hot behind Isaac's eyes. "And you didn't do anything about it?"

The man said, "Fighters always talk about killing each other. It's a business of rivalries."

Isaac asked, "Did you tell all this to the police?"

"Yes, I did. I'm happy to cooperate in any way I can." The man handed Isaac a business card with the longest name he had ever seen, and the title, "VP of Talent Relations," underneath. "Ms. Black has communicated to me that she is looking for work with us. I would like it if she would contact me at her earliest opportunity." He pointed to a handwritten number. "That's my personal phone number, there. Anytime."

"You're *scouting* her from a hospital bed? Fucking shark," Isaac said. "She's in a coma. Get lost."

At the insult, the man leaned his big head in a sideways bow. He waited an extra second, just to show he could, and then turned to go. Even retreating, he scared Isaac a little, but not as much as the open door behind him.

Isaac turned and entered a hospital room for the first time since Chris died.

Lying on the hospital bed next to Kate was a broken woman. Nina looked like a Sumi-e painting gone wrong. Her hair pooled on the pillow like spilled ink. Her face was a wreck of swelling and red and purple bruises. Her eyes were closed.

Isaac knelt beside the woman who had possibly saved his life. He touched her hair. His sweat fell onto her eyelid. Not an eyelash trembled. He wiped it off, smoothed her hair off her forehead. The disinfected air was stagnant. He didn't know what to do. He didn't know who he was, except for in those eyes that were now shut against him.

"Still unconscious," Jackson said.

Isaac hadn't noticed him sitting on the other side of the bed, holding Nina's hand, tubes stuck in it.

Kate turned to look at Isaac. "Will she wake up?"

Jackson said, "The doctor said to wait and see. So we wait and see."

Isaac didn't recognize his own voice. "What do you know about this?"

Jackson's own voice was high and strange, like a bad flute. "I found her in the alley behind her old apartment. I didn't get there in time."

"Was she conscious? Did she say anything?"

"She was already like this. Lying next to that cop on the pavement."

"He wasn't a cop anymore," Isaac said. "They kicked him off the police force for misconduct, excessive force, some crap like that."

"What are those things?" Kate asked, pointing at the fine acupuncture needles in Nina's hands and feet.

"That's to make her better," Jackson said. "Goddamn nurses haven't been in here in over an hour. They love coma patients. So easy to take care of."

In the dim room, fluorescent light from the hall flickered across Nina's face. Isaac's own face throbbed. He wondered how Nina had stood it all these years, the pain of combat. He ran his fingers across the bandaged bridge of her nose, her swollen cheek.

"At least you said you loved her," Kate said.

"She's going to make it," Isaac said.

Tears bubbled to the surface of Kate's face, as if they had been waiting all along. "Is she?"

He reached for her. "Yes," he said into her hair.

Kate cried in his lap for a long time.

Just as Kate's sobs softened, Isaac was startled by a sound from Jackson's direction. There was a sputter, a whining creak, and a throbbing rumble. It sounded like an old, rusted engine grinding to life.

The old man was crying now. He was bent in his chair, holding himself in with his elbows, each sob wrenching from his frame. It looked so painful, Isaac wondered if the man had ever cried before, or if they were witnessing the colossal breakage of a thick wall, built long ago for a purpose, kept for a greater purpose.

Finally, Jackson stopped crying, as painfully as he had started. There were wheezes, groans. Rings had appeared under his eyes. He pulled a blue bandanna from his pocket, blew his nose, and folded it again. Isaac noticed for the first time that Jackson's sleeve was brown with Nina's dried blood. Jackson nodded as if agreeing to something in his head, lower and lower until his double chin rested on his chest. He had fallen asleep.

How could he sleep? Around them were all the sounds of an inner-city hospital during a full moon night. Someone wailed at terrible news. There were shoes running, doctors and nurses yelling gibberish. Once, someone screamed. But it wasn't them screaming, and somehow Isaac found this fact comforting enough to fall asleep, himself.

At some point in the night, he awoke. Kate was gone from his lap. The room was still dark. Nina's chest rose and fell under the stiff, white sheets. The hospital was suddenly silent, as if all the people in Denver had agreed to stop hurting and shooting each other for just a few minutes.

In the dark, Kate was also awake, hovering over Nina's quiet form like a ghost.

"Go back to sleep, Kate," Isaac whispered.

She didn't answer. She didn't look at him. She was somewhere in her head.

By the clinical nightlight, the shadows under Kate's eyes elongated. The weight of a heavy life bent her slight frame in a way that made Isaac want to take her to a place where she could rest until everything in her life felt as distant as a story she read once.

But Kate didn't want rest. For Kate, even sleep was for suckers. She was looking less and less like Chris anymore. A thin layer of his features still covered her face, but beneath that, something fierce was surging up on its own. A peculiar light shone through any available crack—her eyes, her voice, the spaces between her motions. She was rising. She was evolving into something yet unspecified.

"Don't worry," she said. "I can do it this time." Kate grabbed Nina's inert little finger. She shook it and said, "Wake up."

She sounded matter-of-fact, like a mother rousing a child. But Kate was the child.

"Wake up," she said again, louder, more firmly.

Jackson sat up. "What are you doing?"

Kate looked down at the pinky finger in her fist. She pulled it, hard. Then again. Then she bent it backward. "Wake up, Nina. Wake up." She started shouting, "Wake up! Wake up!"

Isaac said, "Kate. I'm so sorry."

But Kate wasn't looking at them. She had stopped shouting, and was staring at Nina's hand in hers, her mouth open. Nina's face was as still as glass, but her hand had formed a fist, with Kate's hand inside it.

"She's moving," Kate said. She swung her hand in the air, and Nina's clung to it. "She's moving!"

Jackson grabbed Nina's other hand and took her pulse, pulling out all the needles and letting them fall to the floor.

Isaac picked up their two intertwined hands and turned them over and over, examining the puzzle of it—Nina's pinky in Kate's fist, Nina's hand wrapped around it. He tested her fingers, but the grip was fast.

"I did it," Kate said in wonder.

"Nina? Can you hear me?" Jackson was shouting in Nina's face. Isaac pushed a twist of hair from her forehead. Under the lids, Nina's eyes twitched a millimeter. She was waking up on her own. Her breath fogged against his.

Jackson turned to Kate and said, "You woke her up."

Kate's face collapsed into itself. She started crying, hard, looking around wildly for somewhere to put her grief and elation. Isaac reached for her, but she instead turned to Jackson. The old warrior started at being touched. Then he held out his arms, and she fell into them.

Isaac touched Nina's chest, found her heartbeat. It was strong under his fingers, and getting stronger. He tried to memorize her body's language, its vocabulary of heartbeats and air. He didn't need any other definitions for love.

He whispered to her, "Your life is not an accident."

He pressed his other hand against his own chest. He listened to their two hearts thumping off-kilter together, beating the most ancient rhythm in the world.

⁓

NINA WOKE UP ALIVE.

She knew she was alive even before she opened her eyes, because she could smell. She smelled her own blood from inside her nose. Beneath that, she smelled Isaac's cologne, Kate's candy smell, Jackson's sour milk sweat, and she could smell fear. She smelled the astringent smell of hospitals and the boiled, burpy smell of cafeteria vegetable medley. She smelled acrylic paint on the wall nearby, the old stench from someone's shoes, dry mouths, bad news. Nina had heard about people who died and were brought back to life. They saw tunnels and light and heard voices from God. But no matter how evil those people were, the afterlife never stank.

So she was alive! How had she pulled that off? She remembered everything. She remembered getting hit and falling down. Even better than that, she could feel herself remembering, the wormhole of her brain flexing and relaxing under her painful but possibly intact skull. She remembered what she had eaten for lunch that day—an apple. She remembered what she had been wearing—gi pants and a T-shirt, although it seemed like she was now naked under some kind of polyester gown.

She reached back farther into her memory, and was surprised to find that she could remember things she had never remembered before. Like learning how to walk, holding onto things, and pulling herself always up, up. She remembered speaking baby talk, and nobody understanding her. She remembered being rammed through a hard, inflexible tube into bright, dry light. *My birth!* she thought, and then immediately forgot it again, forgot remembering it.

Nina cracked an eyelid. Three people stood next to her bed.

Isaac's hand was on her chest. It was a light touch, but it still hurt. His other hand was on his own chest, and he looked up at the ceiling, as if he were taking an oath over her body. His nose was broken, slanting to the left. Black eyes were starting to form, which only made him more brooding and gorgeous. His gaze ticked down, and caught on hers.

Kate was in Jackson's arms. Her soft brown hair curled around her mouth and waved with each breath. Jackson's head was buried in her shoulder.

Nina opened both eyes.

Kate wriggled free and threw herself on top of Nina's body.

The pain was startling. Nina breathed deeply of the little girl's loamy smell, listened to the hollow sound of her breath in her body. Kate was alive and breathing, as simply as she had ever breathed.

Isaac said, "Kate, get off her. She's hurt."

Kate slid off her body with excruciating slowness. Isaac's hands roamed in soft pats, as if he didn't know where to put them on her body—the top of her head, her shoulder, her knee.

Jackson dashed out of the room and was back in an instant, pushing a man in scrubs in front of him. The intern leaned over Nina and shouted into her face. "Nina? Nina? Can you hear me?"

The sound waves from the man's mouth hurt her face. He checked the machine next to the bed and wrote something on a chart. "She seems to be in stable condition," he said to nobody in particular, walking backward. "I'll send someone in as soon as…" but he was out the door before he finished his sentence.

"Goddamn American healthcare," Jackson said.

"How do you feel?" Isaac asked.

What a stupid question. I'm in a hospital, Nina thought. *I feel terrible.* Her chest hurt. Her back hurt. Her cells hurt. A flake of dust fell from the ceiling and hit her forehead. It hurt. "Fine," she rasped.

Jackson said, "They X-rayed you. The doctor said you wouldn't be paralyzed or anything. Can you move?"

She wiggled her toes, her fingers, tried to speak and winced.

"They stuck a tube down your throat for a while. That's why—" Jackson massaged his own throat. He picked up a bottle and squirted water in her mouth. Some of it dribbled onto her neck.

Out the window, there was only a vague light. *Is it today?* she wondered.

"It's four in the morning. You've been asleep for a while," Isaac said.

"Not as long as the last time you got beat up, though," Jackson said. "You're improving your time."

Kate looked at the clock on the wall and said, "Hey. It's my birthday."

"Shit," Isaac said.

"Can you get up?" Jackson asked.

She tried to shift onto her side, but it hurt too much.

"Your chart says that you have some kidney and organ damage, but they stopped the internal bleeding. You have a concussion," Isaac said. "And you've looked better."

"You look great to me," Jackson said. His hand was warm on her shin. His face looked younger, like wrinkled paper smoothed over with a hand. The whirlwind always present just under his skin had calmed to a slight breeze.

Isaac said, "They're running some tests to see what kind of damage we're dealing with. Right now, though, they're calling you lucky."

Nina whispered, "Cage."

Isaac and Jackson glanced at each other. Isaac said, "He died, Nina."

She started to cry. She didn't know why. Kate patted her hand. Jackson plucked a tissue from a box and wiped her nose gently, holding the broken part in place.

"I talked to the police," Isaac said. "They'll just need a statement. When you're ready." These words curled around her head.

"Dead?" she rasped.

"Yeah. Cage is dead, Nina."

"Dead?" she asked again.

Jackson said, "He's in the morgue. Very dead. Broken neck, severed spinal cord. No heartbeat. Not breathing, either. Never coming back. Forever and totally dead."

She couldn't get it, no matter how hard she listened. It was that damn seesaw. None of it made sense, because if Cage was totally dead, that meant that Nina was absolutely and unequivocally alive.

How extraordinary.

Nina lifted her head, and tried to push up from the mattress with her elbows. Everyone scrambled forward to help her sit up. Nina reached for them, and pulled until the world was right side up. It looked all right. From where she sat, the world looked fine.

They all kept their hands on her, as if holding her in place. The air in the room shifted and stilled around them. She looked into their clear eyes. These were her people. Each of them was a galaxy made of blood and sinew, light, and the empty space where love inhabits.

Isaac kissed her hands and said, "I'm so glad you're back."

But I've never been here before, Nina thought.

Nobody moved in the growing light. She wondered if this was how a newborn baby felt, eyes wet, wild, and hurting. Trying, under the scrutiny of a family, to put it all together: breath, body, voice. Heart. Everything you need to join the human race.

ACKNOWLEDGEMENTS

ENORMOUS GRATITUDE TO MARY Evans for never giving up on this book, and to Tyson Cornell for taking a chance on it. Thank you to Alice Marsh-Elmer and Julia Callahan for their beautiful work. Thank you to Andrea Dupree, Mike Henry, and all the supportive faculty, staff, and students at the Lighthouse Writers Workshop. Thank you to Nick Arvin and the late Cort McMeel for helping me with the manuscript. Thank you to Scott Harrison and Ellen Moore for letting me work in your beautiful treehouse. And, forever and always, the most gratitude and love to my husband, JD. I love you.

ERIKA KROUSE has published fiction in *The New Yorker, The Atlantic, Esquire.com, Ploughshares, One Story, Glimmer Train, Story, Shenandoah*, and other publications. Her collection of short stories, *Come Up and See Me Sometime* (Scribner), was the winner of the Paterson Fiction Award, was chosen as a *New York Times* Notable Book of the Year, and has been translated into six languages. Krouse is currently working on a novel and a short story collection, teaching at the Lighthouse Writer's Workshop, and working part-time as a private investigator. She lives in Boulder, CO.